TARGET

LEGEND OF THE IR'INDICTI SERIES, BOOK THREE

CONNIE SUTTLE

Print Second Edition (2018)
Print ISBN: 1-63478-075-2
Print ISBN-13: 978-1-63478-075-9
eBook ISBN: 1-939759-12-9
eBook ISBN-13: 978-1-939759-12-2

Published by:
SubtleDemon Publishing, LLC
PO Box 95696
Oklahoma City, OK 73143

Cover art by Renee Barratt @ The Cover Counts

To Walter, Joe, Larry, Lee, Dianne, Sarah and Mark.
Thank you.

ACKNOWLEDGMENTS

As always, this book is the result of collaboration. If it weren't for the support of my editor, my cover artist and my beta readers, it would be less than it is. All mistakes, as usual, are mine and no other's.

About the Author:
Connie Suttle lives in Oklahoma with her husband and a conglomerate of cats. They have finally banded together to make their demands, which has proven disconcerting to all humans involved.

You may find Connie in the following ways:
Facebook: Connie Suttle Author
Twitter: @subtledemon
Website and Blog: subtledemon.com

ALSO BY CONNIE SUTTLE

Blood Destiny Series:

Blood Wager

Blood Passage

Blood Sense

Blood Domination

Blood Royal

Blood Queen

Blood Rebellion

Blood War

Blood Redemption

Blood Reunion

Blood Destiny Series Boxed Set (Books 1-10)

Blood Recall

Blood Alliance*

Legend of the Ir'Indicti Series:

Bumble

Shadowed

Target

Vendetta

Destroyer

Legend of the Ir'Inditi Boxed Set

High Demon Series:

Demon Lost

Demon Revealed

Demon's King

Demon's Quest

Demon's Revenge

Demon's Dream

God Wars Series:

Blood Double

Blood Trouble

Blood Revolution

Blood Love

Blood Finale

Saa Thalarr Series:

Hope and Vengeance

Wyvern and Company

Observe and Protect*

First Ordinance Series:

Finder

Keeper

BlackWing

SpellBreaker

WhiteWing

~

R-D Series:
Cloud Dust
Cloud Invasion
Cloud Rebel

~

Latter Day Demons Series:
Hot Demon in the City
A Demon's Work is Never Done
A Demon's Due

~

Seattle Elementals Series:
Your Money's Worth
Worth Your While*

~

BlackWing Pirates Series
MindSighted
MindMage
MindRogue
MindMaster*

~

Black Rose Sorceress Series
The Rose Mark

Rose and Thorn

Black Rose Queen

Queen of Thorns and Roses

Future Wars Series

Buffer Zone

Black Zone*

Other Titles from SubtleDemon Publishing:

Malefactor

Transgressor

Underhanded*

by Joe Scholes

*Forthcoming

FOREWORD

A note about the locations in this series:

Cloud Chief, Oklahoma is a real ghost town, located near Cordell, Oklahoma. All of the land is now privately owned and the Cloud Chief community portrayed in this book is fictitious in nature.

CHAPTER 1

*J*osh Barnett was completely lost. He'd traveled from Philadelphia two days earlier to visit cousins in Weatherford, Oklahoma. "Tipping a cow," his cousin Chance said, "will make you an official cowboy." Josh, at fifteen, wanted to earn the Stetson hat cousin Chance offered as an incentive. "Just tip the cow; get a picture with your cell and the hat's yours. We'll go to Landon's Western Wear on Saturday to get it."

"Besides," cousin Alex offered, "If you go on the full moon, you won't need a flashlight."

Josh needed a flashlight. And a map. No distinguishing landmarks could be seen anywhere. He'd been bungling about for hours and he could have sworn a hawk swooped over his head. Hawks didn't fly at night, did they?

Must have been an owl, Josh reassured himself, shivering despite the warm Oklahoma night. Now, Josh had come to a fence. "Don't cross any barbed-wire fences," both cousins warned when they let him out of the car just south of Highway 152. Josh dithered for seconds, wondering what to do. The fence was in his way and he wasn't about to climb over the barbed-wire contraption anyway.

Contraption. A great word to use in Oklahoma. It seemed to go well with dry red soil and tall prairie grass waving in the wind. The picture wouldn't be complete, either, without the occasional armadillo, squashed on heated pavement in the midst of a sweltering Oklahoma summer.

"I'll just go back," Josh decided aloud, turning away from the fence. His cousins had likely played a practical joke on him anyway. The slavering beast that leapt at Josh took the young man's life before he could even scream.

"Aedan, they've found Ashe." Adele Evans slipped into the robe her husband held out for her. She'd been flying over Cloud Chief in her peregrine falcon shape while the full moon slipped across the sky.

"The monster they sent killed a boy who was out wandering through the Barnett's wheat fields," Adele added, wiping wetness from her cheeks. "I tried to get the boy to turn around and go back, but he wouldn't." Her hands trembled while she scrubbed tears away.

"I'll call Marcus and Nathan," Aedan replied, worry in his words as he pulled his cell phone from a pocket.

Flying through the moonlit night as the bumblebee bat, Ashe sent another piercing call. Silent except to the most sensitive of ears, it echoed back within seconds, telling him exactly where the Pack ran.

Salidar DeLuca, a fifteen-year-old werewolf and his best friend, had been running with the Pack for nearly a year. Sali had been so proud last year when three days after his fifteenth birthday, Sali's father allowed him to hunt on the full moon. Sali and Ashe were now nearing their sixteenth birthdays. Ashe was looking forward to driving.

Legally, anyway.

When the last of Ashe's echoes bounced back to him, however, he detected something. Something the wrong size and shape. Changing swiftly from bumblebee bat to mist, he blazed across the fields and farmland that made up Cloud Chief, an official ghost town in western Oklahoma.

The shape he'd detected was moving swiftly on the eastern edge of Cloud Chief, just beyond the spelled fence that kept the paranormal community hidden from humans.

What the? Ashe's thoughts scattered when he saw a mangled body, and then the creature that ran away from it. Terrified, Ashe sent desperate mindspeech to his father. *Dad! I'm bringing something to you. Get Nathan! Please wait in front of the house—I'll drop it there. It killed somebody!*

The creature raced across the prairie below, covering ground quickly. It was no match for the speed Ashe held as mist—Ashe had grown in many ways since he'd learned of his gifts, and he'd honed his misting speed to a fine art.

Swooping down, Ashe turned the monster to mist when he came in contact with it. Ashe felt the fury radiating off the monster as he gathered it inside his mist. What shocked him most, however, were the words that came with the fury.

As yet, Ashe had only met three who could return his mindspeech. None of those three were nearby. This one, though, could return mindspeech easily, if it were interested in a two-way conversation and if it weren't so intent on killing Ashe.

I'll Kill you! It shouted mentally. *Rip your heart out!* It raged. Ashe rushed toward his home, frantically hoping his vampire father would be waiting.

~

"Be ready," Aedan warned. Nathan Anderson, one of two remaining vampires who resided in Cloud Chief, already had deadly claws extended.

"I hear Ashe," Nathan nodded. Ashe had just sent mindspeech to his father and Nathan, who waited for Ashe to drop the prisoner.

Both vampires had learned long ago not to exhibit shock or surprise to an enemy.

When the large creature, longhaired, six-horned and growling, hit the ground before them, Aedan and Nathan went to work.

~

"I've never seen anything like this." Marcus DeLuca walked around the creature. Dawn was only an hour away and Aedan had ordered his son inside the house. Ashe had witnessed the killing of the creature and Aedan only waited long enough to hear where the body of the human victim lay before sending Ashe inside with his mother.

"It looks like a prehistoric animal of some sort. Except for the horns," Nathan observed, lifting eight-inch strands of the monster's hair in curiosity.

"They know where we are," Marcus sighed. "I'll call the Grand Master in a few minutes and see where he wants to relocate the community."

~

"This is the third killing we've seen like this in two years, Director." The Joint NSA and Homeland Security Office had received a tip from an anonymous source, reporting a savaged body found in an Oklahoma field.

This murder joined two others, the first in Tennessee and a second in Iowa. The wounds were very similar in each case and the tracks leading to and away from the body were the same.

Large, cloven hooves were combined with clawed, bear-like paws, as if the hind legs belonged to a bull and the front to a grizzly. Only this time, the prints leading away ended abruptly, for some unknown reason.

Before, dogs had sniffed the scents until they'd disappeared eventually. Not so this time, and Director Matthew Michaels of the

Joint NSA and Homeland Security Department didn't want to show his uncertainty to subordinates.

"Gather the evidence and remove the body," he snapped angrily. His employees rushed to obey. Matt stood in a wide field next to a fence while daylight waned about him, with tall prairie grass blowing around his feet in what seemed an endless wind. The grass surrounding him was already drying in the oppressive heat, though it was barely June.

"Matt, I have information," one of the special agents ended a call on his cell and stepped carefully through the slender, waving grasses.

"I'm almost afraid to hear it," Matt replied. Jasper Hadley, one of a handful of werewolf agents Matt employed, probably didn't have good news.

The special paranormal division of the FBI had been working undercover for nearly forty years. A courageous former Director had gotten the permission of a President to start the whole operation.

Now, sixteen werewolves and ten vampires worked in that division, with the full knowledge and consent of the Grand Master and the Head of the Vampire Council. Only the Director, the President and a few others were aware the division existed at all.

"The killer is dead and not far from here," Jasper said quietly. "You're invited to take a look and we can haul it to forensics afterward, but it won't be anything we've dealt with before. This race," Jasper, rubbed the back of his neck in an agitated manner, "they don't care who or what they kill. Get in their way and you'll likely end up dead. Unless you're a vampire or a small pack of wolves."

"Just what I wanted to hear," Matt grumbled, raking a hand through light brown hair, his hazel eyes surveying the crime scene. "Know where we're going?" he asked, noticing the sun was about to set. One usually didn't notice such things unless one was used to working with vampires. The Director was always aware of sunset times and full moons.

"Yeah. I'll drive." Jasper led the way to a Chevy Trailblazer he'd rented at the Oklahoma City airport. Red-haired and blue-eyed, Jasper was unusual among werewolves, with a light sprinkling of freckles across his nose. Other werewolves always recognized his scent, though.

"Where are we going?" Matt asked as Jasper pulled through a gap in the fence, the vehicle bouncing uncomfortably as they crossed a shallow ditch. The Barnett family had allowed Matt's team to cut the barbed wire fence in order to provide easier access to the crime scene.

Two of the dead teen's cousins had shamefully admitted to playing the practical joke, by sending their city relative out on a full moon to tip cows. A common myth, as it turned out. Cows were not easily tipped, didn't sleep while standing (although they did doze now and then), and if you managed to get one to stand still long enough, would still require several strong friends to help you push it over.

"We're going down the road just a little way—to Cloud Chief; it isn't easy to see the community entrance from the road," Jasper replied to Matt's question.

"I would never have noticed this," Matt turned in his seat. It looked to be solid brush and fencing when Jasper had driven right through it. Matt heard gravel crunching beneath the vehicle, but that hadn't been visible from the country road running alongside it.

"Meant to be that way," Jasper informed the Director, driving slowly over a rough path consisting of gravel lying across ruts, with weeds and grass growing in the center of the narrow trail.

"This is the back of beyond, isn't it?" Matt, a native of Los Angeles, observed dryly.

"I wouldn't mention that to the residents," Jasper said. "This is protection for them."

"I realize that," Matt nodded absently, looking around. He saw two houses as they drove along and would likely see more, but they didn't appear until the truck was nearly past them.

"We'll get the full story when the sun is completely down," Jasper went on.

"Yeah. I figure we will," Matt agreed.

"Son, stay in the house," Aedan warned. "We don't want them to know who brought that thing here or how it was brought here."

Ashe hadn't slept. The day after a full moon was always bad for anyone who shifted. Now, the whole community was preparing to move and it was because of him.

Sali had called three times, asking if he'd heard anything. Ashe figured Sali would know where they'd end up before he would. Sali also asked about the creature Aedan and Nathan had killed, but Ashe had been warned not to talk about it. Sali hung up after a while, completely disappointed.

"They'll come hunting you, Ashe, if they discover you have the talents they want. Misters are extremely rare among their kind. Keep that information secret," William Winkler had warned Ashe and his parents two years earlier.

The fertilized egg his parents had gotten from a clinic so paranormal scientists could splice in his mother's and father's DNA had been carefully planted by a race known as the Elemaiya.

At war among themselves, one faction had seeded fertility clinics with donated eggs in an effort to increase their numbers. Their half-Elemaiyan children could turn out almost as talented as the full bloods.

The opposing side had learned of it and set about exterminating any children born from those donated eggs. The supernatural community of Cloud Chief had protected Ashe for the past three years, after the first attempt on his life when he was twelve. Now, Ashe sat inside his bedroom, depressed and dejected, a half-packed box of books lying on the floor beside his bed.

"At least we learned where the vampire misters originated," Ashe muttered to himself. If a vampire had the least bit of Elemaiyan blood, he had a very good chance of being able to mist or mindspeak. Ashe could do both, in addition to his shapeshifting ability.

Granted, he turned into the tiniest mammal in existence—the bumblebee bat—but it had been useful at times. His echolocation skills were the most helpful while he was in bat form.

"Son, the authorities have arrived, so stay inside your room," Aedan poked his head inside Ashe's door. Tall, dark-haired and gray-eyed, Aedan was quite handsome. Ashe had overheard the older girls commenting on it one day after school. Ashe never thought of his parents in those terms—they'd always been his parents. Nothing more.

Aedan, as vampire, would always appear young. His mother was still in her prime, but as a shapeshifting falcon, she would age. Shifters normally lived more than two hundred years. Ashe didn't like thinking about a time when his mother wouldn't be alive.

"I will," Ashe told his father, setting a handful of books inside the box.

"This isn't your fault," Aedan sighed. "Keep packing your things. We'll talk later."

"All right." Ashe wanted to be someone else right then. Almost anyone would do. He listened while his father climbed the steps toward the ground floor of their home.

"Nice work," Jasper complimented Aedan and Nathan. The creature's head had been neatly severed, with very few additional wounds. Nathan had distracted the beast, swiping its ribs with lengthy claws while Aedan, moving faster than a blur, had stepped in to remove the head. The body was now stored inside the Evans' garage under a tarp until someone could come and remove it.

"I've never seen anything like this before," Matt shook his head in wonder and confusion. "It's half bear, half bull, with extra horns and long hair."

"We hear they're manipulating their own children to make these things," Aedan muttered in disgust. "I've been informed by important vampires that these are the assassins for the Dark Elemaiyan race. They kill the enemies of their own kind plus anyone else they target."

"Are humans targets?"

"Only if they're in the way," Nathan had shown up as quickly as he could after sunset. Now he was answering questions with Aedan.

Marcus DeLuca had come, too, but he wasn't as well versed on the creature as the vampires. He was content to listen.

"And the boy was in the way. How did you know to go after this one?" Matt looked to the two vampires for answers.

"My wife saw the creature first, and then she found the boy, who was a short distance away and right in the beast's path when she flew overhead," Aedan replied. "She swooped down to warn the boy, but he didn't deviate from his path. The result, I believe, of a cruel practical joke gone horribly wrong."

"Yes, I'm fully aware," Matt sighed. "The family is understandably upset."

"As we would be," Marcus said. "How do you intend to explain this child's death?"

"Perhaps a panther, roaming outside a natural habitat," Matt said.

"I'd appreciate it if you'd select another animal," Nathan frowned. His oldest daughter, Cori, set to start her third year of college in the fall, was a shapeshifting panther.

"A bear, then," Matt nodded. Nathan was satisfied with that. After all, half the creature resembled a bear and the community had no bear shapeshifters. "I hope all of you can clear out before we release that information and every person nearby that owns a gun goes out hunting a wild bear."

"We're packing now," Marcus replied. "We have no desire to meet trigger-happy humans." None of them mentioned the real reason they were moving.

"How long do you think you'll need?" Matt asked.

"Give us five days," Marcus said. "I think we can be gone by then."

"I'll hold off on the information—the autopsy could take as long anyway," Matt agreed. "If you need anything from us, get the information to Jasper, here. It'll be our thanks for taking this thing down." Matt toed the creature on the garage floor. "Jasper, call the vampire agents in. They can load this thing up and get it out of here tonight." Jasper was on his cell phone immediately.

"Mom, I really don't feel hungry." Ashe dumped a pile of winter clothing into what seemed like the thousandth box. Adele Evans stood in Ashe's doorway, a concerned expression on her face. He'd been packing all day, fretting over the fact that the community was being forced to move because the Dark Elemaiya had found him again.

The rest of the community wasn't aware that they'd found him two years earlier, when the witch's shield had been breached. Only Ashe knew that. He also knew the reason the Elemaiya hadn't found their way back since then. That had changed quickly two nights before. An innocent human had died, too, simply because he was in the way.

"Honey, you need to eat something."

Ashe wished he were six again and could climb into his parents' laps and let them handle his difficulties for a while. He couldn't. He was an adult or nearly so, but this had dealt a blow to him.

The community had been forced to move from New Mexico when he was five because information was inadvertently shared with humans regarding their existence. Now, the community was being uprooted again, and it was because he was hunted. If the Elemaiya found him, he'd either be killed or enslaved, depending on which side found him.

"Dude?" Sali peeked over Adele's shoulder. Sali had gotten his growth spurt, standing at five-eleven. Ashe, though, was now six-three and likely to pass his father's six-four in another year.

"I thought you'd be packing," Ashe sighed helplessly.

"Almost done," Sali grinned. "I have to start on what Marco left behind next."

Ashe envied Sali's older brother at times. William Winkler, the Dallas Packmaster, offered to pay Marco's tuition to the University of Texas, in Austin. Marco was a year away from graduation and worked for Winkler during the summer. Much to Marcus DeLuca's chagrin, Marco had become an official member of the Dallas Pack the year before.

Cori Anderson still dated Marco, but didn't want to go farther than that until she graduated from the University of Oklahoma. Ashe talked to her occasionally; Cori called him for advice and information now and then.

"Got all the books packed, I see," Sali remarked, surveying the empty shelves. "Dad says the Grand Master called Mr. Winkler. I think they've found a good spot for us," he grinned.

"You're excited about this?" Ashe stared at his friend.

"Yeah, dude. Mom wants a bigger house. Think about it, Ashe. Maybe we'll move somewhere nearer to a city or something."

"How does everybody else feel about this?" Ashe watched Sali's face; his best friend truly was excited about the move.

"Are you kidding? Dori and Wynn are already planning theoretical shopping trips."

Ashe chuckled despite himself. Dori and Wynn still feuded with Sali, but it was turning into a dance of sorts. Ashe never said it, but he wondered which one Sali would end up asking out.

Sali stole their pens and they chased him. He jerked books out of their arms and they chased him. He flipped ears and they chased him, throwing pens and pencils at Sali's retreating back while he ducked in an overly dramatic fashion. Principal Billings had Sali sitting inside his office every other week for tormenting Dori and Wynn.

Ashe's relationship with Principal Billings hadn't improved over the years, either. Billings knew Ashe had tapped into his office computer during sixth grade and Billings had never forgiven him.

Ashe was viewed with constant suspicion, although he hadn't touched Billings' computer for more than three years. The Principal had almost gotten rid of Ashe at one point, thinking to send him to a human school because he hadn't shifted in Transformational Arts class.

Saved by the bumblebee bat at almost the last moment, Principal Billings hadn't appreciated the image he'd presented to the community, flapping arms wildly to fend off Ashe's alter ego at graduation that year.

All of Cloud Chief still chuckled about the incident. Principal Billings growled angrily if anyone brought it up. Nowadays, Ashe worked to stay below the Billings Radar, as he liked to call it.

"What's your mom gonna do about the store?" Sali asked.

"I think Jason and Marcie are coming up to run it while a realtor tries to sell it," Ashe was back to depression. He and Sali had good memories of working at Cordell Feed and Seed.

"You think they'll come before we leave?" Sali looked interested. His Aunt Marcie, much to everyone's surprise, had taken to Jason. They'd gotten married and moved to Denton, Texas, a year and a half after Marcie had come to Cloud Chief. Jason still worked for Winkler, but Winkler was giving him time to help Adele with the store.

"Ask Mom, she talked to him," Ashe said. "Come on; help me get this stuff out of the closet."

"Sali, want a burger?" Adele was back, offering food again. Ashe was dragged upstairs to the kitchen by a ravenous Sali.

"Everything is cleared away," Aedan walked into the kitchen and sat at the table, smiling in amusement as Sali devoured a second hamburger. "Marcus says the final details are being worked out on our next location; the Grand Master has to clear the way with another Packmaster. We won't be in their area, just nearby, I hear," Aedan explained.

"I hope it's closer to a city," Sali said.

"You just want to drive around and impress girls," Ashe teased.

"I'm impressive already," Sali lifted his arms and flexed his muscles. Ashe's mother laughed.

The doorbell rang so Aedan rose to answer it. Marcus and Denise DeLuca walked into the kitchen. "Feel like buying a boat?" Marcus clapped Aedan on the back and grinned.

CHAPTER 2

"Star Cove, Texas?" Ashe was surfing on his computer as quickly as he could. Sali, leaning over Ashe's shoulder, blinked as Ashe checked the maps he'd pulled up. "Here it is." Tapping the screen, Ashe pointed out the small Texas community, just north of Corpus Christi.

"Did Winkler know we'd need a new place?" Sali asked, trying to learn more about their new home by peering at a tiny dot on the map. "Dad said Winkler had a whole development ready to go."

"I'm not sure that was his original intention; it was just convenient, with new housing already built. I think it was an investment," Ashe said. "Dang, I can't get updated information." The online map service didn't have the new addition on satellite imaging, yet.

"But it's near the water," Sali grinned.

"It'll certainly be different from dry, western Oklahoma."

"And your dad will only have to build his bunker," Sali said. "I can't wait. Mr. Winkler says he's sending Dallas wolves driving rented trucks. They'll have us out of here in one night."

"But Dad and Nathan will have to wait and leave when the sun is down. Mr. Winkler says if they hurry, they can drive it in one night. If not, he has a place set up in San Antonio for them to spend the day."

Ashe's frown wrinkled his forehead. He always worried if his dad had to stay somewhere strange. Vampires were vulnerable in the daytime. Any sunlight hitting his father might kill him.

"Come on, they'll be okay," Sali nudged Ashe's shoulder. "See what else you can find out."

"Ashe?" Dori and Wynn walked into Ashe's bedroom, offered Sali a halfhearted glare and stared at the computer screen. "This is where we'll be?" Dori's voice held a hint of awe. "It's right next to the gulf."

"Should be just north of this street," Ashe pointed out Friendly Lane in Star Cove. "Looks to be a good spot to park your boat if you're a fisherman, but the addition is too new to be on the map or satellite yet."

"Wynn and I are going to be next door to each other," Dori poked Sali in the chest.

"Nah, I'll be right in the middle," Sali teased in an effort to stir something up.

"You will not separate us," Wynn poked Sali harder in the chest.

"Help!" Sali flopped onto Ashe's bed in mock fear as two angry female shapeshifters wrestled with him. Ashe worked to hide his snicker as Sali struggled to escape both girls without hurting either.

"Salidar, if you hurt someone," Denise DeLuca warned. Sali's mother stood in Ashe's doorway, hands on her hips while she surveyed the wrestling match. Wynn and Dori stopped trying to hold Sali down and stood back. Sali pointed to himself and proclaimed his innocence, attempting to explain how he was getting the worst of the battle. Ashe worked harder to stifle the laugh.

"Girls, we'll drop you off on our way home," Denise offered, after telling Sali it was time to leave. "Sali still has packing to do."

Wynn flashed Sali a superior smile, flipped her nearly white ponytail in his face and followed Denise DeLuca up the stairs, Dori right behind her. "See ya later, dude. This is gonna be great." Sali waved and walked out of Ashe's bedroom.

"Yeah. Great," Ashe breathed a sigh. A boy had died, an alien race still hunted him and it was likely there were a few Cloud Chief residents who weren't excited about moving. Ashe got up, unfolded another box and went to work on his dresser.

Ashe's fears were brought home the following day. Saturday, June fourteenth had arrived and his mother left him at home to continue packing while she went to Cordell to open Cordell Feed and Seed.

Principal Billings and Larry Garnett, the werewolf English teacher, parked in the driveway and rang the doorbell. Ashe, pulling the kitchen window curtain aside, grumbled to himself when he saw who it was. He also considered pretending not to be at home. Instead, he squared his shoulders and went to lift the garage door.

"Principal Billings, Mr. Garnett, I can make coffee if you want some," Ashe offered respectfully, leading the two men inside the house.

Paul Harris, the former English teacher, had blown up the Evans and Anderson homes three years earlier. He'd led the Elemaiya to Ashe to begin with, but he'd been caught with his Elemaiya conspirators after several murders.

The Pack had delivered justice. Ashe never knew exactly what that was; all he'd known was that Mr. Harris disappeared shortly after he'd been captured and the two Elemaiya had been destroyed by Nathan Anderson, Mr. Winkler and his father.

"We wanted to get the phone number for William Winkler," Principal Billings turned his best frown on Ashe after refusing coffee. Mr. Garnett looked as if he'd like coffee, but followed Billings' lead.

"It's on the Internet," Ashe said as respectfully as he could. *Winkler Security* had a huge website.

"That's the company number. I've left three messages and he hasn't called back."

"He might be busy," Ashe suggested, thinking that if Principal Billings left a message for Winkler, the Dallas Packmaster might put off calling back as long as possible.

"I know he has a private number that will get me right to him.

Marcus is away so I can't get it from him, and Lavonna Anderson said that Aedan might have it."

Ashe didn't like lying. Preferred not to do it if possible. He did it now, facing Principal Billings. "Then Dad may have it. You'll have to ask him." Ashe did have Winkler's private cell number—he'd had it for three years.

"Call if there's trouble," Winkler said, handing a business card to Ashe before leaving Cloud Chief. "Don't give it to anyone else," Winkler grinned and slid into the company van he'd driven from Dallas. Ashe wasn't about to give the number to Billings now. Winkler's private cell number was a secret he'd kept for three years and he'd never had to use it.

"Then tell your father we'll be by after sundown. This is your fault, you know. I don't appreciate being forced to move. *Again.*" Billings and Mr. Garnett stalked out of Ashe's house; Ashe followed to lower the garage door after them. Mr. Garnett gave a half-wave to Ashe while Principal Billings wasn't looking. Ashe lifted his hand in silent reply.

"I got everything in the living room packed up; the bathrooms too, except for what we can pack in suitcases," Ashe told his mother when she came home from work carrying bags of takeout. Ashe recognized the smell immediately; he was going to miss the chicken and dumplings from Betsy's Diner.

"The movers will be here Monday night," Adele sighed. "We'll do the kitchen tonight. We'll have sandwiches or takeout until they get here."

"Mom, Principal Billings came by today with Mr. Garnett. He wanted Mr. Winkler's phone number. Mrs. Anderson told him that Dad might have it, since Marcus was away from home."

"What did he say to you, honey?" Adele, now almost a foot shorter than Ashe, looked up into her son's face.

"He said it was my fault that we have to move. But it's something I knew already," Ashe held up a hand when his mother protested. "I offered him coffee and told him he'd have to talk to Dad about the phone number. He didn't want coffee and left." Ashe didn't say what he really thought; that Billings had come by just to upset him.

"I'll have Aedan call when he wakes. Maybe we can prevent another visit from Principal narrow-minded." Ashe blinked. He'd never heard his mother speak in disrespectful terms about any of his teachers or school administrators.

Cloud Chief was too small to have an official school board, but there were three administrators— Marcus DeLuca, Jonas O'Neill and Nathan Anderson. They represented all three types of paranormals in Cloud Chief: werewolf, shapeshifter and vampire.

One of their jobs was to approve expenses as proposed by the Principal and teaching staff. Mr. Garnett had asked for—and gotten— new computers for the classrooms. Students could now write essays or research information for homework assignments in the new computer lab. It had made things much simpler for the school. Now, all of it would have to be moved.

"Mom, who's packing up the school?"

"They're sending a special truck and a crew just for that," Adele slipped an arm around Ashe's shoulders. "They're going to pack everything and haul it down. Marcus says that the community center Mr. Winkler built for residents in the new addition will be redesigned and used as our school."

"This sounds like a really big expense for Mr. Winkler."

"He'll have this land and all the houses and buildings deeded over to him," Adele said. "It probably won't cover a fraction of the cost, but it'll be something. Besides, he's a very wealthy man. If he couldn't afford it, he wouldn't have offered."

"All right." Ashe pulled the container of chicken and dumplings from the bag his mother had brought, grabbed a fork and started eating.

~

"Looks like things are under control," Aedan glanced around the kitchen later when he came upstairs. Ashe and his mother had started packing the moment they finished eating dinner. Now, half the kitchen was in boxes and labeled. "I'll get the things down from the attic before dawn," he added.

"Dad, Principal Billings came by earlier," Ashe said.

"I know. Marcus called," Aedan held up his cell. "Stop worrying about it, Son. Marcus has already spoken with Billings."

Ashe watched while his father kissed his mother lightly before heading out the kitchen door. He knew what his father, Nathan Anderson, Mr. Thompson and many of Cloud Chief's werewolves were doing; they were patrolling the perimeter, watching for another attack from the Elemaiya.

His father had his cell phone and a walkie-talkie strapped to his belt; everyone was holding their breath, waiting for the Elemaiya to return.

"We followed the mutation, my Queen, but we did not have to eliminate him. Someone from the community did so. We were unable to prevent the human death beforehand, however." Emerald bowed low before his Bright Queen.

"Humans are of no consequence. The boy still lives?"

"Yes, my Queen. And he is approaching age."

Their spy had informed them only recently that there was one remaining child born of their donated eggs. Friesianna was worried, as Hilbah hadn't handed the mother's token to her before he'd died. The Bright Queen had no information on this one, but she pretended that she did—it wouldn't do to appear weak in front of her subjects.

"Good. We know of his shapeshifting ability and that will be most useful when spying on the others. We will wait a bit, to allow things to settle. Our Dark cousins will not send another assassin until the community becomes complacent again. We will wait as well. Until the next full moon. Security will be lowest at that point and we will take him. He will learn what it is to serve me."

"Of course, my Queen." Emerald bowed low.

～

"They're going to separate, once the trucks reach I-40, just to make sure nobody follows," Winkler said. The Dallas Packmaster had arrived, bringing several others with him.

Ashe stared at the man Winkler identified as the Director for the Joint NSA and Homeland Security Department. This was the man who'd taken Director Jennings' place. Winkler called him Matt, as if he knew him well.

Winkler had known the previous Director very well, too, Ashe knew. He wasn't about to bring that up—too many secrets surrounded that information and lives depended upon his silence.

Guards were provided by Winkler Security, and most of those were werewolves, with only a few humans involved. Sali, standing beside Ashe in the Evans' kitchen, told Ashe which ones were actually humans.

"Man, I wish I had your nose," Ashe muttered, thinking how nice it would be to tell by scent exactly who or what might be standing before him. Sali grinned at the compliment.

"As soon as we determine that we're not being followed, we'll head toward the Gulf Coast. Some will go through Houston, some through San Antonio and the smaller trucks will break off at Waco and go through Victoria. They'll come into Winkler Estates on three different days. Take what you need to rough it until your belongings arrive in the trucks." Winkler was addressing at least one representative from each family inside the Evans' kitchen.

"Is everyone ready?" Marcus asked. "Are your bags packed into vehicles? Remember the assigned route and what to watch for?" He gazed around the room at the nodding heads and verbal assents. "Good. Get in contact with Mr. Winkler's team or me if you run into problems."

"I know some of you are stopping in Dallas or Amarillo before going on," Winkler nodded to the DeLucas, who were staying in

Dallas and at the O'Neills, who had family in Amarillo. "Make sure you're aware of your surroundings at all times and don't take unnecessary risks."

"Are we ready?" Marcus stood and pulled the keys to his van from a pocket. Everyone nodded at Marcus' question. "Good. Let's load up and drive."

"Ashe, your father will call the moment he rises and gets on the road," Adele said.

As a security precaution, Mr. Winkler had advised the community to move things up, so everyone was leaving early Monday morning. He'd informed Marcus and the two vampires the night before, creating a flurry of last minute packing. Now, everything had been loaded into huge vans, doors had been closed and locked and werewolf drivers were waiting.

Ashe still worried about his father and Nathan. Aedan's SUV was left in the garage for the two vampires to drive; everyone else was leaving. "Come on, honey." Adele slipped her hand in the crook of Ashe's arm—the others were already outside. Sali was waiting on Ashe, since the DeLucas planned to spend two days in the Dallas area before driving on to Star Cove.

"Mom, I don't remember the house we had in New Mexico," Ashe said, looking around the Cloud Chief residence for the last time. "I remember this house and the one we had here before that the best. This is where I grew up," he added.

"We'll make a new home in Texas," Adele patted her son's arm. "We will." Ashe walked out of the house with his mother.

"It took a move to convince me to get rid of the old Ford," Adele smiled sadly, as she and Ashe loaded into the new, blue Cadillac. Aedan had picked this one out for his wife and given it to her as a gift.

"Dude, call as soon as you get there. I hear the houses have been assigned already," Sali grinned, slapping the passenger side door.

"I will," Ashe grinned at Sali's excitement. Ashe had gotten a cell phone for his fifteenth birthday, as promised. Sali, whose birthday was a month later, got one as well. Now, both were hoping for cars for their sixteenth birthdays. Ashe's was the twenty-second of June and only a few days away; Sali's was the sixteenth of July.

"Drive safely, Mrs. Evans," Sali called out as Adele pulled away from their Cloud Chief home. Ashe waved before rolling up the window.

"Man, I wish we were already there," Ashe sighed, turning to watch Sali climb into Marcus' van. The van was pulling Denise DeLuca's smaller Honda behind it.

"I'm just glad Jason and Marcie were willing to come and take care of the store until it sells," Adele said. "We had some good times here, didn't we?" She gave Ashe a tremulous smile.

"Yeah. We sure did," Ashe agreed.

Ten hours later, the onboard GPS system announced they were nearing their destination. Ashe and his mother had stopped for lunch and then dinner along the way, making quick stops both times. Now, they were less than two miles away from their new home.

"Who's gonna meet us?" Ashe asked, looking all around him. They'd already traveled stretches of road where water could be seen in the distance. Ashe knew it was the waters between the barrier island and the mainland of Texas, but it was water and gulf water at that. On the map, it didn't look as if their new neighborhood was far from the gulf, but that could be misleading.

"Mr. Winkler's Second, Trajan Gibson, will meet us. You know, Trace's older brother?" Ashe's mother answered his question.

"Yeah. I like Trace," Ashe leaned back in his seat. It was nearly nine and the sun had set, leaving them in twilight. "Look, Mom, there's a sign." A lighted sign, painted brown with white lettering, read *Winkler Estates, next right*. Ashe sat up straighter in his seat. They were about to see their new home.

"That man looks like Trace," Ashe said, pointing out a man who stood outside the gated community of Star Cove. The man really did look like Trace. Nearly seven feet tall, he was leaning against a guard shack outside a wrought-iron gate. Adele drove up next to the shack and rolled down her window.

"Identification," the tall man grinned. Ashe knew he liked this man immediately. Like Trace, he moved with an easy grace that spelled martial arts training. Trace had explained to Ashe that he and his brother studied and practiced some of the fighting arts.

"Are you Trace's brother?" Adele asked, handing the tall werewolf her drivers' license.

"I am," he said. "You're the first ones here. When I open the gate, take the road to the right and go all the way to the end. The development is in a long U-shape, with houses lined up on both sides and the boat slips in the center. Yours is next to the last one on the right. If you have any problems or questions, call this number. Name's Trajan." He was grinning again as he handed a business card to Adele.

"Thank you, Trajan." Adele smiled. Trajan punched a button on a remote he held in his hand; the spiked iron gate slid back with a minimum of noise and Adele drove through.

Ashe was doing his best to make out the houses that lined a long, rectangular channel of water. Boat docks extended into the channel at regular intervals. Each home, lit by a front porch light, had a corresponding boat dock.

"Wow," Ashe breathed as he caught sight of the houses lining the street. No two were alike, which is what he expected in an addition such as this. Some were single story while others had two levels.

All of them were landscaped already, with young trees growing in the front yards of most. Built of stucco and painted in different colors, Ashe knew he'd need sunlight to get the colors correct.

His mother was looking just as Ashe was, driving slowly down the street on the right-hand side. Across the water channel, more homes lined the opposite side. Enough for all the Cloud Chief community, Ashe imagined.

"Mom," Ashe's voice held awe. The second to last house was two stories tall, with a nice front yard and flowerbeds waiting to be filled. A three-car garage also waited, while a piece of white paper fluttered on the glass storm door, protecting the blue door behind it. Adele drove into the driveway and shut off the engine.

"This is ours?" She was out of the vehicle quickly and walking toward the front door. The paper had the name Evans on it; Ashe saw that over his mother's shoulder.

"Try the door, Mom," Ashe said. Adele opened the storm door and turned the knob. The door swung inward.

"Sali, you won't believe this," Ashe was going from room to room, his cell phone at his ear, talking to Sali and examining the house at the same time. "It has a fireplace, two living rooms, a study, three bedrooms, a media room and a huge kitchen. Oh, and it has a three-car garage."

"But what does ours look like? Ashe you have to go look," Sali pleaded.

"Hold on, let me tell Mom I'm going outside." Ashe waved to his mother, who was touching granite countertops in the kitchen and opening the oven door of a huge chef's range.

Adele waved at him; she'd heard Ashe's voice. Ashe walked outside. "Dude, we're the second house from the end on the right side of the boat slips," Ashe said, walking swiftly toward the house on the end. "Here's the paper on the last house. Yep, it has DeLuca on it."

"Go inside," Sali begged. "Tell me what it looks like." Ashe walked into the house.

"Wow, dude. Kitchen is really nice. Media room, ditto, except your media room has the fireplace there. Walking down the hall, now. Four bedrooms, Sal. Big ones. Two have their own bathroom. Wait, here's a family room and a study." Ashe was outlining the rooms as quickly as he could for Sali. "And you have the extra garage, too."

"Who's on the other side?" Sali asked.

"Dude, yours is the last house on the right side. Go farther than that and you'll be in the water. Let me go see who's on the other side of us." Ashe walked out of the DeLuca home, shut the door behind him and trotted toward the house on the other side of his new home.

"Sal, you won't believe this; Dori, Lavonna and Nathan are on our other side." Ashe let the paper drop against the door and trotted to the house next to that. "The O'Neills are next to the Andersons," Ashe said, laughing. "This is incredible. I wish you were here."

"Dude, we're going to Six Flags tomorrow, and then Mom's shopping at one of the malls. We'll be there in a couple of days. Hold the fort until we get there."

"Will do," Ashe said. "I'd better go before Mom starts to worry." Ashe terminated the call and slipped the cell inside his shirt pocket. "Wow," he whispered appreciatively, looking around before trotting toward his new home.

"I've got the bags," Ashe pulled both roller bags inside the house. "Have we gotten into the garage, yet? We can pull the car in to unload the rest of the stuff."

"Let's go look," Adele smiled. "I can't wait for your father to see this." Ashe left the roller bags in the foyer while they went looking for the door leading into the garage.

"Mom, look." Ashe toed a metal door beneath his feet inside the third garage. "It's one of those tornado shelters."

"It is. Let's open it." Adele slid the door back, revealing steps that led downward. "Honey, it's huge." Adele walked downward, flipping on a light. "Ashe, there's enough room down here for a bed and a dresser," she said, looking around. Ashe walked down too, taking in the shelter.

"Dad will install a better door, but this was made for him," Ashe nodded.

"You're right. He'll put something better in, but this will do in the meantime. Mr. Winkler already has the houses alarmed; they're just turned off right now."

"Yeah."

"I wish we didn't have to sleep in sleeping bags tonight."

"It'll be fun. Our furniture will get here in a day or two."

"I know. Let's go see if anyone else has arrived."

"All right."

Adele and Ashe walked out the front door and sat on the edge of the wide front porch. "Sali's next door," Ashe grinned, jerking his head to the right. "And Nathan and Lavonna are on the other side of us. The O'Neills are after that," Ashe said.

"Isn't that Ben Billings' car?" Adele pointed at a house directly across the water channel.

"Yeah. That means he either has to swim or go all the way around to harass me," Ashe grinned. Principal Billings was getting out of his car and surveying his large, single-story house with a two-car, attached garage.

"We have a bigger garage," Adele snickered, bumping Ashe's shoulder with her own.

"He'll have garage envy," Ashe laughed. Other cars were pulling up to houses down the block. "Look, there's Mr. Dodd," Ashe said. The History teacher was pulling into a driveway about halfway down on the opposite side. Mr. Dodd's wife and two sons were climbing out of the car, looking around in wonder.

"Greta and Micah are on our side," Adele pointed out. Micah and Greta were getting out of their car about four houses down.

"Not far from the Packmaster. That's a good idea," Ashe decided. "Look—there's Dori and Lavonna." Ashe trotted out to the middle of the driveway and started waving his arms. Adele, laughing, stood up to join him.

"We're next door to each other?" Dori was out of the car and standing beside Ashe in seconds. "Where's Sali?"

"On our other side," Ashe pointed.

"At least we have a buffer in between," Dori said. "Come on. Let's go look at the house." Ashe and his mother followed Lavonna and Dori into their new home. Adele's cell rang as they walked inside.

"We're leaving now." Ashe, with his sharp hearing, listened to his father's voice on the other end.

"Be safe, honey," Adele sighed.

"We will. Have Lavonna and Dori arrived?"

"Just now. They're looking the new house over. Does Nathan want to talk to Lavonna?"

"He does." Adele handed the cell phone over.

"Nathan? The house is beautiful," Lavonna said.

"Good," Ashe heard Nathan's reply. Ashe likely had the best hearing of anyone in the community, including the werewolves. "I hope we'll be there before dawn, but I'll call if we have to stop," Nathan added.

"All right. I'll put Adele back on." Lavonna handed the phone back to Ashe's mother.

"Honey?" Adele said.

"I'm here," Aedan replied. "Just take care and use every precaution until we get there. Did you get a card from Winkler's Second?"

"I did. He said to call if there are any problems. Aedan, we really like the house."

"Good. I'll see you soon." Aedan ended the call.

"Ashe, you have to see this," Dori was hauling him toward the back of the house. A wide cedar deck lay behind Dori's new home, with plenty of space for a party or barbecue.

"Wow, Dori, ours isn't nearly this big," Ashe said, impressed.

"I love it," Dori, her blonde ponytail bobbing and green eyes sparkling, was hopping with joy, her hands clasped together. "I can't wait until Wynn gets here."

"She lives next door," Ashe grinned. Dori squealed with delight.

Dori and Ashe ended up drinking bottles of soda from a cooler while Adele and Lavonna hooked up the coffeepot Adele brought and drank coffee in Adele's new kitchen. "This is so much better than I thought it might be," Lavonna said. "And Corpus Christi isn't far away."

"Mr. Winkler says that the land the Pack will hunt on is near Gregory. The Corpus Christi Packmaster owns the land and has giving permission for the Star Cove Pack to hunt there."

"Wow. It's different, not calling it the Cloud Chief Pack, isn't it?" Ashe observed. He would have to get used to that.

"They were the White Lakes, New Mexico Pack before that," Lavonna pointed out. "We'll adapt. I think Nathan may actually buy a boat."

"There's something I hadn't considered," Adele laughed.

"Can we go to the beach tomorrow?" Dori asked. "I really want to go."

"I'll think about it. I'm hoping the moving trucks will arrive. We can make plans after that," Lavonna replied.

Sapphire stood before the Queen. He did not have comforting news. "What is it?" The Queen snapped. She was adept at reading emotions from close range. Sapphire hoped his punishment would be light for bringing unwelcome information.

"My Queen, I have had word from our paid source," he replied, cautiously testing the air about his monarch. She was in a rage already, best not to delay. "One of our spies reports that the community lies empty, now. The spy also reports that the relocation information was withheld."

Sapphire closed his eyes as he was blown backward with more force than the strongest of hurricanes. The breath left his body with a painful whoosh as he crashed into something solid and unmovable. Sapphire fell unconscious to the ground.

CHAPTER 3

"Nathan we're being followed," Aedan twisted quickly in his seat to check the headlights in the distance behind them. "And they're not professional about it. When we change lanes, they change lanes."

Nathan Anderson drove Aedan's SUV down I-35, near the Oklahoma-Texas border. "Can you tell anything about the vehicle?"

"Not yet," Aedan replied. "There's not much traffic; how about driving dark for a while?"

Nathan grinned at the suggestion, turned off the headlights and sped up. It was a game for them; go dark, speed up and when the vehicle following sped up as well, they'd wait for a dip in the road so the brake lights wouldn't be visible, pull off, conceal the SUV and wait for their tail to catch up. Then they'd come in behind their trackers to see what they might discover about them.

"There's a likely place," Aedan indicated a turnoff past the city of Ardmore. An older highway ran parallel to I-35 on the eastern side, with an exit and an overpass close by.

Nathan slowed down, got off the highway and slipped the SUV into a spot where it couldn't be seen from the highway above. They waited thirty seconds before their tail went by.

A nearly new, red Lexus raced past; Aedan made a note of the make and model as Nathan placed the SUV in gear and spun out of their hiding place, driving toward the access ramp. Leaving the lights off would prevent their newly acquired quarry from noticing that they were being followed by their former quarry.

"Think they'll slow down anytime soon?" Aedan asked as they drove onto the highway again.

"No idea. I'm going to throttle back a little, though," Nathan eased his foot off the pedal, slowing down below the speed limit. The Lexus continued to race along at the same rate, leaving the vampires behind quickly.

"I wonder when they'll learn they've passed us?" Aedan was worried and amused at the same time.

"No way to tell. I think we should choose an alternate route, though. In case they do figure things out."

"Good enough." Aedan punched the onboard GPS and searched for a new route toward their destination.

"Your dad is spending the day in Victoria. They came down using a slower route," Ashe's mother told him when he wandered into the kitchen the following morning.

"He all right?" Ashe asked, pulling the small container of orange juice from the new fridge. They'd brought OJ, sodas and bottled water packed in a cooler. A trip to get groceries was planned for later in the day.

"He and Nathan are fine. They thought they were being followed, so they found a different route. I'm sure they'll be here an hour or two after nightfall."

Ashe was gulping orange juice when his cell phone rang. Sali's picture appeared on Ashe's cell. "Dude, it's barely seven-thirty," Ashe shook his head and answered the call. It wasn't Sali.

"Ashe, this is Winkler," the voice on the other end said. "Wynn has been kidnapped in Amarillo and we need your help."

"Uh," Ashe looked up at his mother, who'd heard the conversation. Her hearing was sharp, just not as sharp as Aedan's or Ashe's.

"How? When?" Adele hurried to Ashe's side.

"Sometime last night," Winkler replied. He'd heard Adele's voice and responded to her question. "They grabbed Wynn's cousin Andrea too, but Andrea was found later at a convenience store, tied up in the back of an old car. She'd been drugged and was still groggy but okay. There wasn't any trace found of Wynn. If I'm right about this, I think Wynn was the target all along. Ashe, I need what you can do to get her back. The O'Neills are about to go crazy and we have to hurry or Wynn might not make it back."

"This is my son, Mr. Winkler," Adele wiped tears away.

"I know, Mrs. Evans. I'll do my best to see he's safe."

"Where does he need to go?" Adele asked.

"We're on my private jet, twenty minutes away from Corpus Christi Airport. Can you get Ashe there as quickly as possible? We're flying straight to Amarillo from there."

"I will." Adele closed the phone while another tear slipped down a cheek. "Honey, get your suitcase," she told Ashe.

"I'll be okay, Mom," Ashe dragged his suitcase toward the garage minutes later. He hadn't unpacked yet, so he'd dressed quickly, brushed his teeth and ran a comb through his hair before hauling the bag from his new bedroom and loading it into the trunk of the Cadillac.

"Your father and Nathan may come if you're gone very long," Adele said, climbing into the car and pulling it out of the garage. Ashe, who sat beside her, shivered. Wynn was in trouble and he itched to get to Amarillo.

"Mom, why would somebody in Amarillo snatch Wynn?" His blue eyes searched his mother's face for clues. "How would they know she was even there?"

"Honey, you have to consider what she is," Adele said. "And somebody could have let it slip, including her cousin. No more questions. See if you can load directions to the Corpus Christi Airport into that gadget."

Ashe had the GPS navigation system programmed after only a minute or two and they were on their way.

"Wow, this is Winkler's jet?" Ashe was impressed at the size of the private aircraft Winkler apparently owned. Winkler walked down the steps of the jet as soon as Ashe and his mother pulled onto the strip where the private planes landed.

"Go, honey. An extra minute could save Wynn's life," his mother hugged him before urging him toward Winkler, who now waited at the bottom of the jet's steps.

"Mom, be careful. Call me when Dad gets in," he waved behind him and loped toward the jet, dragging his rolling suitcase behind him.

"I'll take this," Winkler grabbed Ashe's bag. "Go on up, I'll be right behind you," Winkler instructed. Ashe ran up the steps and stared when he stepped onto the jet. Marcus, Marco, Sali and six other werewolves waited. Ashe was shocked by how many Dallas Packmembers Winkler was bringing with him. It made him wonder how serious the situation really was.

"Dude," Sali hissed when Ashe settled into the comfortable seat beside him and fastened his seat belt, "Winkler thinks something weird is going on."

"You're almost too purty to put out in the scrub," the man pawed at Wynn, who was too terrified to squeak. She'd been snatched, drugged and hauled off to some windowless hole.

Wynn lay on a concrete slab floor, her wrists and ankles cuffed and chained to the cinderblock walls. Her nearly white hair was matted around her face and she'd been sick twice already. Two men had grumbled about cleaning up the mess. This one, shaggy-haired and foul-breathed, was pawing at her after he left a tray of food on the floor, just outside her reach.

"None of that," a voice commanded from the door. "Place the tray closer and get away. We don't want her weak and wasted. The boss wants a good hunt out of this; his client is paying top dollar."

Wynn's head jerked up at the other man's words, her sky-blue eyes searching for some way to identify him. The sun shone behind the man, placing him in shadow; she couldn't see his face.

He wasn't close enough for her to scent either, in her present state; the manacles on her wrists and ankles prevented her from shifting. If she did shift, the thick steel could break bones. That would leave her completely helpless. More than she was already, she amended mentally.

Did her parents have the slightest idea where she was? What had they done with Andrea? Wynn and her cousin had been snatched while walking to a convenience store for a soft drink.

"What did you do with my cousin?" Wynn whispered. Her throat was dry; they hadn't brought anything to drink until now.

"Don't you worry your purty head about your cousin. She's not your concern." Foul-breath was grinning at her. Wynn knew he was werewolf, but this was a kind of werewolf she'd never met; this one was cruel and callous.

"Get out," the man in the doorway commanded. Foul breath moved to obey.

"I'll be back to pick up the tray," he grinned. Wynn wanted to gag.

"Ashe, I'll be blunt," Winkler settled into the seat across the aisle. At first, he'd sat closer to the front, talking with Marcus and two other werewolves. Now he was sitting beside Ashe. "There's a game preserve south of Amarillo. A wealthy werewolf who has been a thorn in the Grand Master's side for a long time owns it. He isn't an official Packmaster, but he runs his own Pack. Rumor has it that any wolf that's gone afoul of the law, human and otherwise, runs straight to him."

Ashe stared at Winkler. Winkler was giving him information? That was unheard of. And it was Pack business, too, which made it all the more surprising.

"His name is Obediah Tanner and the game preserve is his cover. During the day, tourists go through the public portions of his ranch, snapping pictures of exotic animals and feeding the zebras and giraffes. What he secretly does on certain nights, though, is bring hunters in to a closed off section of his ranch. Those hunters pay a great deal of money to hunt things. Not just animals, but humans and shapeshifters, too, if he can get them. We haven't been able to prove anything up to this point; he's very clever and careful. I figure there are plenty of stuffed tigers and elephants in hunters' game rooms because of Obediah Tanner. The rarer the animal, the bigger the payday for Tanner. That means that Wynn would be the rarest of the rare, Ashe. I don't know that there's another living unicorn right now."

Ashe was stunned. Sali, who'd heard it before, still growled at Ashe's side. "Somebody's paying to kill Wynn?" Ashe whispered.

"I think so, as does the Grand Master. He's sending most of the Lubbock Pack in that direction, in case we need backup."

"Isn't there a Pack in Amarillo?" Ashe asked, still feeling numb.

"There is," Winkler nodded, his dark eyes troubled at the admission. "But we fear there may be a leak somewhere within that Pack. That's why I'm going instead of allowing the local Packs to handle this. Weldon knows the Packmaster from Lubbock very well and trusts him. This will be a fast hit, Ashe. We figure they won't hold Wynn very long; it's too dangerous. People will be looking for her. That's where you come in. You'll have to go in as mist. Whatever you do, don't let any of them see you. The fewer who know of that talent, the safer you'll remain. Got it?"

"Yeah." Ashe sat back in his seat, blinking. Wynn's life—if she was still alive—might lie in his hands.

"Good to see you, buddy," Marco sat in the row of seats in front of Winkler and reached back to slap Ashe's knee. Ashe managed a smile for Marco. They hadn't seen much of Sali's older brother since he'd gone off to college and started working for Winkler. Sali said that Trajan had been teaching Marco Karate and Jiu Jitsu.

"Ashe, we'll get this done." Winkler stood, patted Ashe's shoulder and walked toward the front of the jet.

"We've got some good wolves with us," Marco took over Winkler's vacated seat. "Don't worry; it'll be as safe as we can make it."

"This doesn't sound like a quick hit, this looks like a war," Ashe whispered to Sali as they stood on the private airport tarmac in Amarillo. Ashe was watching as sturdy, sealed crates and plastic tubs were unloaded from the belly of the jet. "Those have to be weapons, dude," Ashe hissed.

Sali's eyes turned toward Ashe. "They only let me come since you were coming," Sali said. "Dad wanted to leave me behind anyway."

"Sal, don't worry about it. You're here, now. We'll get Wynn back. They just need to get me somewhere near that game preserve." Ashe clenched his fists.

"Mom, what's happening?" Dori was in tears. Lavonna and Adele had spent the day trying to calm Dori down. Adele wondered if they shouldn't ask for a physician. At times, Dori turned to ocelot and hurled herself at a wall inside her bedroom, yowling and spitting. At other times, Dori was human and weeping. Lavonna almost wished that Denise DeLuca hadn't called. Now, Ashe was in the Texas panhandle, helping the others look for Wynn.

"Honey, Denise promised to keep us updated, but so far there hasn't been any news." It was late afternoon and Dori was terrified.

"We can't expect things to happen this quickly; they have to locate Wynn first," Adele soothed. "But they'll find her. Mr. Winkler is in the security business, honey. If anybody has the talent and resources available, he does."

"But they don't have Daddy and Mr. Evans with them," Dori wept. "Don't they need to be there?"

"Hon, Mr. Winkler may have other resources," Lavonna hugged her daughter close and brushed damp bangs back.

~

"I know you want to go now, but we're waiting for sundown," Winkler knelt beside Ashe's chair. Ashe, Sali and Marco were inside a hotel room. Mr. Winkler had rented half the hotel, in Ashe's estimation. Marco's room was next door, but his and Marcus DeLuca's room connected with that of Sali and Ashe.

"In the meantime," Winkler added, "Try to rest up. You'll need your strength." He stood and walked through the connecting door, closing it behind him. Ashe heard Winkler say something to Marcus DeLuca before they walked out of the adjoining room.

"The waiting is awful," Sali muttered.

"We have to get everybody together," Marco attempted to calm Sali's restless pacing. He'd been fretting like a caged wolf from the moment they'd settled into the hotel.

Ashe had unpacked a few things—mostly toiletries and his toothbrush, before settling into the chair to think. He wanted a computer. He wanted a map to the game preserve. He wanted anything except the waiting.

He'd called his mother when the jet landed, but kept the conversation short. Ashe didn't want to give her more reason to worry than she had already, and sundown was still two hours away.

"Ashe." Marcus was back with a soft drink and a folded map. Exactly what Ashe wanted. The map was one of those printed brochures the tourists received when they visited the park portion of the reserve, but he unfolded it and laid it on one of the beds anyway. Sali and Marco were looking, just as he was.

"This area here, on the southeast side and away from the tourist park, is where we think the hunts take place," Marcus pointed out a blank spot on the map. "That doesn't mean that Wynn is there now.

We figure they keep the animals and others caged somewhere, and release them from an underground location. That's why we can't get anything on satellite during the day. They've caught movement at night, but signals are scrambled somehow after sundown. We want to get to that system, too, if we can, and take it out or disable it."

"You were in the military, weren't you, Mr. DeLuca?" Ashe looked at Marcus.

"Yeah. I was. But not many know that," Marcus tapped the map to get everybody's attention again. "We're going in on the southwestern edge, here," he pointed to a spot near Arney, Texas. "We can move in there without drawing too much attention. Ashe, Winkler will give you an update when we get there. And we'll have backup, too, if all goes well."

"Okay." Ashe nodded.

"Ashe, we expect you to be cautious. Don't risk your life. If I don't bring you home in one piece, I don't want to be the one to tell Aedan."

"Yeah. I wouldn't want to tell him, either."

"You know how much that girl is worth?" Fritz grinned at Cade. "Lester says that congressman paid five mil."

"Congressman, huh? Does he know we're wanted men?" Cade grinned and spat on the ground.

"Word from Tanner is that Congressman Howard might be a wanted man if certain things leak out, if you get my drift," Fritz chuckled.

"So, Tanner's looking to make a little extra money, going the blackmail route?"

"Could be," Fritz agreed. "And that could be worth more than five mil, when all's said and done."

"Better for us. That hacienda in Mexico is lookin' awful good."

"We just need to make sure Tanner knows how much he owes us."

"We'll make sure of it," Cade said, pulling a knife from the sheath at his belt to clean his fingernails.

~

"It's our God given right to bear arms and hunt any animal." Congressman Jack Howard looked quite distinguished—from the threads of gray at the temples of his carefully groomed dark hair to the designer jeans, cowboy shirt and snakeskin boots he wore. He smiled and blew smoke from the expensive Cuban cigar Obediah Tanner offered.

He and Tanner stood inside Tanner's trophy room, which was elaborately decorated with various stuffed heads. In some cases, the entire, taxidermic animal adorned the spacious room. A very rare white buffalo, mounted on a stand, took up the center of Obediah's favorite room. Obediah often used the buffalo's short horns to hang his Stetsons.

"And you're tellin' me this girl is a unicorn? I thought those were myth." Jack Howard blew a plume of smoke toward the ceiling.

"You'll know the truth of it when her head hangs in your lodge," Tanner said, lifting a glass of whiskey to his lips. Tanner was close to six feet tall, with brown hair going a bit gray and a thick mustache that hid part of a scar running from his left eye down to the chin.

Werewolves didn't scar unless the injury was quite severe. Tanner never forgot who'd given him that scar. He'd fought a Texas Ranger-turned vampire a century and a half earlier, near what was now the Texas-Mexican border. Tanner would have liked to return the favor, but he'd been near death when dawn came and the vampire had been forced to seek shelter from the sun.

"I'm looking forward to this," Congressman Howard drained his glass of whiskey. "I haven't been hunting on horseback for a while."

"We're gonna have a great time," Tanner slapped the congressman on the back.

~

Sali was so nervous, Ashe didn't think he was going to get through the night without having a mental event of some sort. "Sali, you'll go straight back to the hotel if you can't stop fretting," Marcus warned.

Sali was confined to a small space between vans in the near-desert conditions of the Texas panhandle. Marco had already grabbed Sali once when he attempted to escape the confining space. Sali had growled viciously at his brother. Ashe, watching the entire incident from nearby, was worried more about Sali than about himself.

Ashe squinted as he scanned the horizon—the sun was slipping down until only a thin, bright crescent hovered in the west. Marcus and Winkler were waiting on someone else to come, and Ashe guessed that twilight was the time for that. Twenty minutes past sundown, Ashe discovered what they were waiting on—two vampires and the Lubbock Pack.

Vans and trucks pulled up nearby, amid sounds of growling engines and swirls of dry dust. Twenty-six werewolves exited vehicles quickly. The two vampires climbed from an SUV and immediately strode in Winkler's direction.

Ashe had never seen these vampires before, but his experience with vampires was quite limited. His father, Nathan Anderson and Old Harold, who'd died three years earlier, were the vampires with whom he was most familiar. After that came Radomir, the vampire Enforcer the Council had sent to investigate Old Harold's death.

One of these new vampires was at least six-six, with pale-blond hair, cut short and spiked. The other was shorter, around five-ten or so, with dark-brown hair. The taller one looked as if he'd seen a lot of life. The other seemed younger and less careworn, somehow.

After a brief conversation with Winkler, the vampires stood calmly while preparations were made all around them. The Lubbock werewolves were handed rifles and other weapons, and then went through a routine check with Winkler and Marcus while Ashe watched in fascination.

"This is Dalroy," Winkler walked up to Ashe and introduced the taller vampire. "And this is Rhett," he nodded to the shorter one. "Dalroy has some history with Mr. Tanner, I understand."

"Bad business," Dalroy nodded. Ashe drew in a breath. This one had to be from the old west; he could tell by the accent. "You're one of the few," he nodded to Ashe.

"The few?" Sali, who'd stopped pacing to stand beside Ashe, couldn't help himself.

"There are only a handful of children approved by the Council," Dalroy explained. "Maybe twenty or so. All born to shapeshifter-vampire parents." Ashe figured he was a part of a very unusual and risky experiment—one approved by the most powerful among the vampire race. It made him wonder if the Council was still allowing vampires to have children.

"It's time," Winkler announced. "Ashe, we want you to go in and see what you can find as mist. The others here are going to come in from the south and take down Tanner's Pack. Not all of Tanner's bunch will be going to the hunt. It's their job to make sure the quarry doesn't escape. Tanner's Pack will be spreading out along the fence and when they get wind of us, they'll be going over or through it if we don't stop them quick."

"Mr. Winkler, it may be easier to find things if I go in as the bat first," Ashe suggested, watching as armed werewolves loaded into several vans, ready to drive to the southern edge of the preserve. "I can detect anything by echolocation," Ashe went on. "I'll change to mist if I find what I'm looking for."

"Boy, can you send the message back if you do? We can go in if we know where to go," Marcus growled. Normally, Marcus wasn't so abrupt. It made Ashe wonder what Marcus had done for the military.

"Yeah. I'll do what I can, Mr. DeLuca," Ashe nodded. "Sali, will you pick up my clothes?" Ashe turned to his best friend. Sali nodded. Ashe turned to bumblebee bat and fluttered for a moment before Marcus' nose.

"I'll be damned," Dalroy whispered. Ashe heard the vampire clearly, as he turned and flew toward the spot Marcus had shown him on the map.

At first, Ashe didn't get anything—he received echoes off a few scattered buildings and fences, nothing more. Traveling farther over the open space of the preserve, his echoes brought back evidence of a few insects and small animals—rabbits and other desert creatures.

Abruptly, two men and horses appeared, their size and shape bouncing back to him quickly. They were close. Ashe kept sending signals and flew swiftly in that direction. More humans on horses emerged right behind the first two. Ashe turned to mist in a blink, blazing toward the horses.

Winkler, there are horses and riders, about half a mile east, Ashe sent. Ashe flew over at least ten men who were mounted. Each man had a rifle with him. Ashe almost froze. They were going to hunt Wynn. They were going to *kill* Wynn. *They have rifles!* Ashe shouted mentally. Ashe didn't know what else to do except follow as the riders took off eastward.

"Watch toward the northeast," one of the riders said, the horse loping easily beneath him, his gait eating up the desert beneath flying hooves. His rifle was pointed upward as he spoke to another rider, who also had his gun at the ready. The others had rifles in scabbards on saddles, but all were ready to arm themselves if needed.

Winkler, Ashe sent, *a man with a bushy mustache said to watch to the northeast.* Ashe slowed, following along overhead as the horses loped along.

"There!" A man shouted beneath Ashe's mist. "I saw a flash of white!" Ashe was suddenly terrified. More than anything he wished Wynn had mindspeech. That would make things so easy. Instead, he did what he could.

Run, Wynn! Run! I'll try to find you! Ashe flew higher, hoping to capture a glimpse of a racing unicorn.

They'd hit her with whips to make her change, and one had zapped her with a cattle prod to get her to run out of the tunnel. Now, Wynn thought she heard Ashe's voice in her mind. He'd told her to run.

Her flanks burning, Wynn ran as fast as she could, ears laid back, gold horn pointed forward, mane and tail flying as her hooves struck the ground as fast as she could make them go. She'd have been weeping as she ran if she were in human shape. The moon was waning but still shone upon Wynn, illuminating her shining white coat. It would make her an easy target.

I see her! Ashe sent. *But their horses are running faster, now. They've sighted her. I have to help!* Ashe cut off the communication, diving down toward Wynn, who was losing ground against larger, faster horses. She wasn't used to running for her life, Ashe knew.

Ashe swooped behind the man who was lowering his rifle, ready to take a shot as his horse ran beneath him. Turning the gun to mist, Ashe snatched it away, causing the man to shout and curse. Dropping the rifle behind him, where it hit the dry soil with a thunk, Ashe watched in dismay as one of the other riders tossed his rifle to the hunter without missing a stride. This one had paid to bring Wynn down. Ashe was going to take him down instead.

Ashe flew forward quickly, gathering the man inside his mist. The man screamed as Ashe dumped him in the dirt, his body rolling across sandy soil and desert scrub before coming to a stop in a cloud of dust. The hunter, unhurt, rose, grabbed his rifle and aimed indiscriminately. Several shots rang out. While the bullets flew harmlessly through Ashe's mist, one of the men racing away dropped off his horse and lay unmoving amid a stand of mesquite.

Choosing to ignore the one who'd been shot, Ashe went after the man with the bushy mustache; his rifle was now aimed at Wynn. Her unicorn's shining white coat could be seen clearly; her mane and tail were flying, her pursuers catching up.

Ashe misted toward the one taking aim as he got a shot off. Wynn fell. Frightened and infuriated, Ashe misted the gun from the man's hands and before he thought, forced his hands to materialize as he hit the man across the face with the rifle butt.

CHAPTER 4

They've hit Wynn! Ashe shouted mentally, blazing toward the white unicorn that was struggling to rise. A bloody smear stood out on her right shoulder. Ashe didn't take time to think, he gathered her inside his mist. The ones with rifles raised behind him were shouting and firing as they pulled their horses to a stop; they'd all seen the unicorn disappear.

Get them! Ashe said to whoever was listening. *I've got Wynn, she's been hit,* he repeated. Rising high overhead, Ashe watched as a storm hit the men below. Dalroy and Rhett had arrived, prepared to take down the hunters.

Ashe had never seen vampires work like this—a whirlwind of dust was raised as men were pulled from saddles and knocked unconscious. Horses galloped away, frightened by the chaos. Ashe knew he didn't have time to worry about any of that; he had to get help for Wynn. He raced toward the vans on the western side of the game preserve.

"Ashe!" Sali was shouting and struggling against Marco's grip while Marco held his younger brother back. Marcus took Wynn from Ashe, who'd reappeared, Wynn in human form wrapped in his arms.

"It's just a shoulder wound," Marcus reassured Sali, who was trembling after Marco released him. Marco grabbed Ashe's clothing and handed it to him while Wynn was laid gently in the back of a van.

"Don't worry, we'll take care of this," werewolf David Lang had come, armed with medical supplies. Wynn was weeping and shivering while Marcus covered her with a blanket and David gave an injection.

"It'll be better if she's calm," he said to Sali, who was struggling in his brother's grip again as he tried to reach Wynn.

"Wynn, it's all right," Sali called, holding out a hand toward her. "We've got you, it'll be all right." Another of the werewolves who stayed behind was calling Wynn's father, Jonas O'Neill, on a cell phone.

"We've got her. She's wounded but it's superficial, I think. Dr. Lang is tending her now." Ashe was still watching David Lang work on Wynn as he pulled his athletic shoes on.

"She'll be all right," Marcus placed a hand on Ashe's shoulder. "How was the fight going when you left?"

"Good, I think," Ashe said absently as he watched Dr. Lang slip an IV into Wynn's hand. Someone else was there, holding up the bag of IV fluid while the wound was cleaned and bandaged.

Wynn, lying in the back of the van while she received treatment, moaned softly now and then, but Ashe felt sure that Dr. Lang had given her something for pain already.

"A bad graze and some superficial wounds on her hips," Dr. Lang said as Ashe crowded close to Sali behind the van.

"I thought you were a paramedic," Ashe said.

"I work as a paramedic, Son. I'm more than a hundred years old. Got my medical license more than fifty years ago. I know what I'm doing. Now, what about you? Got the shakes?"

Ashe was a little shaky but didn't want to admit it. "I'll be okay," he said, watching Sali crawl into the van beside Wynn.

"Sali?" Wynn's voice was weak.

"Wynn, we'll take care of you, I promise," Sali whispered. Ashe heard it clearly. He also saw Wynn grip Sali's hand. Ashe knew he shouldn't have been shocked to see Sali lift the hand and kiss it. An unexpected wave of jealousy hit Ashe, and he struggled with that as he watched Sali comfort Wynn.

"If you need something, even to sleep, let Winkler or me know," Dr. Lang said, patting Ashe's shoulder and bringing his attention back to the doctor. "That was good work, young man."

Ashe nodded and walked to the back of the van, where Sali still held Wynn's hand. "You okay, Wynn?" he asked hoarsely. He'd been frightened out of his wits when the gun had cracked and Wynn had fallen. Now he wanted to be the one holding Wynn's hand.

"I'll be okay," Wynn sighed and closed her eyes.

"Look what we have here," Marcus grinned. Ashe whirled to see Winkler, his six werewolves and the two vampires bringing nine of the ten men out of the game preserve. All were handcuffed in silver chains. One of the men, the one with the bushy mustache, bore wounds across his face where Ashe had hit him. Ashe worried that the man who'd been shot now lay dead in the desert. He shuddered.

"Ashe, what can you tell me about these men?" Winkler asked.

"He's the one who shot Wynn," Ashe pointed to the one with the mustache, "but that was after I took that one's rifle away; he was going to shoot Wynn first," Ashe nodded at the other man.

"Congressman Howard, what do you have to say to that?" Winkler grinned. Ashe gaped. *Congressman* Howard? He knew that name, all right.

"Your son is fine and we have the culprits in custody. The rest of the Lubbock Pack is scouring the compound. Matt Michaels is on his way, and he'll shut the preserve down as soon as he gets here. They'll go over it with a fine toothed comb for evidence, too," Winkler informed Aedan over the phone.

"Wynn was grazed by a rifle bullet, but thanks to Ashe's quick thinking, it wasn't any worse than that. What we haven't figured out is what to do with the esteemed congressman."

"He needs to rot in jail," Aedan hissed. Ashe, who sat on a chair inside Winkler's hotel room, listened to his father on the other end of the call.

"I think he deserves worse. Who knows who or what he's killed before? Dalroy and Rhett are attempting to get information from Tanner. What we learn may not be comforting by any stretch," Winkler observed.

"Let me talk to Ashe if he's there," Aedan sighed.

"He's here," Winkler said and handed the phone to Ashe.

"Dad?" Ashe didn't know what his father was going to say or do.

"Son, are you all right? Did they hurt you in any way?"

"They didn't have a chance. I do want to talk to you when I get home, though."

"About what?"

"About how I came out of my mist partially, to hit that man in the face. The one who shot Wynn," Ashe clarified.

"Son, if my heart were beating, it would have stopped just then. You became partially corporeal?"

"My hands," Ashe admitted sheepishly. "I wasn't thinking clearly, Dad. All I saw was the man shooting and Wynn falling. I was so mad I just did it."

"I'm not quibbling over the results of your actions, but that might have placed your life in just as much danger as Wynn's. Did they see your face?"

"Not until Winkler and the others brought them in. I pointed out which ones were the shooters."

Aedan Evans uttered a word Ashe didn't hear often. "Son, I know you aren't used to this sort of thing, but tell Mr. Winkler, if he's not listening in right now, to have those vampires place compulsion. I don't want any of those involved remembering what you look like or how you did what you did."

"I'll make sure it's done," Winkler said. He was listening.

"Good. I don't want my boy made more of a target than he is already."

"I understand," Winkler replied.

"Dad, tell Mom I'm okay," Ashe said.

"He'll be home in a day or two," Winkler promised. "We'll keep you apprised." Ashe handed the cell back to Winkler, who terminated the call. "You did very well, Ashe," Winkler smiled. "Don't let a bunch of old wolves and vamps worry you too much. Why don't you go see how Sali and Wynn are doing?"

"Okay." Ashe rose and walked out of Winkler's hotel room.

~

"Son, we removed the memory that you did anything at all. From everybody except Marcus, Winkler and Marco," Dalroy was coming out of Wynn's room as Ashe walked up. "I know that's a disservice to you, but the Grand Master, Winkler and your father want it that way. You'll be the unsung hero, I'm sorry to say."

Dalroy gave Ashe's shoulder a comforting pat. Rhett, the dark-haired vampire, nodded to Ashe and followed when Dalroy moved away. Ashe muttered the same word his father had used earlier.

"Ashe?" Wynn said sleepily as Ashe made his way into her hotel room. Dr. Lang was there and dumping an empty syringe into a medical waste bag before stuffing it inside his med kit.

"You okay, Wynn?"

"She's good. Mr. Winkler got there just in time," Sali said, his eyes slightly unfocused. Ashe breathed a troubled sigh. Not even Sali was allowed to remember.

"Good to see you again, Son," Dr. Lang said, rising to leave. "Don't keep her awake too long, young wolf," he told Sali.

"I won't," Sali grinned. The doctor walked out of the room.

"Thank goodness," Sharon O'Neill rushed into the room, Jonas right behind her. "Wynnie, baby, are you all right?"

"Yeah." Wynn's voice was weak. "Mr. Winkler saved me." Ashe sighed, jerked his head at Sali and headed for the door.

~

"Ashe, I see this has upset you. But you have to know that Wynn might not be alive if you hadn't been there," Winkler held Ashe back while everyone else exited the jet the following evening. They'd arrived in Corpus Christi just before sunset.

"Yeah? I hear you got all the credit," Ashe muttered, moving away from Winkler's grip on his shoulder. Ashe climbed down the steps of the jet without another word.

⁓

"I'm fine, Mom. Stop fussing," Ashe tried to fend his mother off. She'd come to get him; his father hadn't been awake when the jet landed.

"Your father wants to talk to you when you get home," Adele said. "Ashe, this is for your protection, honey."

"Yeah. I keep hearing that word." Ashe watched as Wynn, Sharon and Jonas were loaded into the Anderson's car. Dori had rushed to hug Wynn the moment she'd gotten off the jet. Denise had come to pick up Sali, Marcus and Marco, who would spend a few days with his parents before going back to Dallas. Ashe sighed as he watched them drive away.

"Ashe, you did a good thing," his mother said, touching his arm. "Wynn is alive because of that. Be happy that you could help."

"Mom, she doesn't know who saved her. She thinks Winkler did it. And Sali's all over her, now."

"Is that what this is about?" Adele stared at her son. "I guess it had to happen sometime. Get in the car. Your father is waiting, I'm sure."

⁓

Broad-shouldered and dark-haired, the Grand Master stared at one of the captives from Tanner's wildlife preserve. Matthew Michaels, Director of the Joint NSA and Homeland Security Department, had asked the Grand Master to come while they questioned this particular captive.

"He says his name is Wildrif, no last name," Matt told the Grand Master quietly. Weldon Harper, Grand Master of Werewolves, looked

Wildrif over. He didn't seem like much. Certainly not a werewolf; he could tell immediately by the scent.

Wildrif sat in a steel chair set against a steel desk, his head bowed beneath a spotlight, the bright light shining on hair that could have been blond or brown. It hung long and unkempt about his face. Nothing was remarkable about his features, except the eyes.

"The Grand Master," Wildrif said, lifting his head and staring at Weldon Harper.

"How do you know that?" Weldon growled low.

"I'm a Foreseer," Wildrif's eyes were strange as he turned them to the werewolf. Weldon would have described them as crazy eyes. One was brown, the other pale blue. "I might have been useful, but my kind threw me out anyway. They don't keep the quarter bloods, you know."

Weldon had to work to keep from drawing an audible breath. "They threw you out," he nodded instead. He'd heard this before. Once.

"Yeah. No use for us quarters," Wildrif's giggle was tinged with insanity. "We're not immortal. The halves are, but it doesn't pass to the stinking quarters. But they'd better watch out," he giggled again.

"Why should they watch out?" Weldon asked, puzzled.

"*Ir'Indicti*. He's here." Wildrif laughed wildly and at length. Even a tranquilizer failed to calm him down.

"That's all he said? Ear-in-dik-tee?" Winkler pronounced the word phonetically back to the Grand Master. He'd phoned Weldon while pacing inside his private study.

"He spilled all kinds of information before that," Weldon grumped. "Told Matt that he could see the future for Tanner. That's one of the reasons Tanner was always ready for inspections and raids; Wildrif informed him. He didn't see us this time, though. I think it's tied up in that word he used. What do you make of it?"

"I'm not about to track the Bright Ones down a second time," Winkler said. "It'll just force them to follow me and hope it leads to the boy. Aedan placed compulsion on those two who came to Cloud Chief before, and they were blank-eyed when we set them outside the boundary and told them to get lost. Someone's leaking information again; I'd bet money on it. As to what Wildrif said, I'm not sure about that. It may or may not be tied up with Ashe. I'm not going to trouble him with this—he's upset with us at the moment, and understandably so. That poor girl would be dead if we hadn't taken him along, and Tanner would have skated, I think."

"Matt's working on what to do with Jack Howard and his two bodyguards," Weldon touched on a different subject.

"What do you think he'll do?"

"No idea, but I saw two of his vampire operatives walk in when I walked out of their office in Santa Fe."

"I can't wait to hear the story," Winkler chuckled dryly.

"We can't have a congressman just up and disappear," Weldon agreed.

"What about Tanner and his bunch?"

"Matt turned them over to me. They'll be taken care of tonight. The official story is they were caught smuggling illegal animals, which is true—we found all sorts of creatures on that preserve. They're also going to have footage of the piles of drugs found on the preserve that were imported from Mexico and South America. The story Matt will release is that Tanner and his bunch have escaped to Mexico and points south. There'll be a halfhearted search and that's it. No need to waste time or money on it. Matt's putting Wildrif in a mental hospital for treatment. I think he's as crazy as they come."

"I understand," Winkler agreed.

"If you get any information on the Ir'Indicti thing, I expect to be informed."

"I'll let you know." Winkler ended the call.

～

"I realize this feels like a punch in the face," Aedan sat behind his desk and gazed at Ashe. Ashe had followed his father into his father's new study, which was upstairs and overlooked the boat slip between the two rows of houses.

Ashe folded arms across his chest and refused to say anything. "Son," Aedan went on, "this is something you have to learn to live with. You have something special and you're hunted because of it. I have no idea what those creatures would do to you if they find you, but I don't believe it's anything good. This has to remain a secret. You have no idea how much compulsion Nathan and I placed in the beginning, to make the community forget. Now only Marcus, Denise and the Rocklins know, and that's at the Grand Master's discretion. If he told Winkler tomorrow that Marcus and his Second don't need to know, then we'd have to remove those memories as well."

"Marcus was in the military," Ashe turned his head, refusing to look at his father. Everything was turning sour. In the books that lined shelves inside Ashe's new bedroom, the hero might be allowed a bit of satisfaction in a job well done and executed almost flawlessly, in order to save the girl.

This time, the girl thought someone else had saved her and Ashe couldn't talk to his best friend about what bothered him. Not only did Sali not remember that Ashe had saved Wynn, he didn't know any longer that Ashe could turn to mist or mindspeak. Ashe might as well be on a tiny, forgotten island in the ocean somewhere. He couldn't even talk to the seagulls on his imaginary island. Too many sharp ears surrounded him.

"I know Marcus was in the military. And I know you're smart enough to figure that out. Don't let that secret get away, Ashe. You're getting a little taste of what it's like to be vampire. We've kept secrets from the moment we woke as vampires."

"And how long ago was that, Dad?" Ashe stood and walked to the window overlooking the boat channel below. "You won't tell me, will you? I don't need to know. I know I can mist and haul an almost-grown unicorn filly out of harm's way, but I sure can't know how old my dad is. Can I? Are we done with the talk, Dad? Are we?" Ashe, angrier than he'd ever been, snapped at his father.

"Son, I won't place compulsion, because that would destroy our trust. You have to stop this, and stop it now. As of this moment, I'm grounding you until your birthday on Sunday. Sali doesn't come over, I take your cell phone and you're confined to the house and the yard."

Aedan's eyes were red and Ashe had glimpsed the tips of sharp fangs. His father was almost as angry as Ashe. Right then, Ashe didn't care. Pulling the cell phone from his pocket, he slapped it onto his father's desk and stalked out.

～

"I'm grounding him for three days, until his birthday," Aedan sighed. He'd found Adele in the kitchen later, attempting to explain how things hadn't gone very well when he'd talked to Ashe. Ashe's bedroom door had slammed shortly after he'd left his father's office. "I hope that's enough time for him to cool off and see sense."

"This is awful. He feels something for Wynn, I think, and now she not only thinks somebody else got her out of that place, but Sali stepped right in and is getting Wynn's attention."

Adele didn't often disagree with Aedan over Ashe's punishments, but she understood a little of what her son was feeling right then. "It would be different if Sharon's egg had been used. We know now that wasn't the case. Ashe can date Wynn if he wants."

"Adele," Aedan rubbed the back of his neck uncomfortably, "That's not the only thing we have to be concerned about. We have to impress upon that child that he is vulnerable. He needs the protection the community can provide. And he can mist faster than anything I've ever heard of. The Council's misters take a couple of minutes to do it, so it's a weapon of stealth, mostly. They're always busy. The last time I saw Henri and Gervais they looked exhausted, and vampires don't normally get that way. Same with the mindspeakers. Anthony, Robert and Albert are constantly in demand."

"Will he be able to go to college? Do the things he might want to do with his life? Will he?" That question had bothered Adele of late. Was destiny herding her child into a life of complete concealment?

At least she could open a business and run it as human, without fear that anyone would hunt her for the most part. Ashe deserved that anonymity. He deserved the right to go to college and work at something he enjoyed instead of slinking in the shadows. Even vampires appeared human when they walked among mortals.

"I don't know. Certainly he can take courses online."

"But that's not the same. I loved going to college, Aedan. I had friends among the humans and we had fun. Ashe won't get that, will he?"

"I doubt it," Aedan winced uncomfortably. Adele studied her husband's face, afraid to voice her concern. It wasn't time, yet. Ashe would turn sixteen on Sunday. He had two years, she hoped. Perhaps a few beyond that. What happened then might determine many things in Adele's (and Ashe's) future.

"I guess I won't be taking Ashe on that shopping trip, then, since you grounded him," Adele walked away from Aedan. "I have no idea what he wants for his birthday, and don't tell me that Wynn, her parents and Mr. Winkler don't owe him, Aedan. A lot of people do." The front door slammed behind Adele Evans, leaving Aedan in the kitchen cursing softly.

"Dori, Ashe has been grounded. He won't be doing anything until Sunday." Adele had decided to walk around the neighborhood. Dori, sitting on her front porch, had gotten up to talk with Adele as she wandered past.

"Cori will be here on Friday," Dori said. "She knows Marco is here, and she wants to see Ashe, too."

"She won't see Ashe until Sunday, Dori. Nobody will."

"Mom said she'd take us to the beach on Saturday," Dori was still trying to get around Ashe's punishment.

"Dori, don't ask. Ashe got in trouble and now he's being punished."

"All right." Dori trotted back to her yard, leaving Adele to walk alone again.

~

Ashe heard the phone ring, and then listened while his father answered it. He'd heard the front door slam moments earlier and was learning now which parent had left the house. "Sali, Ashe has been grounded until Sunday. You may not call or visit until then," Aedan said. The phone was hung up seconds later.

Ashe sighed as he unpacked his suitcase, tossing dirty clothes into his hamper and putting the rest in drawers or hanging it inside his new walk-in closet. He'd gotten the second-largest bedroom, which had its own bath and a small walk-in closet inside it. Nothing needed to be cleaned yet and he had nothing new to read. Sighing, Ashe pulled his battered copy of *The Fellowship of the Ring* off the shelf and flopped onto his bed to read it again.

"Ashe, are you coming down for dinner?" His mother poked her head inside his bedroom door an hour later.

"Not hungry," Ashe turned a page.

"You have to eat something. I know they didn't serve lunch on Winkler's jet."

"Don't mention that name to me, Mom." Ashe still hadn't looked at his mother.

"Honey, I understand you're upset. You have to eat and Mr. Winkler is doing what he thinks is best for you. He's not a bad man, Ashe. Besides, I wanted to talk to you about what you want for your birthday. I have soup and sandwiches downstairs. Come and eat."

"Not hungry, and I don't want anything for my birthday."

"Son, you will get up now and go downstairs to eat." Aedan stood in the doorway beside his mother, his eyes red and power in his voice. Ashe blinked at his father. Was he trying to place compulsion?

"Nice try, Dad. I'm not hungry and I don't want anything for my birthday."

~

"Nathan, I gave him the strongest I had on the second try, and it still rolled right off him. I don't know what this means," Aedan paced in front of Nathan. They'd gone to Nathan's garage and shut the door so Lavonna and Dori wouldn't hear.

"What would it mean if he were human, Aedan?" Nathan was trying to get Aedan to view the incident objectively.

"That would mean one thing, but he's not human."

"And what if that's exactly what it means?"

"I will not allow anyone to touch that child. Ashe will not become vampire unless he wants it. I'm telling you now to respect my wishes in this. I do not want this getting to the Council. They already know too much about him. Radomir promised he would hold off on telling Wlodek that Ashe can mist and mindspeak, because Radomir owes Ashe blood debt. You and I know how tenuous that promise might be."

"I know," Nathan nodded. "They won't conscript until he's eighteen at the earliest, so you have two years, at least."

"Do you want your girls looking eighteen forever? Do you? You know that anyone turned below the age of twenty will look that way for eternity. That law needs to be changed to twenty at the very least. Twenty-five if I had my way."

"We don't get to make or change the laws that govern our race, Aedan. The Council and the Aristocracy do that."

"I'm eight hundred sixty-seven, and they still treat me as a child most of the time. Even Adele doesn't know how old I am. I don't want to frighten her or Ashe with that."

"Father," Nathan sighed. He so seldom called Aedan that. Hadn't called his vampire sire that in a very long time. Nathan was nearing six hundred, and Aedan had never abused his vampire child. "Father, you fret too much over this. Let it go. You know I will keep this secret, but I cannot control what Radomir or Winkler do or say. I think Radomir liked Ashe very much, else I think the Honored One would already have come to test Ashe himself."

"He's just a boy," Aedan muttered, dropping into a folding chair Nathan had placed inside his garage.

"I know. It's too bad that Adele couldn't conceive on her own—that a fertilized egg had to be procured to birth your son. He is yours, Aedan. Never forget that. Just as Corilyn and Dorilou are mine."

"He has my stubbornness, that much is certain," Aedan's Irish accent showed at times.

"I wasn't going to bring it up, but since you freely admit it," Nathan grinned.

Ashe had no cell phone and Sali and the others couldn't visit, but he still had his computer. He booted it up to go looking around the area that way. He also had email from Sali, Wynn, Dori and Cori. Then he came across something from someone he didn't recognize. He almost didn't open it. Afterward, he could never say whether he thought it a good thing or a bad thing that he did.

Greetings, the message began. *I am your grandfather.*

CHAPTER 5

*Y*ou are not obligated to me, the message continued, *but I must take the opportunity to warn you while I may. Trust no Elemaiya. They may offer many things, but those offers conceal lies. On both sides. Above all, do not reveal yourself to them. All will attempt to kill you should you do this. I cannot offer anything to you and past this message, you must mistrust me as well. The Queen has forgotten me for many years, but she will come soon and I must obey. I leave you with these final warnings: Make them fear you, grandchild, and beware the Diamond at the shining.*

I grant the love you are due,

Your grandfather

"What the?" Ashe couldn't finish the sentence, he was so shocked. "How did you find me? Bloody 'ell," he quoted one of his favorite lines from a movie.

Ashe didn't have many listed in his email address book so he set about transferring those to a new email address and deleting his old one. After all, hadn't the one who'd contacted him said not to trust any Elemaiya, including the one sending the message? Ashe took him at his word. Before he deleted everything, however, he printed a copy of the message and slipped it inside the dictionary on the top shelf of his library.

"Time for bed," his mother's voice floated from down the hall. She knew Ashe would hear. Frowning grimly, he shut down the computer and went looking for clean pajamas.

~

"The Corpus Christi Packmaster has offered us space for a garden, and she has also offered summer jobs for anyone sixteen and older," Adele said Friday morning as Ashe sat at the kitchen island, eating a bowl of cereal.

He'd gotten up before his mother because his stomach was growling. Adele had given the cereal an irritated frown before going to the stove to prepare an omelet. Now she sat opposite Ashe and was chattering away, although Ashe hadn't spoken, preferring silence except for the clinking of his spoon in the bowl and the sound of the cereal crunching in his mouth.

"What kind of work, you ask, and a female Packmaster?" Adele was asking the questions Ashe was considering, so he kept chewing. "Her name is Shirley Walker, word has it she can stop a speeding bus one-handed and she owns cotton fields, grapefruit, avocado and peach groves. She needs help with the peach and avocado harvests. And no, cotton isn't picked by hand any longer. Machines do that."

"Knew that already," Ashe said before he thought.

"And here I thought you'd lost your ability to speak," Adele gave a small smile. "You need more than a bowl of cereal, Ashe."

"I can make my own eggs," he grumbled, dipping up the last square of cereal and a half-spoon of milk.

"Then make eggs," Adele said. "You need more than that; you haven't eaten since early yesterday." She nodded at the now empty bowl. Ashe picked it up and walked to the new dishwasher. The appliance was nicer than the one they'd had in Cloud Chief. He then went to the fridge and pulled out the carton of eggs. His mother had gone to the grocery store, Ashe saw. The refrigerator was full.

"When do I start? If the Corpus Christi Packmaster hires me, I mean?"

"I wanted to take you in for your driver's exam on Monday; I found out where to go," Adele offered a real smile this time. "And don't stand there and tell me you don't want your license."

"I do." Ashe cracked an egg into a bowl, followed by a second. Briefly, he beat the eggs with a fork; he liked scrambled eggs without milk added. Turning on the burner beneath the skillet, Ashe waited patiently for it to heat up properly before pouring in the beaten eggs.

"Then we'll go on Monday. There's a bookstore not far from the Corpus Christi Department of Public Safety. You can take your driving test first and go looking for books after that. Shirley Walker says Wednesday is soon enough for people to come and interview. She realizes we're still settling in."

"How did you find out about that?" Ashe stirred eggs in the skillet, watching them cook.

"Marcus, of course. Shirley contacted him as soon as he arrived, I think."

"How much does it pay?"

"Minimum wage, but that's still good for anyone without prior work experience."

"I have prior work experience." Ashe did—he'd worked afternoons, weekends and summers at Cordell Feed and Seed.

"Ashe, that was unofficial. You didn't get a real salary and paid no taxes. This is a chance to do both those things. Plus, Shirley's groves are guarded by werewolves."

"Fine." Ashe raked cooked eggs onto a plate, set the skillet on the back of the stove and turned off the burner. Grabbing the salt and pepper, he walked back to his seat at the island. "How many hours per day? What are the working conditions?"

"I think it won't be more than eight hours, but that's a guess, Ashe. Harvests are unpredictable, as you know. I miss our vegetable garden."

"The tomatoes were coming along," Ashe nodded. They'd had to leave their garden in Cloud Chief. Ashe loved fresh tomatoes.

"I know, honey," Adele sighed. "And your father doesn't want to purchase another business here until the old one sells."

"I understand that," Ashe nodded and scooped scrambled eggs into his mouth. "Were you going to do the same thing this time?"

"I've checked out the market; there are several shops around doing the same thing. I don't think another feed and seed would be a wise investment."

"And the beaches are glutted with souvenir and clothing shops," Ashe agreed. He'd already checked that for himself.

"I see you've done your homework," Adele smiled. "But there isn't a bookshop in Port Aransas. I think it would have to be a new and used, with a coffee shop and free wi-fi, but I think we could make it work. Especially if we sold soft drinks and treats, too. The space can't be too large or the rent won't be cost effective. So we'll have to make wise use of a small shop."

"How long will it take to sell the old store?" Ashe asked.

"I don't know hon. Jason called and said somebody came by yesterday, but he thinks it was just a tire kicker."

Ashe smiled at his mother's vernacular. A tire kicker was someone there to look only, more than likely. It came from the car sales industry, he imagined.

The doorbell rang while they sat together, dreaming up ideas for a bookstore near the beach. "I'll get it," Ashe said, sliding off his barstool.

"Nobody said I couldn't visit," Marco walked in with Marcus. Adele, who'd followed Ashe, gave Marco a hug. He grinned at Ashe's mother. "You may not want to hug me when I tell you what I came for," he was still grinning. "But I have to make a phone call, first." Marco hit a number on speed dial. Ashe heard it ring on the other end. He also recognized the voice when it picked up. *Winkler.*

"Mrs. Evans is here, Mr. Winkler," Marco handed the phone to Adele.

"Mrs. Evans?" Winkler said. Ashe could hear every word clearly. Marcus stood by, listening in.

"Mr. Winkler?" Adele said. "What can I do for you?"

"I hear Shirley Walker wants to put your son to work in the groves."

"She has offered jobs to the kids who are sixteen or older. Ashe turns sixteen on Sunday."

"I want to offer a job to Ashe as well. And it won't be twelve-hour days in the heat at minimum wage."

"Mr. Winkler, that sounds dangerous to me."

"It shouldn't be. He'll be working at the house with me. Seems word slipped out that he hacked into someone's computer before he was twelve. Now, I won't name any names, but those kinds of skills are valuable to me. I like to know which banks I provide security for are vulnerable. I'd like to give Ashe a crack at them and see if he can get past their electronic security, among other things. Send him to me for the summer, Mrs. Evans. He'll be constantly surrounded by my own security guards and paid a lot better. Talk it over with Ashe and your husband. I'd like an answer by Sunday evening, if that's possible."

"I was going to take him for his driving test on Monday," Adele sounded stunned.

"He can take it there or here. It doesn't matter. And I'll make sure he doesn't get into trouble."

Ashe stared at Marco, who gave him a grin as he took the phone from Adele.

"Ashe, do you want to do this?" His mother's golden-brown eyes searched his face.

Ashe considered it for a moment. It only took that long, after all. "Yeah, I think I'd like to try it."

"I think we'll have a sit-down soon and talk about hacking into computers, young man," Adele added. Marco laughed. Ashe knew the information had been passed from Cori to Marco, and then from Marco to Winkler.

Ashe had hacked into Principal Billings' computer—twice—because Cori asked him to. The first time had been to check her math grade, not to change it, and the second was to look into Randy Smith's file that Billings had on his office computer. Billings knew about the first time. Likely didn't know about the second. Ashe wasn't about to own up to that.

"Look," Ashe reached out and tapped the front of Marco's shirt, causing Marco to look downward. Ashe flipped Marco's nose as he did so. Marcus burst out laughing.

~

"Son, I know you're still upset." Aedan sat on the end of Ashe's bed. It was Friday night and Ashe knew that Marco had taken Cori, Sali, Dori, Wynn, and two others to see a movie in Corpus Christi. They were likely going to eat while they were out, too. Ashe was missing it.

He sat against the headboard of his bed, arms crossed over his chest while he examined the socks he wore. The white cotton stuck out against the faded black of his old jeans. He'd need new ones soon —these were getting short.

"If I allow you to work for Mr. Winkler, you have to obey him. Just as you would your mother or me. The only reason I'm allowing this is that Mr. Winkler's wolves can likely protect you as well as you'd be protected here. Nobody will suspect you're there, I think. I'll tell Mr. Winkler that if this doesn't work out to send you straight home. Is that clear? Screw up, Son, and you'll be right back here having another talk."

"I got it, Dad." Ashe still wasn't looking at his father.

"Your mother is still fretting over your birthday. She wanted to invite friends over, but didn't know if you'd want that."

"I don't." Ashe was ambivalent about it, but he stubbornly declared otherwise. He'd seen Sali, sitting in Marcus' van, his arm around Wynn when Marco drove away.

"Then we're back to what you might want or need for your birthday."

"I need new jeans. These are short," Ashe forced the hem on one leg down as far as it would go with the opposite toe.

"I know you're still growing, Son. I'll see what Adele wants to do. You'll leave Monday evening; Mr. Winkler's sending the jet. Marco will go back with you. That leaves time to get your license on Monday, providing you pass the test."

Ashe didn't say anything, he just nodded. He'd already gone through the Texas driver's education program online throughout the day. He fully intended to get his license on the first try.

"I know I made a mistake, attempting compulsion. I broke a promise I made to myself when I did that," Aedan sighed, staring out Ashe's window.

Ashe figured his father could see everything outside that window quite clearly, although it was completely dark outside. "We have to trust one another, Ashe. You need to trust that I'm doing the best I can for you. To keep you safe and keep the family safe. I let my anger get away from me, and that's not good. The only excuse I have is that it frightens me when somebody hauls you off to who knows where, and you risk your life to save someone else. I wasn't awake to be consulted on the matter and you have no idea how frustrating that is to me."

"I know it frustrates you, Dad. I've been watching you for nearly sixteen years," Ashe mumbled. He had. His father didn't show emotion much of the time, so when he did, Ashe paid very close attention.

"I know. I like to think you get those observational skills from me," Aedan smiled wryly. "And as a vampire, I didn't think I'd ever get a child. Not in the traditional sense, anyway. I can't truly describe how I felt the moment they placed a tiny baby boy in my arms almost sixteen years ago. Overwhelmed is the best word I can come up with. I thought I might break you, you were so small. Barely eight pounds, I think, and when vampires can bend steel with their bare hands, you can imagine how frightened I was, holding something that fragile."

"Dad, I don't like fighting with you."

"I don't like fighting with you or your mother. It hurts too much. Right now, your mother is barely speaking to me."

"Everything is my fault, Dad. The move, the whole compulsion thing that you and Nathan have to do to keep me hidden—all of it. It's because of me."

"Wynn would be dead if it weren't for you. We'd never have caught James' killer if it weren't for you. Paul Harris would have watched

Randy Smith die by Pack Law and taken pleasure in it. He had that poor human girl murdered because Marco was showing interest in her. He never showed it, but he was racist in the extreme."

"He tried to kill you," Ashe sighed, uncrossing his arms and flexing his fingers.

"And Nathan and Radomir."

"Yeah. And now, nobody can know what I am and I have to hide."

"We have to keep you safe. I know these things don't sit well with you, but we made a commitment when we said we wanted children. If that means keeping you hidden, then that's our job."

"That sounds like jail to me." Ashe picked at a worn spot on the left knee of his jeans.

"Do a good job for Mr. Winkler, Son," Aedan didn't respond to Ashe's statement. Instead, he rose and stretched. "It could lead to something better someday." Aedan walked out of Ashe's bedroom, closing the door behind him.

Saturday might have been one of the worst days Ashe had ever been forced to endure. Marco took Cori (who'd just come from college in Oklahoma), Sali, Wynn, Dori and a pack of others to the beach in Port Aransas.

Ashe wanted to go so badly he could taste it, and he'd be flying to Dallas on Monday night. He hadn't gotten to stick a toe into gulf water yet, and he was likely going to spend the summer away from his new home.

"Honey, I'll take you shopping in Corpus tomorrow. You can buy new clothes for your birthday and we'll go to the bookstore afterward," Adele stuck her head out the patio door. Ashe was sitting in a lawn chair on the back deck, staring at the tall, wooden fence that blocked the nearest housing addition from view.

"Okay," Ashe's voice failed to conceal how depressed he was.

"It's over tomorrow. We'll go out and have a good time."

"Yeah." Ashe sounded listless, even to his own ears. Had he hoped to get a car for his birthday? He knew he wouldn't get one now. His dad wouldn't allow that. Ashe couldn't drive around like the others.

He'd come to the conclusion that nobody would let him out on his own. He was going to be secluded and guarded for the rest of his life. The talk the night before had cleared the air somewhat, but Aedan hadn't given Ashe much hope that he'd be allowed freedom like Sali and the others.

"Ashe, I can't say that I know exactly how you feel," his mother came to sit in the chair beside him. "Because I never had to worry about most of those things. Right now, we just want to see you reach adulthood alive and in one piece. You'll have to humor us a little, honey."

"Mom, I can't live in a vacuum the rest of my life. You might as well shoot me now," Ashe muttered.

"I hope things are better for you when you get to Dallas. Your father is worried."

"I am, too. Does that mean I can't have any fun? Ever?"

"We could still have a party tomorrow night."

"I don't want one. I just want to go to the beach with the others. Or to the movies or out to dinner without a parent. It's not that I don't love you," Ashe was quick to say. "But it's different."

"I know." Adele stared at her lap. "I don't know what to do, Ashe. I truly don't." Adele rose and went inside the house.

"He's miserable." Adele said. Aedan had just climbed out of the storm shelter inside the garage. "He wanted to go to the beach or to the movies with the others and he's cooped up in the house. I know you grounded him, Aedan, but if you decide to do that three days before his birthday ever again without consulting me, you and I will have a little chat afterward." Adele stalked away from her husband.

Of course, it was raining on his birthday. Of course. Ashe watched as the world outside his bedroom window drowned in a pouring rain. "Gloomy. Dreadful. Dismal. Melancholic. Ominous." Ashe muttered a litany of words that fit the day and his life. Still grumbling, he stepped inside the shower. Dressing afterward, he muttered more words. "Miserable. Disconsolate. Depressed." Ashe combed back his brown, slightly curly hair.

"Happy Birthday, honey." Adele dropped an envelope beside Ashe as he sat at the kitchen island, crunching away on cereal squares.

"Thanks," Ashe sighed, hoping his mother wouldn't think him ungrateful.

"Aren't you going to open it?" His mother went to find something for breakfast. Ashe slipped the card from the envelope. The card was very nice, signed by his mother and father. The gift card that slipped out was nice, too—a hefty amount from a major electronics store.

"We thought you might like a laptop, since you're going to Dallas for the summer," Adele smiled. Ashe stared at the gift card. It would buy a laptop, a carrying case and perhaps a few extras, too.

"Mom—uh, thanks," Ashe was almost speechless. A car would have made him truly speechless, but this was pretty good.

"And take a look at this," Adele turned on the small television in the kitchen, tuning it to one of the continuous news programs. "It'll be on in a few minutes; they recycle the stories every half hour or so," she pulled the pancake mix out of the pantry and began to put ingredients together for breakfast. Ashe watched the news, most of which he'd heard already, until it came to what he considered *the* article.

"Congressman Jack Howard was rescued today after a hunting accident in Colorado," the news anchor said while an inset video showed the congressman being helped off a helicopter by two rescue workers.

"One of the two bodyguards hunting with him at the time was accidentally killed in the same incident. The three men were caught in a rockslide while tracking elk," the newscaster went on. "Many questions have been raised over the congressman's hunting elk out of season." The article ended there.

"Hmmph," Ashe muttered. "Congressman Jack Howard shot his own man."

"He did?" Adele turned to Ashe, a shocked look on her face.

"After I dumped him in the dirt when he was about to shoot Wynn," Ashe nodded. "He jumped up and just started shooting at everything. I saw another man fall off his horse. I figure that's the one who got killed."

"Ashe, you knocked the Congressman off his horse?" Adele was aghast.

"He was about to shoot Wynn. What did you want me to do?"

"Did he see you?"

"He didn't see a thing. Neither did the other guy. He was the one who grazed Wynn. You know—the game preserve owner?"

"Marcus says the Grand Master took care of that one himself," Adele sat down again, pancakes forgotten.

"I'll make breakfast for you, you look pale," Ashe got up and started making pancakes.

CHAPTER 6

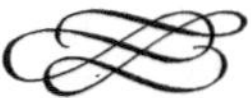

"I like this one," Ashe pointed to a laptop at the electronics store. They'd gone there first. The sales clerk was telling Ashe what it would do, but Ashe already knew that. He picked out a case for it next, plus a few extras. The mall was next, for clothing.

"I like these," Ashe turned in front of the mirror, looking at the black jeans he'd tried on.

"Those look good," Adele agreed. "How about three pairs of those, and four of the denim?"

"Sounds good," Ashe said. A few shirts went into the pile of clothing on the clerk's desk, with packages of socks and underwear.

"You're growing out of everything," Adele said, smiling up at her son. Ashe slipped two pairs of cargo pants into the pile. His mother shrugged and allowed it.

"Where would you like to get lunch?" She asked after loading bags into the car.

"Seafood?" Ashe asked. This was a coastal town, after all. Seafood should be everywhere.

"Let's go to Port A," Adele suggested. That's what the locals called Port Aransas. The small town was mostly a fishing village, but tourists came for the beaches and condos that lined the highway throughout the barrier island. It was also where Adele wanted to put her bookstore.

Victoria's Restaurant was the one Ashe picked—it was right on the water and boats passed by on their way to the gulf. Ashe had grouper for lunch while his mother had locally caught shrimp.

"This is really good," Adele bit into a butterfly shrimp.

"Mine, too," Ashe said. They'd served his grouper with a brown butter sauce that he liked very much. They drove through town afterward, looking for space that might be suitable for a bookstore. They found two spots, one next to a souvenir shop, the other beside a restaurant.

"I think I like the one by the restaurant better," Adele said, writing down the realtor's phone number.

"Yeah. Tourists who come to the other location will be inside the souvenir shop instead," Ashe agreed.

"I was thinking the same thing," Adele said. "Let's go take a peek at the water." The beach was two blocks away and driving was allowed on the sandy expanse. They passed all sorts of vehicles as they made their way down the public beach in Port Aransas.

"Look, Mom, that's incredible." The sun had peeked from behind the rain clouds earlier, and now tourists were putting up umbrellas and laying their beach towels on the sand. Ashe saw people his age running into the water with Boogie Boards while younger children played in the sand or waded in shallow water. Tiny birds raced this way and that on stick-like legs, calling out in piping voices while searching for food.

"I hear they have a marine biology program at the college in Corpus Christi," Adele said, watching the birds.

"That sounds interesting."

"I agree. If I hadn't gotten my degree in business, I might have gone into that or veterinary science," his mother sighed.

"Either would be a good choice," Ashe agreed, craning his neck to watch three people flying kites in the sea breeze, the long, multicolored tails floating in the wind.

"Let's go back on the ferry," Adele grinned. It would be a longer journey backtracking through Corpus Christi.

"Yeah. I've never been on a ferry before," Ashe grinned back. That's how they ended up parking the car on the ferryboat, which held twenty vehicles. Adele shut off the engine and she and Ashe climbed out and stood at the rail while the ferry swished through the water to the other side.

Seagulls called out and brown pelicans flew past as the salt-scented wind blew Ashe's hair askew. "Look—dolphins," Ashe's voice was reverent when he saw dolphins swimming beside the ferry. "Mom, this is so cool."

"I think so, too," Adele laughed.

"Dude," Sali was standing in the driveway, his hands stuffed in the pockets of cutoff shorts when Adele pulled in.

"Dude," Ashe nodded at his best friend.

"Is there cake later?" Sali asked.

"Around seven," Adele said. She'd stopped to allow the garage door to pull up.

"So, what's up?" Ashe hauled bags from the trunk, hiding his surprise at Adele's words—he hadn't expected anyone to be invited for a birthday celebration after he'd said no. Sali grabbed a share of the parcels and followed Ashe inside the house.

"Wynn and me," Sali began, reddening at the admission.

"Yeah, I saw," Ashe grumped. That wasn't the best thing to say to Ashe after being quarantined for three days.

"Dude, you don't like Wynn?" Sali settled bags of clothing onto the kitchen island.

"I like Wynn just fine," Ashe said, carefully laying the bag that held his laptop box on the granite-topped island. "Sali, I hope you're happy." Ashe's voice held a bit of pain.

"Marco said he'd take us to the beach tonight to look for crabs," Sali said, oblivious to Ashe's discomfort. Ashe blinked at Sali. Would he refuse an outing because he didn't want to see Wynn with Sali?

"Sounds like fun," Ashe said instead.

"Good. We'll go after cake," Sali grinned.

"And ice cream," Adele added, smiling at Sali. "Salidar, tell your parents and Marco that they're welcome, too. Bring Wynn and Dori if they want to come. And their parents."

"Dude, is this what you got?" Sali was impressed with the laptop when Ashe pulled it from the box.

"Yeah. Let's go to my bedroom and hook it up," Ashe grinned.

"Take these bags of clothing with you; we need to wash some of it before you leave tomorrow night," Adele stopped both boys from racing up the stairs.

"You're leaving tomorrow night? Where are you going?" Sali grabbed a handful of bags.

"Didn't Marco tell you?" Ashe gaped at Sali.

"No. What was he supposed to tell me?"

"We wanted to make the announcement tonight over cake and ice cream," Adele said. "So you'll just have to wait until then," she gave Ashe a meaningful look.

"Okay," Ashe couldn't hide his disappointment. "Come on, let's hook up the computer and see if it works." He and Sali clumped up the stairs.

"Dude, I can see the gulf from my bedroom," Sali said, looking out Ashe's window. Ashe could only see the back yard from his. "You need to come see the house."

"I saw it, remember?"

"Did you?" Sali gave Ashe a quizzical look.

"Yeah. Remember, I called you, when Mom and I got here first? You asked me to go check out your house. I told you about that bedroom, dude."

"Must have forgot," Sali said, shrugging. "Anyway, Marco got the bedroom that looks down on the back yard. He says he doesn't care, since he won't be home much."

"He's a member of the Dallas Pack, Sali. That's his home now."

"Yeah. I know."

"He's still your brother. That won't change."

"But I like him loads better now. He takes us places and we actually have fun together."

Ashe didn't want to remind Sali of the rivalry between Sali and Marco when he was younger. Sali had been in constant competition with his older brother, it seemed.

"I'm going to take the driver's test tomorrow morning," Ashe said.

"I want to come."

"They won't let you in the car while I take the test."

"I don't care. I'll wait with your mom."

"If she doesn't care," Ashe said. "And as long as you don't make fun of me if I flunk it."

"Me?" Sali pretended to be hurt, a finger pointing at his own chest.

"Don't give me false commiseration," Ashe teased.

"You're not even going to give me credit for knowing what that five-syllable word means, are you?" Sali took the computer cord from Ashe and plugged it into an outlet.

"Sali, I learned long ago that you're smarter than people think. And that pretty much includes all of Earth's population."

"What, you're not venturing past our own solar system?"

"Well, maybe the Wookiees don't think you're smart, but they haven't met you yet."

"Wookiees are shapeshifters," Sali reopened an old argument.

"Nope. Chewie wouldn't go around bumping his head on stuff if he was. He'd just go back to humanoid or whatever and forego the bruises."

"Says the guy who turns into a bat. A teeny, tiny bat."

"Do not dis the bat," Ashe said, booting up the computer.

"Come on, you weigh less than a dime, man."

"And I can make you whine with pain when I send out echolocation signals," Ashe reminded his friend.

"If you're close enough," Sali pointed out.

"Ashe?" Cori's voice floated up the stairs.

"In here, Cori," Ashe called out. Cori walked in, went straight to Ashe and gave him a huge hug.

"He's out of the slammer now," Sali sang off-key.

"I don't consider house arrest the slammer," Ashe grumped when Cori let him go.

"Got one of those ankle bracelets?" Sali asked.

"Monitors," Ashe corrected. "Dad thought about it."

"What did you do, dude?"

"Talked back," Ashe admitted unwillingly.

"Gets you every time," Sali nodded sagely.

"Is this the birthday present?" Cori looked Ashe's new laptop over.

"Yeah."

"Nice."

"Sali?" Wynn's voice, this time. Ashe breathed a sigh. Sali poked his head out of Ashe's bedroom door.

"In here," he said. Wynn walked in, followed closely by Dori.

"How's your shoulder?" Ashe asked.

"Fine. How did you know about that?" Wynn's hand went to her right shoulder.

"Word gets around," Ashe muttered.

"Ashe, show me the house," Cori grabbed his arm and hauled him out of the bedroom.

"She doesn't remember anything," Cori hissed. They stood inside the hall bathroom.

"I'm surprised you remember," Ashe muttered.

"Dad," Cori said.

"Oh." Ashe hadn't thought about that. Nathan would certainly know what happened to Wynn. His memories hadn't been removed like everyone else's.

"Dori doesn't know, either, so don't let it slip, okay? Dad wouldn't tell her because she and Wynn are so close."

"Yeah. I get that," Ashe said. "Cori, what do you know about that?"

"That you were there. I can figure out the rest for myself."

"Thank God." Ashe wrapped his arms around Cori and squeezed her hard, lifting her off the floor.

"Hey, now," Marco stepped inside the bathroom.

"Just thanking Cori for the birthday gift," Ashe laughed, slapping Marco's shoulder. Ashe was taller than Marco, although Marco was more solid. Ashe was still thin.

"It's not anything I need to worry about, is it?" Marco teased.

"Not in the least, lummox," Cori hugged Marco. "Ashe just needed a little moral support, that's all. He's been locked up for days."

"Homemade cake is always better," Dori said later. Denise and Marcus had brought burgers and hot dogs to grill and the whole thing turned into a neighborhood party. Ashe got a gift card from Sali, so he could add music to his MP-3 player. A T-shirt came from Dori and Wynn. Cori and Marco gave him a hat.

"See, you look like Frank Sinatra now," Cori grinned.

"Stylin'," Ashe grinned, running a finger along the brim.

"You'll look good in Dallas, dude," Marco said.

"Dallas?" Sali was quick to pick up on Marco's comment.

"Ashe is coming to Dallas to work for Mr. Winkler over the summer," Marco made the announcement. "Mr. Winkler appreciates his computer hacking skills."

"Are you kidding me?" Sali huffed. "He breaks into Billings' computer and he gets a job?"

"Sali!" Ashe hissed. Marcus, Adele and Denise all looked at one another before bursting into laughter.

"Something amusing?" Aedan appeared, Nathan not far behind. Adele looked at her husband and broke into fresh peals of laughter.

"I wish your father could be here," Adele said the following morning as she, Ashe and Sali waited for Ashe's name to be called for the driving test. The written exam had gone very well, but the driving test came next.

Ashe had giant butterflies in his stomach. Giant *mutant* butterflies, in his opinion. He'd practiced a parallel park before going to Corpus Christi for the test. Doing it at home was certainly not doing it for the testing officer, though. Ashe waggled a leg nervously as he waited. The plastic chairs in the waiting area weren't comfortable, either, making his discomfort more pronounced.

"You'll be fine, honey," Adele tried to calm him. Ashe's name was called. He rose, cast a helpless look at Sali and followed the officer.

"Nice car," the officer commented as Ashe climbed in on the driver's side of the Cadillac and buckled his seat belt. Ashe drove out of the parking lot as instructed, made turns, changed lanes after looking over his shoulder, stopped properly at stop signs and lights and was then instructed to get on and off the highway. He drove back to the testing facility afterward for the dreaded parallel park. Nervously chewing his lip, Ashe pulled alongside the front curb, looked behind him and began turning the wheel.

Ashe watched later as the officer made notes on his clipboard. Did he pass? The man wasn't saying anything.

"Congratulations," the officer handed Ashe a piece of paper. "You passed. Turn that in to get your license." Ashe whooped, causing the officer to chuckle.

"I don't care what it looks like, I can drive," Ashe grinned. Sali had examined Ashe's photograph on the new license, turning it upside down at one point and telling Ashe it didn't look a thing like him. "You have to pass yours next, dude," Ashe poked at Sali.

"Mom, he's touching me," Sali complained good-naturedly.

"Two bags are enough, Mom," Ashe said later as his mother helped him pack. Adele worried that he wouldn't have enough clothing for the summer. Ashe felt bad that they were leaving before his father was up, but Winkler's jet was waiting for him and Marco. "Give Dad a hug, okay?" He'd spent the afternoon packing while Sali watched.

"Your ride's here," Marco walked into Ashe's bedroom as the last bag was zipped up. Marcus was waiting outside in his van—he'd offered to drop them off at the airport. Sali couldn't hide his envy as bags were loaded in and Ashe climbed into the van with Marco.

"Call when you get there," Adele said, trying to hold back tears.

"I will. I'll be okay, I promise." Ashe closed the door, then waved at Sali and his mother while Marcus pulled away.

"Man, that was hard," Ashe mumbled.

"Always is," Marco said, looking at Ashe over the back of his seat.

The trip was uneventful and they landed in Dallas less than two hours later. Winkler and two other werewolves were at the airport to meet Ashe and Marco.

Ashe recognized Trajan right away. He didn't know the other wolf.

"This is Gene Powell," Winkler introduced him. Gene offered his hand and Ashe took it. "Shapeshifter, huh?" Gene said, nodding to Ashe.

"He's cute when he shifts," Marco teased, holding his thumb and forefinger about an inch apart.

"No kidding?" Gene said. Ashe went pink.

"Hey, now," Trajan elbowed Marco. "You don't haze the new help right away; you wait till they don't suspect anything and then do it." Ashe followed the others to a Winkler Security van waiting near the jet, wondering just what it was he'd gotten into.

"This room is yours," Winkler showed Ashe into a spacious bedroom on the third floor of his three-story mansion located between Denton and Dallas. The house was secluded on a four-acre tract, with a high concrete and stucco wall surrounding it. Ashe dumped his bags on the bed and looked around.

"You'll get up at six, work out for an hour with Trajan and Marco, shower, eat breakfast and then come to my office down on the first floor. We'll talk then about what I want from you," Winkler grinned. "Hungry?"

"A little," Ashe admitted.

"Good. Let's go raid the kitchen. Anything is up for grabs unless the cook puts a note on it," Winkler said. Ashe followed Winkler down the stairs to the first floor.

Two of the largest stainless-steel refrigerators Ashe had ever seen hummed in the kitchen. "The cook comes in around five to start cooking for the day. The guard switches at six-thirty, so breakfast starts at six. There are three shifts of guards and it might be a good idea to get to know all of them in case you need to go in or out."

Ashe nodded while Winkler started piling containers of ham, turkey and salami in his arms. Winkler grabbed the mustard and mayonnaise and then went looking for bread.

Ashe had a sandwich and soft drink with Winkler, all while listening as Winkler described the guards and informed him that Marco and three others slept in the detached guesthouse. Trajan and a few other werewolves had rooms inside the house.

"You'll get weekends off unless we need you for something," Winkler said. "You'll get paid every two weeks, but that'll go into an account your mother set up for you at a bank in Corpus Christi. Don't worry, I'll see that you have spending money," Winkler grinned. "Come on, let's get you to bed."

Ashe stuck his dishes inside the dishwasher before following Winkler upstairs. Later, he settled into bed, watching television for a while—the bedroom had a TV plus a docking station/alarm clock for his MP-3 player. Ashe sighed, shut off the television and closed his eyes.

"Uh, okay." Ashe watched Trajan lift weights.

"Come on, you don't want to be a string bean forever, do you?" Trajan set the heavy weights down and pulled Ashe toward a lifting bench. "We'll start you out light and you can work your way up," he said.

Ashe was flat on his back on the bench after stretching to Trajan's specifications. He worked with weights for half an hour before Trajan sent him out to the grounds to run laps with Marco.

"You do this every day?" Ashe huffed beside Marco.

"When I'm here. Trajan was an athlete in school. You don't get away with much around him."

"Uh-huh." Ashe shook his head. "How far do you run every morning?"

"Around three miles, I think," Marco replied. "You'll get in shape pretty quick. You're used to walking around Cloud Chief."

"I sort of miss it, even though the gulf is nice," Ashe said.

"Tough to let the old place go," Marco agreed.

"Had enough?" Trajan slapped Ashe on the back when he and Marco came in panting after the run. Ashe just nodded. He was too winded to speak.

"Don't forget to stretch again before getting in the shower," Trajan called out behind Ashe, who was heading toward the stairs as fast as his rubbery legs would take him. Ashe showered, dressed and went to breakfast.

"You the kid?" A gruff old werewolf examined Ashe from head to heels.

"I guess," Ashe said, piling bacon onto a plate. Breakfast was served buffet style and everybody helped themselves.

"Don't get in the way," the werewolf growled and moved away from Ashe.

"Okaaay," Ashe muttered.

～

"Mr. Winkler?" Ashe knocked on Winkler's office door after breakfast.

"Come on in," Winkler said, pointing to a chair in front of a huge desk. Ashe stared at a large photograph hanging on the wall behind Winkler's desk. It showed Winkler, sitting beside a beautiful woman with strawberry blonde hair. In the photograph, Winkler was smiling at her.

"Taken twenty-four years ago," Winkler said, turning to look at the photograph.

"Who is that?" Ashe asked.

"The love of my life," Winkler said. "She's dead now."

"Sorry," Ashe mumbled.

"Maybe I'll tell you about that, someday. Someday. Now, let's get down to business."

Ashe was led to a computer in an adjoining room and given the name and address of a bank. "Tell me everything you can about this bank by five o'clock," Winkler grinned and walked out again. Ashe began by pulling up the website for the bank.

"So, what can you tell me?" Winkler poked his head in the door a few minutes after five.

Ashe held out a piece of paper to Winkler. "I got the name of the President right off, and then went looking into his stuff. I got these numbers after hacking into his personal account," Ashe grinned. "I saw an information page where the birthdates for his kids kept switching around. Some listed month, day and year, others listed day, month and year, and the last ones listed year first and then month and day. These last ones got me into some sort of system inside the bank."

"You're kidding," Winkler whistled and went to sit at the computer. He plugged the numbers in, just as Ashe had, and sure enough, he got through. "Ashe, if you'd known what to do, you could have transferred bank funds to another account," Winkler said. "And it only took you eight hours to do it."

"Knew I shoulda set up that offshore account," Ashe joked.

"If you want, you can grab a drink and get in the pool out back," Winkler said, lifting his cell phone from a pocket. "I have to make a couple of calls."

"Okay," Ashe nodded and walked out of the room.

A handful of werewolves lounged around the pool when Ashe walked onto the patio. A tub filled with beer, ice and soft drinks was sitting next to a potted palm. "Any water in there?" Ashe asked as he went digging through the ice.

"Yeah. Keep digging," the wolf sitting closest to the tub said. Ashe kept digging and did find a bottle of water. "You the shapeshifter kid?" The wolf asked.

"Yeah. I guess I am," Ashe replied.

"Name's Grady," the man held out his hand.

"Uh," Ashe wiped his cold, wet hand on his jeans before taking it. Grady laughed. "My name is Ashe," he said, shaking Grady's hand.

"Well, Ashe, don't take any crap offa any of these guys. You let them bully you around and that's all you'll get." Grady sipped his beer.

Ashe nodded and went to find a seat elsewhere. Ashe drank his bottled water quietly and watched the others. Six wolves sat around the pool, including Grady. Grady had reddish-brown hair and muddy brown eyes. The werewolf squinted in the sunlight while enjoying his drink and watching the others. Two of the remaining five looked like brothers, both with dark hair and gray eyes. They talked quietly in a shady spot at the end of a loop in the pool.

Winkler had spent a lot of money on the pool, Ashe figured; it was irregularly shaped, with palms, tropical plants and flowers surrounding the flagstone border. Ashe didn't listen to the conversation the brothers were having—that wouldn't be polite.

Instead, his eyes wandered to the last three, who were lined up in lounge chairs. Those three were as different as they could possibly be. One had hair nearly as black as Winkler's, with dark eyes and a heavy forehead. The thick, bushy eyebrows set at an angle lent an ominous look to his face. The nose and mouth were certainly overshadowed by the brow and facial hair.

The one sitting to his right was shorter, perhaps five-six or seven. He also had nearly white hair, which was an anomaly in werewolves and his silvery blue eyes watched the others surreptitiously. The last werewolf was brown-haired, brown-eyed and wouldn't stand out in any crowd.

They all sat up straighter when Winkler walked through, however. Ashe figured it was the respect the Dallas Packmaster was due. Winkler came right to Ashe and sat in the empty chair beside him.

"Kid, you just scared the hell out of a bank president," he grinned. "I'm sending a crew in tomorrow to get his system upgraded and change all his codes. I don't think he'll be using his daughter's birthdays for security codes anymore. And I told him to change the password to his personal computer more often." Winkler slapped Ashe on the knee. "Good work. Better than I expected. Dinner's at seven-thirty." Winkler rose and walked back in the house. Ashe shrank down in his chair as all six werewolves stared at him.

CHAPTER 7

"Only the twenty-fifth of June, second day on the job and already making money for Winkler Security," Trajan had Ashe lifting a hundred pounds over his head. "But that doesn't mean anything in my dojo," Trajan snickered. "In here, you belong to me."

"That's," Ashe huffed a little, struggling to lift the weights, "not scary or anything," Ashe lowered the weights. He was lying flat on his back on the weight bench again while Trajan supervised his weight lifting.

"Yeah, I'm plenty scary," Trajan leered at Ashe. Ashe wanted to laugh but didn't. Trajan, at six-eleven, was still something humorous to see when he made faces. "Come on. I want you lifting two hundred before I send you back home. Gotta get you in shape to fend off cyber pirates."

"Does your job description include harassment?" Ashe asked, hefting the weights up again.

"Sure does," Trajan grinned. "Three more of those, and then we'll do some squats."

"Man, I still ache from yesterday," Ashe grumbled.

"And you'll ache more from today. Come on, two more, now. Get with it."

"Is he always a slave driver?" Ashe asked Marco later as they ran laps.

"Trajan doesn't fool around in the gym," Marco said. "And thanks to you, I'll be one of the team sent to the bank this morning to install the new equipment and get them updated. If you could break in after only a few hours, anybody else could get in after a day or two. They were setting themselves up," Marco blew out a breath. "The bank president kept saying that the old system we installed six years ago was still good. Winkler told him it was outdated and could be breached with modern technology. The boss was right, as usual."

"I guess so," Ashe panted.

"This one probably won't be possible, but take a crack at it anyway," Winkler gave Ashe the name of another bank, this one in Idaho.

Ashe smiled. His mother called Idaho the potato and onion capital of the world, which was great if you loved potato pancakes. Sali lived for the days when Adele actually made them. Ashe would call, Sali would run to the house as quick as he could and wait patiently until Adele served them up.

"Will do, boss," Ashe said, nodding at Winkler. Winkler laughed and slapped Ashe on the back.

Ashe lined up behind Grady for the dinner buffet that evening. He hadn't made much progress on the project Winkler assigned earlier, but he wasn't ready to give up on it yet. When Ashe had given an update before going to dinner, Winkler just smiled and gave the go-ahead to keep trying. Ashe was working on the problem in his head when the grumpy werewolf he'd met at breakfast the first day walked up and stood behind him.

"Rookies need to be at the back of the line," the werewolf rumbled. Since Ashe didn't know his name, he thought of him as Gruff. Ashe, following Grady's advice, didn't move or say anything. He thought it best to just ignore Gruff and hope he gave up on his quest to belittle and demean.

"You hear what I said, boy?" Gruff jerked Ashe around by the shoulder. Ashe had three inches on Gruff, but Gruff was wider, heavier and definitely meaner.

"Put your hands on the boy again and I'll take it as a challenge," Trajan had Gruff's collar in his hand, his face inches from the older werewolf's nose. Ashe stared as Gruff slunk back from Trajan. "Turn around and get your dinner, Ashe," Trajan said. Ashe whirled and rushed forward to reach the buffet line.

"It's Trajan's job to keep peace in the ranks," Grady said when Ashe sat at the long dining table after grabbing a glass of sweet iced tea and setting his plate of food down. "Orville will back off or he'll be punished," Grady added. "But don't get any ideas about baiting him. Or anybody else, for that matter."

"I don't do stuff like that," Ashe was still shaken over the incident.

"Orders are for you to drink at least one of these a day," Marco set a protein drink in front of Ashe before sitting beside him. "It'll help build you up a little. You're just too skinny, dude." Marco grinned, taking the sting out of his words.

"Yeah. I get that," Ashe said, shaking himself.

"Orville tried a little bullying," Grady nodded toward Ashe, who was popping the tab on the protein drink. "Trajan took care of it."

"If I were the toughest wolf in the room, I still wouldn't bother Ashe without knowing what I was getting into," Marco said innocently. Grady ignored the comment and Ashe, hoping the whole thing would go away, cut into his hamburger steak.

"Ashe, get up boy. We need you." Trajan shook Ashe's shoulder. Ashe, heart pounding from being wakened from a sound sleep, blinked in confusion at his alarm clock beside the bed. It read three-thirty, the red numbers blurring a little as he struggled to wake.

"Come on, get dressed. We have to be at the airport in half an hour." Ashe, fully awake now, snatched clothing up and dressed as quickly as he could. Trajan was rushing him out the door before he could get his shoes on.

"You can do that in the van," Trajan's voice held concern. Ashe caught the worry from Trajan, his heart pounding double time in his chest. He tried to ask Trajan what was going on, but Trajan hushed him.

Winkler was waiting inside the van as Trajan and Ashe climbed in. Two others that Ashe didn't recognize were there as well. One was driving while the other sat in the back with Trajan and Ashe.

"We have a situation in D.C.," Winkler said. "Matt called. We're going in. I just hope we get there in time."

"But," Ashe said. He thought it would take hours to arrive at the nation's capital. He revised that thought when he saw what waited for them at the airport. A military jet sat there, the engines revving as Trajan, Winkler and the unknown werewolf hauled Ashe across the tarmac and up the metal steps to the jet. Seating was limited and there was barely room for all of them inside the tiny space.

"We'll break the speed limit going in," the unknown werewolf muttered grimly as he strapped himself in.

Ashe, looking around for his own seatbelt, found the ends, pulled them together and clicked them across his lap. Ashe blinked at Winkler, but Winkler's eyes were closed. Figuring that the Dallas Packmaster didn't want to be disturbed, Ashe sat back while all kinds of potential situations raced through his mind.

Unmarked patrol vehicles met them at the D.C. airport, as did Director Matthew Michaels. "Are you sure this is a good idea?" The Director walked up to Winkler and peered around the tall werewolf at Ashe, who stood in the early-morning light, shoulders hunched and hands in pockets. Trajan had an arm loosely draped around Ashe's shoulders.

"It's the best we have, Director," Winkler said. "If it doesn't look good when we go in, we'll come right out and let the regular forces have it."

Ashe sat in the back of a limousine between Winkler and Trajan while the Director, sitting beside the unnamed werewolf, outlined the problem for Ashe. "The British Embassy has been taken over by terrorists," he explained. "They tried the same thing with three other embassies at the same time, but were only successful at this one. There are quite a few dead at the other venues, including the enemy, but those embassies are now secure. Only the Brits are in danger, now. We gather that there are at least seven terrorists inside the building; four were killed before they gained entrance. Right now, everyone inside that embassy is in danger, if they haven't been killed already."

"Ashe, you're going to carry Trajan and some of the Director's men inside; they'll try to take out the terrorists," Winkler said. "Don't put yourself in danger; we'll show you a map and you'll drop your cargo where Matt says to drop them. Understood?"

"Uh-huh," Ashe felt shaky as Winkler and the Director outlined what they wanted. A map of the embassy interior was spread across the hood of a police cruiser, safely parked behind crime scene tape.

The lights were on in the British Embassy, but nobody was visible behind the windows. Someone had a representative from the terrorists on the phone, but they were refusing any sort of negotiation at that point.

A covered porch with square columns lined the front of the building, which was built in a wide U-shape. Ashe couldn't begin to describe how many national agencies and security personnel were outside the British Embassy in the early-morning light.

The media had been kept away from the site and Ashe was thankful for that. He didn't want his mother to see his image plastered all over national television, especially since she thought him safe in Dallas—he'd talked to her shortly before he'd gone to bed the night before. A light breeze ruffled Ashe's hair and flipped crime scene tape tied to vehicles and convenient traffic signs. The day promised to be a warm one.

"We think this is the safest place to make the drop," Matt made sure Ashe knew the proper room and the floor number inside the building as he bent over the map. The small room Matt indicated held copy machines and other office equipment. "Now," Matt went on, "these are the ones you'll take inside." Matt jerked his head at six men who stood nearby. "All of your jobs are on the line if you breathe a word on how you got inside," he spoke to the six operatives, all of whom stood at attention beside him. "Remember your non-disclosure agreements," Matt reminded them.

"Yes, sir," all six said in unison. Ashe knew they must be military, maybe Special Ops or something. He also figured that nobody would tell him anyway, so he didn't ask.

"Boy, now's the time. Get them in there pronto," Matt ordered.

"Yes, sir," Ashe nodded and went to mist. The six operatives and Trajan weighed nothing as mist. Ashe quickly found the designated room inside the embassy. He also found three bodies inside the room when he dropped his seven passengers. One of the dead was a young woman, who looked to be a secretary or assistant. The other two wore uniforms and were obviously security guards.

Ashe was supposed to come right back out of the building and join Winkler while they waited for the ones left inside to do their job. After seeing the dead woman, her throat viciously slashed, he decided otherwise. What would they do? Send him home? Ashe followed over Trajan's head.

His hearing still as sharp as it ever was, he heard voices on the lowest floor toward the front of the building. He'd dropped Trajan and the others on the second floor.

Footsteps sounded on the stairs. At least two people were walking up. Did Trajan hear them? The six operatives had scattered in other directions, looking for terrorists and survivors. Ashe hovered right behind Trajan's shoulder as the tall werewolf stepped inside a room, concealing himself beside the door.

Ashe realized Trajan was waiting for the two to come upstairs. Pulling a pistol from his jacket pocket, Trajan waited for the terrorists to walk past. Except they didn't. Instead, a grenade rolled right up to the doorway where Trajan stood. Ashe shrieked *grenade!* mentally and then gathering Trajan inside his mist again, rushed down the stairs ahead of the two who'd tossed the grenade.

Ashe didn't know where the six operatives were, but there was sudden shouting and screaming as at least a dozen prisoners, tied up and sitting on the lower-level floor, had a grenade tossed in their midst by another captor.

Desperate, Ashe gathered the prisoners up as well, somehow leaving the grenade sitting on the floor. It and the one above stairs detonated one right after another as Ashe shot skyward, going straight through the roof with fourteen screaming people inside his mist.

Somehow, Winkler had found a bullhorn and was shouting through it. "Meet at the New Zealand Embassy," he yelled, his voice magnified by the device. Ashe, unsure where the New Zealand Embassy was, made a complete circle, confused.

Then Winkler and the Director began pointing in the proper direction before climbing into a squad car and skidding away. Ashe followed overhead until the car pulled up before another, smaller building nearby. Ashe zoomed right through the walls, making his passengers shriek again before dropping them all in an entryway.

Screaming and crying, still bound and in a tangle, the hostages were attempting to wriggle away. Trajan, however, grabbed Ashe as soon as he reappeared and held him in a tight bear hug. Winkler, the Director and several others rushed in and began untying the hostages.

"This is gonna take some 'splaining," Ashe muttered. Trajan gave him an extra hug and let him go.

"Ashe, I know I don't have to tell you to keep this quiet; national security is on the line," Winkler said inside an office later. "Matt can be counted on to keep your secrets—he already knows about Amarillo."

Winkler went on to tell Ashe that the hostages were being debriefed inside the same building, and Ashe learned that three of the six operatives had been found alive inside the rubble of the British Embassy. Ashe had done as much as he could, but felt bad for the ones who hadn't survived the attack.

"Mr. Winkler, something set those guys off—the terrorists," he said. "I think they knew we were coming, somehow."

"The Director thinks the same thing, Ashe," Winkler nodded. "But that's for him to solve. We've done what we came to do. Would you like something to eat or would you rather rest for a couple of hours before we find a ride home?"

"Can I do a little of both?" Ashe held his stomach, which had been growling for half an hour. It was nearly ten in the morning, Eastern Daylight Time. Trajan had gone in search of coffee for himself and Winkler.

"Lie down on that sofa," Winkler pointed to a sofa against the back wall of the office. It held a desk, the sofa and two chairs. "I'll see if I can get somebody to find food." Winkler walked out the door. Ashe flopped down on the sofa with a sigh, removed his shoes and curled up on it.

"He's sixteen, and you'll be opening a can of worms with the vampire and shifter communities if you try it now," Winkler pointed out. Matt was already talking of recruiting Ashe. "I have him for the summer, but that won't be true if his parents learn what he's doing right now. I'll take him back to Texas, but he'll be a flight away if something else comes up, Director."

Matt had to be satisfied with that. Ashe was underage and the President would have a fit if he found out who'd done the rescue. "All right, but do everything you can to keep him with you for the rest of the summer. Damn. If I could just keep that kid," Matt shook his head.

He'd been impressed with the Amarillo thing. This was achieving the impossible. He and the President had been on the phone with the British government following the rescue at the Embassy. The official explanation was that the Special Ops team had gotten everyone out.

Later, a bit of well-placed compulsion from two of Matt's vampire operatives would ensure that the victims' stories matched that explanation.

"What can I offer in payment, besides giving you a ride back to Dallas?" Matt asked.

"The kid hasn't had breakfast," Winkler grinned.

Matt shook his head later as he watched Ashe devour French toast plus ham and eggs over easy, with a glass of orange juice. "He's still growing," Trajan said softly.

"I can't do a lot right now, but here are a few souvenirs from the White House," Matt handed a duffle bag over with an official seal on it. Ashe took it, surprised that he'd gotten anything.

A private jet waited on them this time, with more comfortable seating. Winkler herded Ashe up the steps, with Trajan right behind Winkler. The unknown werewolf was noticeably absent this time. Ashe blew out a breath and looked around quickly before boarding the jet. He'd never been to Washington, D. C. before and hadn't gotten a chance to see much of it this time.

"Come on," Winkler placed a hand on Ashe's head to duck it below the top of the door.

"Ashe gets to sit in an air conditioned office and we're picking peaches in the humidity," Sali grumbled.

"Hey, you volunteered. And we get paid for this," Dori peeked around the trunk of a peach tree and wrinkled her nose at Sali. Wynn was still recovering, so she was at home with her parents.

Several others from the community had taken the job in Shirley Walker's peach and grapefruit groves. A rush of wind blew past them, rustling the leaves and bending the trees, but it was gone almost as quickly as it arrived. Sali was grateful for the cooling wind; it was oppressively hot in the South Texas groves.

"Mom?" Marcie stared at her youngest son. She hadn't recognized the red Lexus that pulled up in front of Cordell Feed and Seed, but she recognized the two who'd climbed out of it.

"Honey?" Marcie was crying as she hugged Jackson Pruitt to her. Her oldest, Dustin, stood nearby as his mother wept and held onto Jack.

"Marcella?" Jason walked into the shop from the back; he'd been working in the greenhouse.

"These are my boys," Marcie stood back from both of them. "Boys, this is Jason Landers. My husband."

"Yeah. We heard," Dustin nodded respectfully to Jason.

"Boys, did your father allow this visit? And how did you find me?" Marcie wiped her cheeks with a shaking hand.

"We heard from somebody in Phoenix that you'd come here. Dad wouldn't tell us."

"Honey, your father will be livid."

"I don't care. I've already sent word to the Grand Master about him," Dustin muttered, a look of anger crossing his face. "And I sent photographs. He has my email address. If he forces us to go back, then he isn't much of a man. Besides, Jack will be eighteen next year. Dad can't do anything after that."

"You're still members of the Phoenix Pack," Jason warned. "There's protocol, Son. I'll have Winkler contact the Grand Master, too, but these things can take time to sort out. Especially if the Packmaster files his own complaint."

"Honey, I'm just worried your father will try to cause trouble," Marcie sighed.

"Mom, something's going on. I heard from Bob Greer that Dad didn't throw a big fit when we left, but a few days later something happened and he tore the house apart. I don't think we had anything to do with that, but we also don't know what caused it."

"Jason, I think we need to get the boys to Dallas as soon as possible," Marcie said, turning imploring brown eyes on her husband.

"I think so, too. Let me see if I can get Trace or somebody else up here to take over until the shop sells. I'll make some calls." Jason headed toward the office at the back of the store.

"He's a good man," Marcie said. "We'll get this sorted out. Are you hungry? There's a really good restaurant around the corner."

~

"Take the rest of the day off, Ashe," Winkler said. "Work out with Trajan and Marco, but that's it," he added. "That'll give you a long weekend. Marco can take you out later if you want to see Dallas." Ashe had slept during the trip back to Dallas, but still felt tired.

"I think I'll get in the pool for a little while and then go to bed for a nap," Ashe said, yawning wide enough to crack a jaw.

"That sounds great. I have to return some calls, but the pool sounds good." Ashe waved at Winkler's words, yawned again and headed toward the stairs and his bedroom.

~

"My Queen, how may I serve you?" Rabis bowed low before Friesianna.

"I have not forgotten that your gift is Foresight," the Elemaiyan Queen snapped. "I need your talents now."

"My Queen, what has happened to Hilbah?" Rabis knew very well what had happened to Hilbah. Hilbah was weak as a *Miriasu*, one born with Foresight. Hilbah's greatest talent had been telling Friesianna what she wanted to hear instead of the truth.

Hilbah's unexpected death at the hands of a human criminal left the Queen without a Miriasu. Rabis was the only remaining choice. He'd stayed away from the Queen's camp for centuries. Now he would be forced to return and serve her.

"I have a task for you, Rabis. One of our half-children must be brought to me. Of all those we made, only he has failed to hear the call and come to us."

"Is he of age?" Sixteen was considered an adult among the

Elemaiya. "I heard that many half-children have been killed by our Dark cousins."

"Of course, he is of age. I would not ask otherwise," the Queen's temper was rising.

Rabis knew not to push her. He took in her beautiful, hand-embroidered silk gown and the crown she'd wrested from her predecessor centuries before. Friesianna had never been a proper Queen. Someday, Rabis knew, she would pay a price for her treachery and for subsequent mistakes made through the years.

That time has not come as yet, more's the pity, Rabis thought sadly. Because Friesianna held Le'meruh, what many Elemaiya termed the rare ability of extreme compulsion, Rabis was compelled to obey her. He was faced with cowering before her now and performing the duties of a Miriasu.

"I will serve my Queen gladly," Rabis lied, bowing low.

"As you should," she snapped. "Come. We have little time."

"Come on, you can do better than that," Trajan watched as Ashe bench-pressed one hundred twenty pounds. Ashe was doing it—barely. "We've got leg presses after this," Trajan was back to torturing him, it seemed, and Ashe was still expected to run afterward with Marco.

"Trajan, I have another one for you. Maybe two." Ashe knew that voice.

"Jason?" Ashe said, working to get the weights up again.

"Young man, I heard you were drafted," Jason's face appeared above Ashe. The old werewolf was smiling.

"Currently undergoing torture," Ashe hissed out a breath.

"He's so mistreated," Trajan muttered sarcastically. "Who's this?"

"Marcie's youngest, Jack," Jason introduced someone else Ashe couldn't see. "And her oldest, Dustin, is parking his car. He'll be in shortly."

"I can take both of 'em, if that's what you want."

"I do, but Dustin is past twenty. We'll have to ask."

"Good enough. Let me know," Trajan agreed. "Ashe, all the way up," Trajan said, watching Ashe wobble the weights.

"Jackson Pruitt, but everybody calls me Jack," Ashe took the hand offered to him when Trajan let him up from the weight bench. Jack was dark-haired like his mother, with the brown eyes common to Marcie and Denise's family.

"If you're done, Ashe, get to those leg presses," Trajan rumbled.

"Dude, are you sure you want to do this?" Ashe hissed loud enough for Trajan to hear. That earned a flip to the ear from Winkler's Second. Ashe was pretending permanent harm as he walked toward the contraption where he'd do leg presses.

"Looks like fun," Jack said, sealing his fate.

"Mr. Winkler, Dom was involved in something, I know it," Marcie said. She and Jason sat inside Winkler's spacious office. "He went out of town at least once a month. At first, I thought it was another woman, but I don't think that was it. Several times, I found evidence that he'd been to Mexico. I knew better than to say anything, though." She had known better; Dominic Pruitt had beaten her throughout their marriage. If her father had known what Dom Pruitt truly was, he'd never have consented to the marriage.

"Why don't you let me work on this?" Winkler steepled fingers beneath his chin. "I'll do some credit card traces and such. We'll see what we can find. In the meantime, I'll call the Grand Master. If he'll approve a temporary transfer for your boys, we'll get this sorted out."

"Thank you, Mr. Winkler. You have no idea how much this means to me."

"Jason, you can move those two boys into a bedroom upstairs if you want. Nobody will get to them unless they can get past all my guards."

"Thanks, Mr. Winkler." Jason stood and nodded to his Packmaster.

~

"Grand Master, Pruitt may be part of the supply chain that Tanner had going. Those drugs and most of the animals had to come through Mexico."

"You know we don't have a good way to police some of the Packs in Mexico," Weldon Harper growled over the phone. "It's just too dangerous in some areas. Most of them obey, but there are outlaws. It wouldn't surprise me if Tanner wasn't funding them through his illegal hunting operation. I didn't get as much as I'd like from him."

"Too bad he's dead," Winkler muttered. "Do you have anyone who can track Pruitt?"

"I've got one of my trackers in. Do you have anyone I can put with him? If you do, I'll fly him through Dallas."

"I can send Grady."

"Good. I'll have Clayton on a plane by tomorrow."

~

Ashe stood in line outside the theatre complex in a Dallas suburb with Marco, waiting to buy tickets to a summer action film. Ashe was hoping Trajan would come along, but Winkler's Second had work to do. Jackson Pruitt had come, though.

Ashe wasn't sure what to think of the young werewolf; Jack wasn't Sali, whom Ashe had known all his life. New friendships were always difficult for Ashe. He had to find something to talk about, so common ground might be discovered.

Jackson at times seemed distracted. Haunted, perhaps. Nevertheless, Winkler had handed Marco a wad of cash and told him to take Ashe and Jackson out to dinner and a movie that Friday evening. Dinner had been at a popular steakhouse, and then they'd driven to a nearby theater.

"So, you're a shapeshifter," Jackson said as Marco asked for three adult tickets at the window.

"Yeah." Ashe stuck his hands into the pockets of new jeans. He didn't feel comfortable talking about the bumblebee bat in private. Talking about it in public, albeit quietly, made Ashe particularly uneasy.

"Don't say those things in public." Marco placed a hand on Jackson's arm before handing out tickets for the film.

"Didn't mean to make you uncomfortable," Jackson became defensive.

"Would you talk about yourself in public?" Marco's low growl at Jackson surprised Ashe. Marco seldom became so upset. Not since high school, anyway.

"Sorry, man," Jackson hung his head.

"Come on, I'll buy popcorn," Ashe sighed.

"That wasn't bad," Marco said as he, Ashe and Jackson walked out of the theatre two hours later. The action adventure film had been more entertaining than Ashe originally thought. As they walked, Ashe searched the parking lot for their vehicle; Marco had borrowed one of Winkler Security's unmarked vans to drive to the restaurant and theatre. Winkler's business owned a fleet of them; most marked with the logo, a few not.

Lights mounted on tall, steel poles illuminated the parking lot as they made their way toward the van, but the large lot was still dim to Ashe's eyes. Ashe slid the side door of the van back, preparing to climb in while Marco and Jackson loaded into the front.

"Hold it right there," two men with guns climbed out of a car parked next to the van. "You," one of them, a tall man with close-cropped hair, waved his gun at Jackson, "get in the car and nobody gets hurt."

Marco, standing on the opposite side of the van, growled. That spelled one thing to Ash—Marco wasn't growling low; this was an angry growl from one werewolf to another.

"Shut up or you'll die," the other werewolf snapped at Marco. This would-be kidnapper was shorter and shakier than the one with short hair.

"Don't hurt them, Hicks," Jackson had his hands up, pleading with the shorter male. Ashe had seconds, perhaps. His gaze was locked on Hicks' gun, which was pointed at Marco. He could try to get Marco on the other side of the van and then attempt to pick up Jackson, or he could grab both werewolf assailants at once, since they were very close together.

Marco, I'm getting them. I'll take them back to Winkler's kitchen. Have somebody meet me there, Ashe sent. He then went to mist and lifted both Hicks and his shorthaired partner before racing toward Winkler's home.

CHAPTER 8

"What the?" Jackson shouted as Ashe and both men from his father's Phoenix Pack disappeared.

"Shut up and get in the van!" Marco yelled, jerking his cell from a pocket. Climbing into the van and starting it, he had Winkler on the phone as he raced out of the parking lot.

"Winkler, two wolves were here trying to grab Jackson. Ashe is bringing them to your kitchen. They're both armed! Gotta go." Marco punched the end call button and screeched out of the theatre parking lot with Jackson hanging on, frightened and shaking in the passenger seat.

"What happened?" Jackson shouted as Marco raced toward the highway.

"Can't talk," Marco hissed. "Just hold on and I'll try to get us there in one piece."

"Don't hit Ashe," Winkler growled at Trajan and three other guards. He and Trajan were the only ones who knew how Ashe would arrive.

The others were blinking in confusion at an empty kitchen. All five were armed with rifles.

Winkler wished at that moment he had mindspeech—he'd tell Ashe to release his prisoners in the floor and remain mist so he wouldn't be placed in danger. "And don't kill unless you're forced to," Winkler added. "We need to do some questioning."

"What are we looking for, boss?" Grady cast a puzzled glance at the Dallas Packmaster.

"They'll be here soon enough," Winkler said. "Raise your rifles and remember what I said."

Ashe barely paid attention to the two werewolves inside his mist. He was worried over the same thing that concerned Winkler—getting shot if he appeared in the kitchen with the other two. He was almost there; he could see the roof of Winkler's mansion. *I'll drop them in the kitchen*, he sent to Winkler. *I'll stay mist and meet you in my bedroom.*

Ashe thought that best, in order to keep anyone else from seeing what he truly was. *And to keep from being shot*, he added to himself. His passengers screamed in terror when he flew through the roof of Winkler's home, then screamed twice more as he dropped through the ceilings of two more floors. *Get ready!* Ashe shouted mentally and dumped two werewolves on the kitchen floor. Gunfire erupted behind him as he zipped through the house toward his bedroom.

Winkler came upstairs with Marco half an hour later, shirtless and with a bandage on his right shoulder. Ashe wanted to slink away. He'd gotten the Dallas Packmaster injured.

"It's nothing," Winkler sighed at Ashe's expression. "We've got them locked up."

"They're from the Phoenix Pack. The shorter one recognized Jackson," Ashe said. "I think they were trying to kidnap him."

"Probably," Winkler agreed. "Trouble is; Dominic Pruitt isn't in Phoenix right now. His Second is running things and he says Dominic didn't tell him where he was going or when he'd be back. Now, as a Packmaster myself, that's generally a problem. If Trajan doesn't know where I am and can't get in touch with me, then I've been kidnapped or I'm dead. I don't think Dominic Pruitt is either one of those things. As soon as Hicks and Burton are conscious again, we'll ask questions. The Grand Master wants to know what those answers are, and pretty quick."

"Is Jackson okay?" Ashe slid off his bed.

"He's fine—his mother and Jason are talking to him now," Marco said. "He's not sure what he saw, and some of the wolves downstairs are asking questions."

"What was I supposed to do?" Ashe sighed and paced.

"What you did. Ashe, we'll have to keep Jackson hidden until we know the threat from his father is over," Winkler explained. "And that may mean a move." Ashe watched the Dallas Packmaster closely. Lines of pain formed around Winkler's mouth.

"Doctor Lang available?" Ashe asked, suddenly concerned.

"He'll stop by when his shift at the fire department is over," Winkler said. "I'll be fine until then."

"Just a graze," Marco agreed. "Bullets bounce off the boss."

"Good," Ashe said. "I'm sorry, I didn't know where else to take them."

"Son, you did fine. Stop worrying about it," Winkler patted Ashe's shoulder. "Want anything to eat or drink?"

"Come on, we'll find a sandwich downstairs," Marco coaxed.

"All right." Ashe walked downstairs with both men. He was sitting at the kitchen island having a roast-beef sandwich when David Lang walked in. Winkler didn't even stop eating while Dr. Lang cleaned out the wound and bandaged it again.

"I'd ask if you wanted something for pain, but I know better," Dr. Lang laughed.

"It'll be healed in the morning," Winkler waved the doctor-turned-paramedic off. "Now, what I really wanted to say, Ashe, is that since

Dominic Pruitt knows where we are, we'll be traveling to my beach house in Port Aransas tomorrow. We'll stay there for a little while, I think, until we can get this sorted out. You'll get to see your parents and friends on weekends if you want. I'd prefer that you stay at the beach house with me during the week. It's right on the gulf, so it shouldn't be a hardship."

"And you won't be getting out of your exercises, we have a weight room there and you and Marco can run on the beach," Trajan walked in, grinning. "How's the shoulder?" He asked Winkler.

"Fine." Winkler huffed. "Grady is meeting someone here tomorrow afternoon, so he won't be traveling with us. Pick at least six to come along, and let Jason, Marcie and her boys know they're coming too. Those two didn't know where Pruitt was; he just called and sent them after Jackson. So, we're at a loss, still, on that end."

"Will do, boss." Trajan set about making a roast-beef sandwich for himself, asked the doctor if he wanted one, made an extra and set out soft drinks for both.

"I sent Orville to Cordell," Trajan grinned. "Trace will head down to Port A as soon as Orville gets there. Gene's coming and I have Ace, Gabe, Spencer and Nick all packing bags. Told Marco to come along, too. Just in case."

"Sounds good," Winkler agreed. "Never hurts to have an extra or two. Jason and Marcie will move into one of the extra houses in Star Cove. Put Ace and Gene in next door to watch those boys of hers."

Trajan nodded. He was on the boss' wavelength. Winkler hadn't gotten as far as he had or stayed alive because he trusted or believed everybody. Plus, the Grand Master wanted Winkler closer to the border, in case there was trouble. Winkler's jet would be parked at the Corpus Christi Airport and kept at the ready.

"We'll leave first thing in the morning. Have those two from the Phoenix Pack ready to go to the Grand Master before then."

"Already taken care of," Trajan nodded. "Got six of ours going with them in one of the bigger vans. Did you get everything out of them that you wanted?"

"With a little help," Winkler nodded. "I asked Wlodek for a little fanged assistance. Since somebody was already in the states that I know, he dropped by. Looks like he's gonna be with us for a little while. At Wlodek's orders." Trajan noted the set of Winkler's mouth and didn't ask questions about the why of it.

"Where is he now?" Trajan asked instead.

"Grabbing a few supplies," Winkler said. "He'll be here before dawn and we'll transport him in a body bag. He'll look like luggage."

"Until sundown," Trajan snickered.

"Yeah. There's always that."

"Dad, Marcie's boys came to Dallas," Ashe informed his father. He'd called his father's cell, since his mother was likely in bed already. It was after midnight and Ashe had just finished packing for the trip. "And then two of their father's wolves showed up to kidnap Jackson, who's still seventeen. Winkler and the Grand Master want him hidden and out of harm's way until they can get everything sorted out, so we'll be down there in the morning. Winkler's putting Marcie, Jason and her two boys in one of the empty houses in the new addition, and the rest of us will be staying at Winkler's beach house in Port Aransas. I'll get to come home on weekends if I want."

"Son, how bad do you think the Phoenix Packmaster wants that boy?" Aedan wanted to know how much security they'd need at night in case Dominic Pruitt discovered where his youngest son was being kept.

"I'd say he wants him back pretty bad; he sent two wolves with guns after him." Ashe didn't want to tell his father about his involvement in the incident. Or about the trip to D.C. He'd let Winkler handle that. If Winkler wanted.

"Where are those wolves now, Son?"

"Chained up and on their way to the Grand Master in the morning," Ashe said. "I think he wants to do more questioning."

"Son, we've missed you. It'll be good to have you back."

"Yeah. I missed you, too."

Ashe stared at what looked to be a body bag that Trajan and Marco were loading into the jet. It wasn't going on with the luggage; this was carried into the passenger section of the jet and they were handling it carefully. Several locked coolers were also loaded onto the jet.

The blond werewolf with ice-blue eyes was coming, as was Gene, whom Ashe had already met. He was also introduced to Gabe and Spencer, the werewolf brothers, and Nick, a short, black-haired werewolf he hadn't seen before.

Gene had taken charge of Marcie, Jason, Jackson and Dustin. Dustin wanted to be called Dusty, and Ashe thought he was doing his best to fit in with Winkler's Wolves. It made him wonder if Dusty wanted to become a permanent member of the Dallas Pack. Trajan promised to start training Dusty in martial arts with Marco soon. Ashe guessed that he'd have to be stronger and in better shape before Trajan considered him for that sort of training.

After landing in Corpus Christi, Ashe climbed into a van with Winkler's entourage. The blond werewolf loaded into a second van provided by the Corpus Christi Pack. The body bag was hefted into Winkler's van, along with their luggage.

"How's my little sister?" Winkler said to the werewolf driver.

"Just fine," the driver grinned.

"Ashe, this is my brother-in-law, Sam Sheridan, Jr.," Winkler grinned at Ashe, who sat behind Winkler in the second row of seats. "He and his dad own a lot of land south of Corpus Christi."

"We grow a lot of fruit and vegetables," Sam grinned at Ashe as he backed out of the parking space. "We just don't compete with Shirley on the cotton."

"Nice to meet you," Ashe nodded to their driver. He hadn't known until then that Winkler had a sister. Ashe was happy to sit back and watch Corpus Christi fly past, and then the waters of the gulf as they drove over a high bridge to reach Mustang Island.

He gasped, though, when Sam pulled off the road that ran through the island and onto a private drive. The drive led to a beach house that fronted the gulf. Ashe had seen this house from the road when he and his mother had driven past days ago. The house was enormous, with a large, two-story detached garage. It didn't surprise him that Winkler owned something so nice.

"You'll sleep in the main house," Winkler told Ashe, watching while Trajan took charge of the body bag, just as before. Trajan and Gabe carried it to the steps leading to the apartment over the detached garage. "Come on, I'll show you which bedroom is yours and you'll have your office right next door."

"I have an office?" Ashe grinned.

"Yep." Winkler slapped Ashe on the back. "But it's Saturday, so you're off. Feel free to unpack or do laundry. We don't have much of a staff here. I'll bring in a cook and a housekeeper for the big stuff, but your laundry and bed making is your job on the beach."

"That's okay, I do it at home," Ashe said.

Ashe gaped at the view through the glass doors of the media room. "Dang," he breathed. "That is awesome." Winkler led him down a long hallway on the second floor.

"You get the bay view," Winkler said, opening the door. Ashe walked into the bedroom, which had its own bath and a view of tall grasses on the western side of the island. A thin strip of water lay beyond that, between the island and the mainland.

"That's the ship channel," Winkler explained when Ashe asked. "Ships come through all the time. They haul oil in for the refinery just outside town. Plus some of the Navy ships travel through—Corpus Christi has a Naval Station, although mostly they handle the Navy jets and planes."

"Sounds cool," Ashe said, dropping his bags onto the bed.

"Your office is downstairs, beside mine," Winkler led Ashe down the steps and through another hall. Winkler had the office with the gulf view; Ashe could see the guesthouse from his. It didn't matter; if he wanted to see water, he only had to go to the kitchen, the media room or just go outside and take the wooden walkway to the beach.

"I like this, Mr. Winkler," Ashe breathed.

"Good. I like it too. Now, why don't you grab something to drink from the fridge and go out to the deck? Watch the waves roll in until lunch?"

"Sure." Ashe followed Winkler to the huge kitchen, where a short, bald man who introduced himself as Jimmy was busy preparing a meal. Winkler got a soda with Ashe and walked out to the massive deck behind the media room.

"This is one of my favorite spots," Winkler settled into a cushioned rattan chair. Ashe sat nearby, setting his soda on a glass-topped table beside the chair. He watched waves pile up on the beach while tourists walked past and brown pelicans and seagulls flew by, calling out in flight.

"Do they always fly like that?" Ashe watched a line of brown pelicans flap by, so close he could almost reach out and touch them. It looked as if they were playing follow the leader.

"A lot of the time," Winkler grinned. "You'll see a few of the white pelicans, too, but they're not as common here. I've invited your parents and your friends over tonight for a cookout," Winkler went on. "I think your father will come after sunset. The rest will be here around seven."

"Thanks," Ashe said.

"Come on, you can do this," Marco was forcing Ashe to run in the late afternoon sun. Ashe had his shirt off, sunscreen slathered on and was working to keep up with Marco and Trajan. They ran easily on the beach, and Ashe watched as bits of shell and a stray jellyfish or two blurred past as he forced himself to take longer strides.

"See, those long legs can work for you," Trajan grinned. Ashe knew the nearly seven-foot werewolf was playing with him and could likely leave him behind and stranded if he wanted. "And tomorrow, you'll be in the weight room again at seven."

"What sport did you play in school?" Ashe was breathing hard.

"Basketball mostly," Trajan said. "Got a scholarship. Had to turn it down. Can you see me out of town at a scheduled game during the full moon?" Trajan shook his head. "So, now I take all my frustrations out on my trainees."

"You went to a human school." Ashe didn't make it a question.

"Ashe, most werewolf children do. A lot of those kids don't know what they are until they go through the change the first time. I gotta tell you, the werewolf kids in those experimental communities turn a lot faster than those in the human schools. Dad says it's because they know what they are from the beginning. The rest aren't told because the secret is too hard to keep. Some don't turn until they're eighteen or nineteen. I think it's instinct—the wolf knows it's not safe."

"Wow, Trajan. How old were you?" Ashe hoped he wasn't prying.

"Seventeen," Trajan replied. "Trace didn't turn until he was eighteen and about to graduate. It was hard, spending that last year in high school, suddenly realizing I was something else and couldn't ever play pro like I wanted."

"Trajan, I'm sorry about that," Ashe said. And he was. He felt a bit of kinship with Winkler's Second at that moment. Ashe was worried that he'd never be able to attend college, or do much of anything that called attention to himself. He was hunted and he could never forget that.

"Kid, I think you know how I feel," Trajan said and ran ahead.

Ashe took off his shoes when they reached the stretch of sand in front of the beach house and walked into the water. "This is a long way from Cloud Chief, isn't it?" Marco said, wading in beside him.

"Yeah. Do you ever talk to Randy Smith?" Ashe asked, gazing out over the horizon. The water stretched before him as far as he could see.

"Every now and then, by email. I think Cori talks to him more often than I do," Marco sighed. "He's working for a newspaper in Chicago, now."

"He could write really well," Ashe agreed. He'd seen the essay Randy had written at age thirteen.

"Still can. Graduated with honors from the University of Illinois. His dad, Terry, was from that area. Dawn sent him up there because Terry's brother lives in the area. Dawn went back to the Santa Fe Pack, last I heard. She stays in contact with Randy. Anyway that's what Randy tells Cori."

"I hope he's all right," Ashe said. "I was hoping I'd hear from him once in a while, but never got anything."

"Ashe, I think that's not his fault," Marco whispered. Ashe thought about that for a moment.

"Compulsion," Ashe sighed.

"Yeah."

"I think that word is worse than cursing to me," Ashe said. "It worries me that someday, nobody will remember who I am except the vampires. And that frightens me." It worried Ashe, too, that it might drive a wedge between him and his father.

"I hope that doesn't happen," Marco said. "It's bad enough that Dad asked for Sali's memory to be altered."

"Marco, I can't talk to Sali about any of this stuff anymore," Ashe allowed the defeat to come out in his voice. "I've been isolated from my best friend. I don't know how they could think I'd feel anything other than angry about that."

"Ashe, if there comes a day when I don't remember any of this stuff, I just want you to know that it wasn't my idea, and that before that happened, I thought you were probably the most amazing shifter I'd ever met."

"Thanks, Marco." Ashe felt a flush creeping into his cheeks, but he ignored it, turning his face into the breeze coming off the water.

"Ashe!" Adele gave him a hard hug when she walked into Winkler's beach house later. Ashe had taken a long shower before dressing in clean jeans and a T-shirt. He walked around barefoot, thinking he probably needed sandals—that's what Winkler was wearing around the house.

Sali, Marcus and Denise were hugging Marco before Cori got to do the same. Sali, looking tan from working in the peach groves, grinned at Ashe. Wynn had come with Dori and Lavonna, and she was staying close to Sali's side.

Ashe observed Dori, thinking at first that she watched Wynn. That wasn't the case. He realized after a while that Dori's eyes followed Sali everywhere, with bare longing on her face. Silently he railed against the injustices life dealt.

The cook had prepared barbecued ribs and chicken for the crowd, with potato salad, baked beans, rolls and apple pie for dessert. The food was good; Ashe sat at a table with Sali, Wynn, Dori, Marco and Cori, eating and talking. Cori had her cheek against Marco's arm after a while and Marco smiled down at her. Ashe sighed.

"Winkler, I think I could smell this barbecue from fifty miles away," a new voice announced as steps sounded on the wooden deck. Ashe turned to see who it might be. The man was around Winkler's height, with black hair, gray-blue eyes and a wry smile. He clapped Winkler on the back. Hard.

"Anthony Hancock," Ashe whispered, leaning back in his chair, completely stunned.

"He doesn't use that name anymore," Marco said softly. "It's Tony Rockland, now."

"I did a history report on him—how he was killed by terrorists," Ashe said, staring at the former Director of the Joint NSA/Homeland Security Office.

"A vampire happened to be there when his hotel was bombed," Trajan knelt beside Ashe's chair. "I wouldn't mention any of that stuff unless he says it's okay. He works for the Vampire Council, now, but Tony and Winkler knew each other before all that."

"He's a vampire." Ashe's voice held bitterness.

"Yeah."

Aedan Evans and Nathan Anderson arrived less than half an hour later. Both nodded respectfully to Tony Hancock. Ashe couldn't think of him with a different name—Ashe had hero-worshipped the man who'd reportedly died while tracking terrorists. Now he was just another vampire who could place compulsion.

He was dressed well in designer clothing, too. It wasn't a suit but the shoes were Italian, Ashe knew that much. His father had a few pairs of shoes inside his closet that were quite expensive. These looked to cost more than that and the slacks Tony wore were likely tailored and hadn't ever seen the inside of a department store. It appeared that working for the Council paid very well.

"I think I'll go for a walk on the beach," Ashe said, rising from his seat.

"Want to go, too, Cori?" Marco smiled at Cori, who still leaned against him.

"Yeah. Let's go."

Sali, Wynn and Dori ended up going, too. Ashe was halfway down the steps leading to the beach walkway when a strange voice filtered into his head. *Don't get lost, Ashe. I don't want to be forced to look for you.*

"My Queen." Ruby bowed before Friesianna. "Our paid source gives a location in Texas, but it has been watched closely. The child is not there. Perhaps they are hiding him."

Friesianna cursed. "This is untenable," she hissed. "That boy is ours. We will force them to hand him over."

"Perhaps more difficult than you might imagine," Ruby, one of the Queen's four Jewel Sentinels, replied carefully. He had no desire to anger the Queen. "The community is guarded and shielded. Three witches placed a braided shield—difficult for one of ours to unravel."

"Then send two. Or three. I don't care how many. Get inside and get something for me that I can use as leverage."

"Of course, my Queen." Ruby bowed low and backed away.

"Child, I realize you owe this debt. It is because you owe it that you will not be punished as severely for keeping the information from me. I have the boy under surveillance, now. I hope you realize what an asset he will be."

"Father, I beg you not to conscript. He will do as you ask, as long as you ask, I think." Radomir lifted his eyes to Wlodek, Head of the Vampire Council.

"You know the law. There is already much rumbling in the Council about this."

"I know." Radomir silently cursed the two who'd witnessed Ashe's ability in Amarillo, Texas. They were obligated to report in detail to the Council. Now, Wlodek knew of his attempts to conceal Ashe. While he wouldn't be punished as severely, perhaps, he'd lost his sire's trust.

Blood debt was blood debt, however; Radomir would be dead if not for Ashe Evans. He also knew Ashe's father would never consent to conscription. There was a way around this, but Wlodek and the Council might not see it. Anthony Rockland had been sent to watch Ashe. "You intend to tie up one of ours over this?" Radomir asked instead.

"The boy is being threatened by those fool Elemaiya. They think to snatch him away. They'll throw him as fodder before their enemies, when we could make much better use of his talents. Calm yourself, child. This will come out best for us, you'll see."

$\mathcal{A}$ she wasn't about to say anything to the others. There was only one conclusion he could draw, though—Tony Hancock could mindspeak. That meant he had Elemaiyan blood in some measure. He was vampire, though, and Ashe didn't want to draw more of Tony's attention than he could help. He also felt a bit of guilt for taking off down the beach without greeting his father, but he had. Now he walked over wet sand while the gulf waters rose and fell around his ankles.

"You're a million miles away," Cori was suddenly beside him, Marco right behind her. Ashe had walked ahead of the others, hands stuffed in his pockets, mind working furiously.

"I wish I was a million miles away," Ashe mumbled, kicking at the water. His jeans were wet to the knees from the surf splashing around his feet.

"Ashe, you don't mean that," Cori looped her arm in his.

"Yes I do, Cori." How could he explain that the Council had likely sent someone to keep an eye on him? That troubled Ashe. Why would they be interested in him, unless they wanted something?

"I've got your arm; you're not going anywhere without me," Cori smiled up at Ashe, her blue eyes playful.

"Then Marco has to come along, too, I guess," Ashe said.

"Yeah. Marco has to come, too. Come on, Ashe. You're here with us now. This is a wonderful moment. Share it with us instead of getting lost in your head."

"Yeah, dude. There's more to life than hacking computers," Sali poked Ashe as he and Wynn walked by. Sali had an arm draped loosely over Wynn's shoulder. Dori, looking lost, trailed right behind them.

"I think your mom would like it if you went home with her and your dad tonight," Cori said, pulling Ashe along with her. She now walked with her arms linked with Marco and Ashe. "Wynn's parents are having a party for Marcie's boys tomorrow afternoon. They put an aboveground pool in the yard, so it'll be a swimming party."

"So, they're getting right into the whole beach thing," Ashe said, staring out over the gulf waters. The moon was in its dark phase. A few lights from the shore shone weakly on the water.

"Dad's thinking about buying a boat," Cori grinned. "He let it slip that he used to live in a fishing village in Wales."

"And might have made his living off the sea," Ashe sighed. "And Dad won't tell me a thing about himself." Ashe kicked at the water.

"I've always thought he was older than Nathan," Marco offered. "Just by the way he did things. Cori's dad has always seemed more relaxed. That's a good thing, since Cori's such a handful." Cori removed her arm from Ashe's and smacked Marco lightly on the shoulder. Marco laughed and hugged her.

"Is there anything you want to bring home with you?" Ashe's mother asked later when Ashe and the others came back from their walk on the beach.

"No, Mom, I think I've got everything I need for one day," Ashe said. Trace had just come in—he'd driven from Oklahoma to Corpus Christi and looked tired. Ashe gave him a smile before walking out of the beach house with his parents.

"Good to see you, Dad," Ashe said. Aedan gave Ashe a rare grin and patted Ashe on the back as they walked toward the SUV parked out front.

"Wow, the patio furniture is amazing," Ashe liked what he saw when his mother proudly led him to their patio when they arrived.

"Got it yesterday," Adele said. "Your father and Nathan helped put up the O'Neill's pool. It's ready to go for the party tomorrow. What can you tell me about those boys, Ashe?" she changed tack quickly, asking about Jackson and Dustin Pruitt.

"I think there's a problem with their dad, and I think that's affected Jackson," Ashe answered truthfully. "He's a little strange at times. Tried to ask me about being a shapeshifter in public, once. Marco got onto him and there wasn't anybody close enough to hear."

"That's not good. Denise tells me he hasn't turned yet."

"Trajan said something about that earlier—he told me that the wolves who go to public schools sometimes don't change until they're eighteen or so. Jack's not eighteen yet. Trajan says that the wolf knows it's not safe, or something like that."

"Marcus and Jason are probably going to work with him," Aedan sighed, sitting on the glider with Adele. "And Marcus says Jason may ask to join the Star Cove Pack so the boy can try to fit in with the Pack. There's a college in Corpus, if he wants to attend after he graduates from high school."

"I've been thinking about that," Ashe said.

"Son, you've got two years yet," Aedan began.

"No, Dad. Not for me. For Mom. There's a school here that has a marine biology program. Mom said the other day that if she hadn't gone into business, she might have chosen that or veterinary medicine. Mom, I think you should go back to school. If you want to." Ashe gave his mother the most serious look he could. Adele blinked at him in surprise.

"Honey, I just never—gosh, that might be fun."

"Yeah, I think you'd be great at it," Ashe said. "Either of those things, actually."

"Is that something you might want, Adele?" Aedan stared at his wife.

"Well, the sale of the store could pay for my tuition, and I might be able to test out of a lot of things."

"Adele, I will pay for this if you want it," Aedan hugged Ashe's mother.

"I'll check the college out next week," Adele said, smiling. "It really does sound like fun."

"And then I can ask if you have any homework," Ashe grinned.

"Revenge, honey?" Adele laughed.

"Maybe."

"Somebody told me there was home cooking," Winkler laughed when he, Trajan, Trace and Marco walked into the O'Neill's home the following afternoon.

"There is; it's potluck," Sharon O'Neill said, taking the bags of soft drinks and ice that Trajan and his brother handed over.

"Hey, Trace," Ashe, who'd come through the kitchen with Sali to get paper plates and plastic cups, greeted the werewolf who'd come to Cloud Chief twice to help out.

"You get taller every time I see you," Trace chuckled. "Tell me where to put this." He held up two bags of ice.

"There's a big cooler on the patio," Ashe said. "Follow me." Ashe led the way through the O'Neill's family room and through the patio doors where the pool party was in full swing. A volleyball net was strung across the pool and there were at least ten teenagers slapping a ball across the net.

"You'll pay for your day off tomorrow," Trajan grinned at Ashe. "I've got Ace ready to work with Jack and Dusty. We'll have a weight room and a few other things installed in the school building. It's time Principal Billings started paying more attention to physical education."

"I wouldn't say that to his face," Ashe grinned. "But you can." Trajan laughed. Ashe helped Trace get the bags of ice emptied into a cooler, then stuffed sodas into the ice.

"You gettin' in?" Trace nodded to the pool.

"Are you kidding? Ashe has knobby knees. He won't even wear shorts, most of the time," Sali grinned.

"Is that why you show up to lift weights in jeans? We have to fix that," Trajan said. "Your knees can't be knobbier than Trace's. He'll wear shorts tomorrow. I'll get some for you tonight on the way home, and we'll get weight-lifting gloves, too. You're gonna need 'em."

"Fine. If you buy shorts, at least get cargo shorts," Ashe pointed a finger at Trajan.

"I'll buy two pairs, if you'll wear exercise shorts to work out in."

"Deal," Ashe grinned. "As long as you don't make fun of my knees."

"Who's making fun of your knees?" Cori walked in with Marco. Ashe lifted an eyebrow; it looked to him as if Cori and Marco had been doing a little kissing.

"Everybody," Ashe said. "You see how I'm worn down and oppressed, don't you?"

"And it's stunted your growth," Marco laughed. Ashe was a good three inches taller than Marco, and likely to get taller.

"It's gonna be a great summer," Trace slapped Ashe on the back and grabbed a plate before heading to the buffet.

Ashe went through the books on his bookshelves later while Sali, Wynn and Dori lounged on his bed. He pulled a couple of paperbacks off the shelf that he hadn't taken to Dallas with him and stuffed those inside his backpack.

As an afterthought, he also pulled the dictionary down that held the note from the one calling himself his grandfather. He zipped up the backpack after that and hefted it over his shoulder.

Winkler, Trace and Trajan were taking him to Winkler's beach house, with a brief stop at a department store in Aransas Pass, first. Trajan was determined to buy the promised shorts and gloves.

"You ever played this before?" Trace held up a popular video game when they got back to Winkler's beach house.

"Used to play with Sali and Larry Campbell," Ashe said. "But they got tired of losing."

"I think the gauntlet just got thrown," Trajan said. "Come on, Marco and I will take you two on. We'll see who loses now."

"You're on, bro," Trace flipped on the giant flat screen hanging on Winkler's media room wall.

"What's going on?" Vampire Tony Hancock walked in and sat on a nearby sofa.

"I'd ask if you wanted a soda or something, but I know better," Trajan said.

"I'd just have to cough it up later. Discreetly, of course," Tony replied. "I've played this game," he added. "When my surrogate sire wasn't looking. He thinks it's a frivolous waste of time."

Ashe blinked at the former Director of the Joint NSA and Homeland Security Department, wondering what a surrogate sire was and why Tony had one. Figuring that he wasn't likely to get that question answered, he turned back to the video game.

Tony Hancock had been vampire for twenty-two years. Ashe knew exactly what his date of death was in the official records. He'd died at age thirty-seven, so he'd be fifty-nine now and didn't look a day past twenty-six.

"Watch this, we're gonna save the universe," Trajan grinned, loading up the game. Trace did well enough against his brother, but Marco was working as hard as he could against Ashe. With Ashe, it was as if he always knew the enemy's moves before they were made. Trajan and Trace sat back and whistled as Ashe obliterated cyber creatures, one after another.

"Here, my arm's tired," Ashe handed the controller off to Trajan while his avatar died on screen.

"Holy crap, kid, did you even have your eyes open there at the end?"

"Don't know," Ashe shrugged. "Now you know why Sali won't play against me anymore. If he wants to play, he invites Larry, Jeff and

Hayes over." Ashe named off the other male students in his and Sali's class. "I'm going to bed. If you want a rematch sometime, let me know." Ashe rose from his seat on the floor. He couldn't help himself as he walked out of the room. *How much Elemaiya blood do you have?* He sent to Tony Hancock.

I'm an eighth, Tony returned. Ashe was shocked that the vampire even answered.

~

Honored One, the child is more than talented. He seems intuitive, if that is the proper term. I'd say it borders on Foresight, actually. Is there more information available on the Elemaiya? I never received anything, as you know, and they do not bother with anything less than half-bloods. If there is anyone you know who might be able to provide information, I'd appreciate any assistance with this. It will help me determine what his full talents are, I think.

-Anthony.

Tony closed his laptop and sighed. The boy was only sixteen. He hoped Wlodek would give him more than two years before sending someone to collect him. The rule of conscription was at times a harsh one. If the vampire race found a human who would enrich their race, the normal rules of turning could be ignored.

That's how brothers had been turned—mindspeech and misting ran in families. The Council's two misters were brothers, as were the two other mindspeakers. Tony had mindspeech but no blood siblings. They'd have been turned quickly if he'd had any.

Tony had been adopted as a baby by his werewolf mother. He had a stepbrother—Deryn Alford, a werewolf in the Denver Pack. No werewolf had ever become vampire. They also didn't have the misting or mindspeech ability that a handful of vampires held over the centuries.

Tony was surprised to get a return email so quickly from the Head of the Council, the message causing his cell to vibrate. Tony read it from his phone rather than opening his laptop again.

Will contact my eldest, the message read. *He will know if anyone will—W.*

"Yeah, he'd know, all right." Tony deleted the message and went to walk the beach.

~

"You promised to bring the boy," Obediah Tanner's brother stared at Dominic Pruitt.

"He took off with Dusty. I'll get him back. He'll learn what it's like from this end of things," Dom snorted.

"You know we need him and more like him to haul this stuff across the border," Ezekiel Tanner snapped. "All we have is older males, and half of those have bullets lodged in their bodies. They can't run as fast anymore."

Dom didn't want to point out that Obediah and Ezekiel had chased away or killed any females who'd associated with the rogue Pack, which was located just across the border in Mexico. It prevented any young wolves coming from that Pack. This was a lucrative business, but they worried about recruiting from any of the Grand Master's Packs. Somebody would surely pass the information along and the Grand Master would send his Trackers with an army of wolves and vampires at their backs.

Dom, Obediah and Ezekiel had smuggled drugs and contraband for years. Dom was searching for a good location to set up another game preserve—the one Obediah ran had brought in huge payoffs from wealthy clients, in addition to being the perfect place to hide smuggled drugs until they could be distributed throughout the United States.

Hunting on the preserve had been Obediah's idea—the shapeshifters had no form of government to protest against the practice, so it was easy to kidnap a rare one here and there. There was no shortage of well-paying hunters either, who jumped at the invitation to take them down.

Dom and Ezekiel both realized that Obediah was likely dead now, after the raid on his game preserve—neither had heard from him since.

Dom hadn't heard from the two wolves he'd sent after Jackson either, and he was getting worried. Jackson hadn't turned yet, but that could happen anytime. He'd informed Jack of what he was shortly after his mother took off.

The boy hadn't taken it very well, but he'd come to like it soon, Dom was sure of it. The boy would make a good runner, too, if they could get him back. He'd thought to recruit Dusty, but his oldest son had too much of his mother in him.

Dustin. Just the thought of him made Dominic growl. Dom had given up on his oldest son. Jackson liked the expensive cell phones, toys and the Corvette his father had bought for him recently. With the promise of wealth, Jackson could be convinced to run drugs as a wolf.

All it took was a specially made harness, loaded with sealed bags of illegal substances. Money would replace the drugs in the bags, once the receivers on the U.S. side of the border were reached.

Border guards were less likely to aim at what they saw as a wolf or coyote. It was easy for them to slip through. The bullet wounds came mostly from farmers and ranchers, worried about their livestock.

"I'll get the boy back," Dom promised. "Maybe we can hit that supernatural community, too. Should be enough young wolves to be had there, plus the kids who turn into larger shifters. They can carry as well as a wolf can."

"What?" Zeke stared at Dominic Pruitt for seconds before the idea took root. Dom recognized the light in Zeke's eyes as he weighed the merits of Dom's suggestion. "Do it," Zeke said, nodding curtly. "We can snatch those old enough. They'll learn quick enough what it's like to live on this side of the border."

"How are the plans coming along on taking William Winkler down?" Dom asked. He'd gotten wind from some of Zeke's rogues that something was in the works. Zeke hadn't shared anything, yet, though.

"That plan is taking shape," Zeke growled. Dom was wise enough to recognize that growl—it meant Ezekiel Tanner wasn't prepared to share information yet. He was angry, though. Angry that Winkler had been instrumental in his brother's takedown. Dom kept further questions to himself. After all, he had plans for William Winkler too, and he was keeping that information to himself.

"I don't think any normal person will get into this bank," Ashe handed over what he had to Winkler the following afternoon. The bank in Boise had been a difficult system to crack. Ashe had noticed that his usual ability to crack puzzles and such was much sharper, now.

Perhaps it was because most puzzles didn't provide much of a challenge to him. Now, when Winkler set these things in front of him, he could almost see a road map to his destination if he just closed his eyes and concentrated.

"Kid, this is frightening," Winkler said, going over the information in the folder Ashe handed to him. "I'll tell you what; go find something to eat while I make a call or two."

"Okay," Ashe stretched and rolled his shoulders to work out a few kinks. He'd gotten stiff, sitting in a chair most of the day. "Do I have time for a quick run on the beach?"

"Take Marco or somebody with you," Winkler nodded.

"All right." Ashe wandered down the hall toward the media room. "Who wants to go out for a run?" He asked. Trace, Trajan and Marco were in the kitchen for an afternoon break. Keeping the grounds and surrounding beach patrolled and safe was their job, as well as that of Gabe, Gene and Spencer.

"I'll go," Trace offered. "Just let me finish this glass of water. You ought to have some too, before we head out. It's hot and muggy out there." Ten minutes later, Trace and Ashe were running down the beach. Trace was nearly as tall as Trajan and he ran with an easy lope, even in the sand.

"You know, Trace, I've been thinking," Ashe said. "When those two wolves found us in the theatre parking lot in Denton, they were parked right beside the van we drove."

"They might have been following you," Trace said.

"Yeah. I guess. But what if that isn't true? What if they had a trace on Jack's cell or something? Besides, I think Marco might have noticed if we were followed. He's pretty careful."

"Yeah. Well, I'll mention it to Winkler and see if he wants to check into that," Trace said. "Come on; see if you can catch up with me." Trace took off at a faster pace.

~

"Let's go do a little checking for bugs," Winkler said, once Trace mentioned what Ashe had said. "Probably should have done it to begin with. Just didn't credit Pruitt with that many brain cells."

"Yeah, well, even the dumbest of us have our moments," Trace agreed.

"Then let's go see if Pruitt had a moment. Bring the equipment and the others. We'll find out."

"Okay."

~

"Does he have his cell with him?" Winkler asked Marcie, who wore a worried frown when Winkler, Trace, Trajan, Marco and Ashe walked into the house.

"It's charging up on the kitchen counter; Jack went down to see Larry and Jeff at Jeff's house. They seem to be getting along pretty well."

"Check it," Winkler jerked his head at Trajan. Ashe stood by, watching in fascination as Jack's cell was checked. Trajan grimaced as he cracked the expensive phone's case and then used tweezers to lift out a tiny chip.

"Lookie here," Trajan handed the chip to Winkler, who had a small plastic bag ready.

"Can we look through the rest of his things?" Winkler asked Marcie, who now wore a horrified expression.

"Look through everything. Get every bit of that crap away from my son," she insisted. Winkler and his team went through the rest of Jackson's things, finding one more chip in a duffle bag shoved inside his closet. "This can't be happening," Marcie moaned. They checked Dusty's things as well, but failed to find anything.

"We'll destroy these," Winkler promised as they walked out the door.

"Good. I'm not telling him," Marcie said. "I'll let Jason know, but that's it," she added.

"I'll send somebody else to stay with Ace and Gene," Winkler nodded. I'll call Nathan and Aedan when the sun sets. We all need to be on guard in case these things got past the shields those witches put up."

"Jack's been outside the community several times, so they could have picked up a signal then," Marcie was wiping tears. "Keep them away from us, please. I don't want any of them near me or my sons."

"We'll do our best, Marcie. Jason's tough and Gene and Ace are two of my best. I'll send Nick over, he's good, too. Just stay calm, all right?"

"Yeah. Thank you, Mr. Winkler."

"Good call, Ashe," Winkler said, once they'd loaded into the van. "Now, Trajan, what do you think we should do with these?" Winkler held up the small plastic bag, which contained the locating chips.

"I have an idea," Trajan grinned.

"Dude, that's just nasty," Ashe said when Trajan returned to the coffee shop after using a strong adhesive to glue the chips to the underside of a police cruiser parked outside.

"We'll let Pruitt argue with the kind officers driving that car—if he catches up with them and wants to," Trajan shrugged.

"My contact said to give this to the boy," Wlodek's eldest vampire child handed a small volume over. Wlodek, black-haired and black-eyed, was born Greek nearly three thousand years earlier. His eldest living vampire child, sitting across from him now, was Roman at birth and more than two thousand years of age.

"This looks new," Wlodek observed, taking the book.

"It is a translation, so I had the loose papers bound and covered."

"Then express my gratitude when you see him next."

"I will. He also said to exercise caution, and not to play with fire."

"More vague warnings? I am not surprised." Wlodek turned the book over in his hands.

"You know he can't interfere. Not directly. He says it's part of a larger volume, and that this is the most he could give."

"I understand." Wlodek sighed.

"He also says that Radomir should not be punished. He acted honorably, and you will see that for what it is one day."

"Shall I let him have my seat as Head of the Council as well? He desires to make my decisions for me?"

"No, father. I think he wishes to keep you from making a terrible mistake."

"Very well. I will look through this first, and then hand it over to the boy."

"Good. Is there anything else?" Piercing blue eyes twinkled and white teeth flashed in a brief but brilliant smile at the Head of the Council.

"No, child. Thank you for doing this so swiftly."

"You are welcome, father."

CHAPTER 10

"Nick is headed to Star Cove to provide extra protection for Jackson and Dusty," Marco said the following morning over breakfast. Ashe recalled that it was Tuesday, July first. The full moon was eleven days away.

"Trajan says that Jack hasn't turned yet," Ashe said, rotating an arm to loosen up his right shoulder. Winkler's Second had made him do extra reps in the weight room before sending him out for a run with Marco and Trace. Trajan had then disappeared into Winkler's office for a private breakfast meeting.

Ashe realized that Trajan had a serious job as Winkler's Second, but he couldn't help but like the tall werewolf or his younger brother, Trace. He also liked Jason Landers, Jackson's stepfather, very much. The old cowboy was more than one hundred fifty years old and treated everyone with a courtesy that Ashe didn't see in many people.

"You think Jackson might turn this time?"

"Maybe," Ashe always hedged his bets. "Tell Ace and Jason to be careful, okay?"

"Werewolves aren't in the habit of saying be careful to fellow werewolves, but I'll see what I can do," Marco grinned, biting into a piece of crispy bacon.

"All tough guys," Ashe nodded.

"Darn tough," Gabe and Spencer, werewolf brothers, wandered in from guard duty and sat at the breakfast table, helping themselves to the food laid out. Ashe liked both werewolves, and decided he appreciated the fact that gruff and grumble Orville had been asked to tend the store in Cordell instead of coming to the Gulf Coast. Orville hadn't liked Ashe from the beginning.

❧

"Here's your assignment for today, courtesy of Matt Michaels, our friend in Washington," Winkler handed over a few pieces of paper. "And he warns you that this information is secret," Winkler grinned.

"Okay, I'll look through it," Ashe agreed, walking into his office. Ashe was shocked to see Congressman Jack Howard's name on the papers, with a suspected offshore bank account. "Wow," Ashe breathed, eyebrows lifting as he booted up the computer.

❧

"Mr. Winkler, just tell Mr. Michaels that I was particularly motivated on this one," Ashe handed over the paperwork two hours later, complete with passwords and codes to a bank account in the Cayman Islands.

The esteemed congressman had millions stashed away and hidden, according to the records. Ashe didn't know what else the congressman had, but regular deposits from a business in South America had shown up.

"Ashe, you're beginning to frighten me," Winkler grinned, belying his words.

"Mr. Winkler, I would never do anything like this on my own, unless it was necessary to save a life. You have to believe me when I say that," Ashe said.

"And that I will believe," Winkler said, raising his cell and punching a number on speed dial. He motioned for Ashe to sit while the call went through. "Matt?" Winkler said when the phone was answered.

Ashe heard the Director's voice quite clearly. It made him wonder if he knew that the former Director-turned vampire, Anthony Hancock, was staying with Winkler. Winkler gave information on Congressman Howard over the phone and Mr. Michaels was pulling information up on his own computer.

"Got it," Matt Michaels was laughing. "I'll get a team on it now. Our congressman may go down faster than he ever thought possible. I'll keep you posted. Tell that kid I owe him." The phone went dead.

"I'm thinking about taking college courses," Adele pushed the information she'd printed off the computer toward Denise and Sharon.

"Marine biology?" Denise lifted an eyebrow and handed the sheet of paper to Sharon.

"Ashe will be off to college or doing something else in two years," Adele sighed. "I can open another business or do this. I still haven't decided."

"Marcie's looking for something to do; she says Jack wants to find another Pack after he turns eighteen," Denise pointed out. "I think she and Jason liked running your store in Cordell."

"Yeah. But there's plenty of those businesses in this area already," Adele said, sipping coffee. "Ashe and I were looking at opening a small bookshop on the beach in Port A. If I buy another business, that's what I'll probably do."

"Jonas and I will likely buy another farm when Wynn graduates and goes off to college," Sharon said, handing the flyer back to Adele. "It's what we know best, and it hides us well enough when we turn."

Sharon turned to a palomino mare and Jonas became an eagle. Wynn's unicorn came from her mother's side of the family. A great-great-great grandmother had also been a unicorn, but they were so rare as to be the myth everyone believed. If Obediah Tanner and Jack

Howard had succeeded, then there might not have been a legacy to pass down to another child, someday.

"Where does Jack want to go?" Adele asked. Jack had just finished eleventh grade in Phoenix and would be a senior when school started again.

"No idea. Marcie says at times he appears confident and seems to know what he wants. At others, he looks haunted. Now, I've got a good guess as to why that is, but I won't spread that rumor until I know for sure," Denise said. "Marcie and Jason are taking Jackson to Corpus Christi to buy clothes. He barely got out of Phoenix with a suitcase and a duffle bag. Ace and that other one, Nick? Is that his name? Are going too."

"How are Sali and Dori doing in Shirley Walker's groves?" Adele asked.

"Fine, when they're not in trouble horsing around. I think they got into a fruit fight with Jeff, Hayes and Larry. Jennifer Campbell was mortified when Larry's pay was docked for destroying peaches."

"After all those years of Wynn and Dori fighting with Sali, now she's dating him," Sharon O'Neill shook her head. Adele sighed again, and this time it was for Ashe.

"Come on, quicken your pace," Trace and Marco had Ashe running along the beach again before dinner. "You just sit in a chair all day. You'll shrivel up, man," Trace grinned. They'd run a mile down the beach, now they were nearly back to the beach house. Ashe felt a buzzing in his head and jerked to a stop.

"What's that?" Trace and Marco had stopped beside him. Ashe had seen something on the deck of the beach house, just before he'd heard the whine.

"Bullets!" Trace snapped. "Marco, move!" Trace and Marco took off at top speed for Winkler's deck. Several things were moving there, Ashe just couldn't make them out. He heard shouting, though, and then saw Trajan forcing his body through the glass doors at the back of the house, a rifle in his hands. Another whine and Trajan was knocked backward.

"No!" Ashe shouted, and then somehow, in some way, without ever turning to mist or becoming the bumblebee bat, Ashe was on Winkler's deck and gathering Trajan into his mist.

Be careful! He shouted mentally to Marco and Trace, who were still running toward the deck. Ashe had arrived in a blink. Three men in sand-colored camouflage were on the deck, assault rifles in their hands.

The bullets that now flew through the broken panes of patio doors flew straight through Ashe's mist. One of the assailants went down. Trace, as a huge black wolf, hit another of the attackers viciously, nearly biting through an arm and forcing the man to drop his gun.

The other was now aiming at Trace when Marco hit him as a wolf so gray he was nearly black. Only a patch of white at his throat told Ashe it was Marco.

Winkler, bleeding from a shoulder wound and backed up by Gene and Gabe, who'd also been hit in the right arm and left thigh, raised rifles. The remaining attackers were down in seconds after two shots rang out. Ashe dropped Trajan into a rattan chair as carefully as he could.

"You okay?" Ashe waited for Trajan to open his eyes. The wound was on Trajan's right side and blood flowed sluggishly from the injury.

Winkler was cursing and kicking one of their assailants. He also heard the name Nick. Several times.

"What happened?" Ashe grabbed a towel from a stack the housekeeper kept on the deck in a basket, in case anyone wanted to swim in the gulf. Pressing the towel to Trajan's wound, he knelt next to Winkler's Second.

"Betrayal, that's what," Winkler came to examine Trajan's gunshot wound. "Spencer's dead. Marco, see if you can get Shirley Walker on the phone. One of her wolves works as a nurse at the hospital in Corpus. We need him. Pronto."

"Did they just walk in the front door?" Ashe asked, pressing the towel harder against Trajan's side to curb the bleeding. Trajan grunted in pained response.

"Nick did. Spencer didn't know not to let him in," Winkler cursed again. "Two came in with him and killed Spence. These three came around the back and started shooting into the house. Trajan and I got the two in the house; one of us wounded Nick, too. If you hadn't gotten here when you did, Trajan would probably be gone as well. Thank goodness Gene got suspicious and followed Nick when he left Star Cove."

"Marco and Trace got those guys, I just picked up Trajan before they could shoot him again," Ashe was shaky but didn't want to show it.

"They're on the way," Gabe pocketed his cell phone. Ashe watched Gabe. He'd just lost his brother, in addition to being wounded.

"No more questions right now," Trajan opened his eyes and blinked at Ashe. Ashe nodded his understanding. Marco was on the phone, talking with his father when Trajan passed out again.

The werewolf nurse who worked at the hospital showed up half an hour later, but he couldn't get the bullet out of Trajan until Anthony Hancock rose for the evening.

"My surrogate sire is better at this than I am," Tony muttered, forming a long claw on a single finger. "Hold him down," he nodded at Trajan, who was breathing shallow breaths.

The nurse had given him something for pain and washed out the wound, but hadn't attempted to remove the bullet. Ashe hadn't been told to stay away, so he watched in frightened awe as Tony Hancock dipped his claw into Trajan's flesh and flipped the bullet out in seconds. It bounced across the tiled floor of Winkler's media room, coming to rest against an expensive, hand-woven rug.

"Now we can fix this," the nurse sighed and went back to work on the wound. Winkler had been patched up, as had Gabe—those bullets had either grazed or gone through. Ashe knew that feeling, having been shot when he was twelve.

"You all right, Son?" Aedan walked in with Marcus.

"Yeah. Dad, I was never in any danger. We went for a run on the beach—Marco, Trace and I. Mr. Winkler got attacked while we were gone. We just came up at the end."

"Is this the end of it? Do you think there are more out there?" Aedan asked.

"No way to tell," Tony Hancock said. "But we'll certainly look into the matter. Would you like to place compulsion on Nick, so we can get answers?"

"Absolutely," Aedan nodded. Winkler, Tony, Marcus and Aedan all left the room.

"Damn," Trajan sighed.

"You're in no shape to go running after them right now," the nurse said, pushing Trajan back onto the sofa when he attempted to rise.

"Ashe," Trace jerked his head toward the back doors, which were still broken, with glass hanging in shards from the frames. Ashe followed Trace to the deck.

"Get me in there, Ashe," Trace whispered. Ashe blinked at Trace before going to mist and hauling the werewolf into Winkler's private office. Nick was cuffed with silver and tied to a chair when they arrived. Gabe stalked around the prisoner, growling even in human form. Ashe, holding Trace within his mist, hovered in a corner of the room.

"Now, you will tell me everything and you will be truthful about it, won't you?" Aedan leaned down, looking Nick in the eye.

"Yes," Nick said, nodding slightly.

"Who sent you?" Aedan asked.

"Dom Pruitt. He knows you have his boys, Winkler. He says you stole his family. He wants you dead. Paying a lot for it, actually. He said to kill you first and then grab the boys."

"No loyalty, Nick?" Winkler growled.

"Offered a lot," Nick winced.

"What do you think I might have paid to have the information brought to me?" Winkler asked angrily.

"What else did he offer you?" Aedan asked. "What did he promise?"

"Home in Mexico. On the water. Anything else I wanted, in exchange for your head." He stared at Winkler.

"Anything else?" Aedan asked.

"That's all I know."

"Gabe, he's yours," Winkler said. When Ashe saw Gabe pull the pistol from his waistband, he flew straight through the ceiling, dumping Trace on the roof before flying over the waters of the gulf.

~

"Your father wasn't happy that you took off," Winkler was waiting inside the media room when Ashe walked in just after daybreak the following morning. The patio doors had been boarded up and the blood washed from the deck and the floors inside the house.

"Yeah. I figured," Ashe said. "Trajan okay?"

"He's fine. Sleeping it off. He'll be healed up in a couple of days."

"Where's Nick?" Ashe watched Winkler. Would Winkler lie? His dark eyes never wavered from Ashe's face.

"Sleeping. With the fishes," Winkler replied. "Shirley sent somebody who has a boat."

"Ah."

"Ashe, in this business, it's unavoidable. Vamps, weres and shifters don't have normal lives. We like to protect our kids, but the talented ones get thrown into it early."

"I've already been informed that I won't have a normal life," Ashe sat on the opposite end of the sofa Winkler occupied.

"The trick is to keep as much as possible as normal as possible. Last night was definitely not normal. My wolves are extremely loyal as a rule. Every now and then, there's someone who thinks money might be more important. I handed Nick to Gabe because Nick killed Spencer. That's the worst kind of betrayal. It would have been more honorable to call Spencer out and offer to fight, instead of convincing him to trust Nick enough to allow him inside the house."

"Yeah," Ashe dropped his head in his hands. He hadn't slept. He'd been misting, flying as the bat or hopping—his newfound talent of jumping from one place to another—all night.

"Come on, you can call your mother and we'll both talk to her, and then you'll go to bed for a while. Trace and Marco are taking the early shift. They have to deal with getting glass replaced in the doors."

"How are you going to explain that?" Ashe studied the boarded up frames.

"Werewolf-owned glass company," Winkler said. "You'd be surprised at how many werewolf businesses are out there. We have our own phone directory. Shirley called him last night. He said he'd be out around nine."

"So, what's gonna happen to the one who hired Nick?"

"Ashe, we're working on that, all right? Most of my wolves don't know as much as you do right now. In the meantime, I have to get my Second back on his feet."

"Yeah. Trajan asleep right now?"

"Want to check? I'll let you take breakfast in if you want."

"I will." Ashe went to see Winkler's cook. Jimmy was preparing a meal in the kitchen as if nothing had happened. Ashe got two plates of food on a tray and went to Trajan's bedroom on the second floor.

"He said no coffee," Ashe set the tray down on Trajan's bedside table. Trajan had asked for coffee the moment Ashe walked through the door after knocking.

"Who?" Trajan was grumbling.

"The cook. You know—Jimmy."

"I'll have a talk with him later. Kid, I've got to find a way to stop getting rescued by you."

"I'd hope you'd do the same for me. Or Sali or Marco or Winkler."

"Yeah. Hand that plate over, I'm starved." Ashe handed a plate and a fork to Trajan, who'd slid his legs over the edge of the bed so he could eat.

"Your mother," Winkler handed his cell to Ashe after walking into Trajan's bedroom.

"Mom, I'm fine," Ashe said right away. "I was nowhere near the grassy knoll." Winkler threw back his head and laughed.

"Ashe, do I need to come over there?" Adele asked, worry in her voice.

"I think everything is under control. Everything all right there?"

"Yes, things seem to be fine. Another werewolf showed up to help Ace guard Marcie's boys, but that's it. One of Shirley Walker's, I think." Winkler was nodding—he knew about it already.

"Good. I guess Dad made it home okay?"

"Yes, but he was worried about you."

"I only went down the beach a little way. Nobody saw me, I promise."

"Are you sure you're all right?"

"Yeah. I'm fine. Really. And so are Mr. Winkler and Trajan."

"All right. But if anything like that happens again, you'll come straight home. Do you hear?"

"Mom, don't worry, okay? I'm fine."

"I'll be bringing in more guards, Mrs. Evans," Winkler promised. He knew she'd hear.

"Fine. Ashe, your father will call tonight when he rises."

"Okay."

"I love you, honey."

"Love you, too, Mom." Ashe flushed. Winkler and Trajan both grinned.

"Here's your mail, Adele." Denise handed over the stack of mail she'd gotten from the Evans' new post office box. Nobody in the community had mail delivered to their homes. It was safer that way. Mailboxes were lined up outside the housing addition, but those only received advertisements and flyers addressed to occupant.

"I got a card from Dawn Smith," Adele lifted the postcard so Denise could see. The photo on the front depicted a famous chapel in Santa Fe.

"What does she say?" Denise asked.

"Doing fine, hope the move went well," Adele read. "Randy heard from Cori that you had to leave Oklahoma. Sorry to hear that. Love to you and yours—Dawn."

The card had been addressed to the old post office box in Cordell. Dawn knew it would be forwarded.

"That was nice of her," Denise said.

"I wonder if she'll ever marry again," Adele sighed, setting the card on the kitchen island.

"I don't know. She and Terry were so close; I think it did major damage when he was killed and then Randy was almost killed, too."

"Randy would be dead if Ashe hadn't pulled him away."

"Too bad nobody else remembers that, including Dawn and Randy," Denise agreed.

"It's just too dangerous—too many people would come looking for Ashe. I wish there was some way we could protect him better, so he can lead something close to a normal life. Want a cup of coffee, Denise?" Adele went toward the coffeepot.

Ashe blinked at the television screen. And then blinked again—he was still half-asleep. Winkler had gotten him up to see the breaking news on all the television stations.

"Congressman Howard cannot be located," the journalist reported on a popular, twenty-four hour news program. "The Justice Department has warrants out for his arrest, for investing campaign funds in South American casinos and other illegal enterprises, with profits funneled to an offshore account. It seems that the congressman may have been tipped off and chose to leave town before arrests could be made." A photograph of the congressman, coming back from the supposed elk hunt in Colorado, was shown on the screen.

"I think he's running to Pruitt and Pruitt's contacts in Mexico," Winkler muttered. "If he makes it past the border, we may never get our hands on him again. If my hunch is correct, Pruitt was helping Tanner—with a lot of things. That means Howard knows of Pruitt and vice versa."

Ashe's hands were balled into fists. The congressman had tried to kill Wynn. He wanted to curse. "That creep. We should have taken care of him when we had the chance," Ashe snarled.

"We don't always get what we want, and criminals go free every day," Winkler said gently. "Don't let it worry you. He's likely out of the country, and Wynn is safe."

"But what about other shifters? There have to be some in Mexico, right?"

"I'm sure your father would say we can't let that upset us. Howard was likely doing this for a very long time inside this country. Now he's an outlaw and hunted. Hopefully, he'll be too busy hiding to do a lot of hunting of his own from now on."

"He's still a creep, and a murderous creep on top of that."

"I don't think I've ever seen you this upset before, Ashe," Marco sounded surprised. He'd come in to watch the news program with Ashe and Winkler.

"You didn't see him, Marco. He was going to take pleasure in killing Wynn, and he knew what she was. He knew she was human most of the time. He was so determined to kill her, even after I knocked him off his horse, that he grabbed his rifle and fired off a shot without looking. He killed one of his own guards."

"There are people who know what we are. Howard likely had that information from Tanner. They don't think any part of us is human." Trajan was not only out of bed, he was eating a sandwich as he walked into Winkler's media room. Ashe was still fuming when his cell phone rang. He checked caller ID—it was Sali. Ashe mumbled a greeting.

"Dude," Sali said, "you're not going to believe who came home for the summer."

"Who's that?" Ashe grumped.

"Jeremy Booth," Sali replied. "And Chad Hollis is with him."

CHAPTER 11

"Arch nemeses Chad Hollis and Jeremy Booth? Chump and Wormy?" If Ashe thought his day couldn't get any worse, then he was very wrong. "Does Cori know?"

Not only did Chump and Wormy hate Ashe, Cori and Jeremy hated one another with a capital H. Ashe agreed with Cori's sentiments concerning Jeremy—Ashe didn't think there were many redeeming qualities in Jeremy Booth.

Jeremy had given Ashe a black eye, too, when Ashe had responded to one of Jeremy's insults at age twelve. Jeremy had hurled a terrible insult at Ashe, and Ashe hadn't taken it well.

"Yeah," Sali answered Ashe's question. "Man, I thought she was gonna march over to the Booth's house and punch Jeremy in the face," Sali chortled. "She'd probably get Chad, too, if he didn't duck and run."

"Good old Chump," Ashe grumbled. Chad Hollis wasn't any better than Jeremy; in fact, he was probably worse. For three years, he'd blamed Ashe for his mother's death when Ashe had nothing to do with it. He'd also set a mobile home on fire two years earlier, when he and Jeremy had attempted to frighten the human families and their half-human children who'd come to Cloud Chief for protection.

Chad and Jeremy had gone to the same college in Arkansas after

135

graduating from Cloud Chief Combined. They'd both called Ashe *empty*, the worst insult one could level against a shapeshifter, before Ashe revealed the bumblebee bat.

They'd gone on to ridicule Ashe for shifting to such a lame and wimpy animal, before reverting to calling him empty again.

The act of compulsion played a large part in the difficulties that seemed to follow Ashe everywhere. Ashe had breathed a very relieved sigh when Chad and Jeremy had gone away to college.

For the past two summers, they'd worked at jobs in Little Rock. For some reason, they'd decided to take the summer months off this year. Jeremy's parents had adopted Chad since he had no living relatives, and Marcus received funds from the Grand Master to help support him through college.

"Ashe, you'll be here, they'll be there," Marco said softly. He and everyone else inside Winkler's media room had listened to the conversation. Holding any sort of private communication around werewolves, vampires and shapeshifters was nearly impossible. They all had exceptional hearing.

"I'll be home on weekends," Ashe sighed. Sali heard Marco's comment, and then Ashe's reply.

"I'll help you punch them if they call you empty again," Sali offered. "They don't get to dis the bat. That's my job."

"They call you empty?" Winkler lifted an eyebrow.

"Yeah." Ashe nodded at Winkler. "Sali, I need to go." Ashe hung up before Sali could say good-bye. "I'm going to the beach." Pocketing his cell, Ashe headed for the doors that held newly replaced glass panes.

"I'll come," Marco rose from his chair.

"Marco, I need a little time," Ashe said and shut the door behind him.

"Let him go," Winkler motioned Marco down again. "I think he'll be all right. Just in case, Trace, can you watch him from the deck?"

"Yeah." Trace walked out the door and settled on one of the patio chairs.

"I've disagreed with Dad a lot over the years, but taking Sali's memories away that Ashe can do most of what he does? That's just lame." Marco rose and went to join Trace.

"I agree with Marco," Trajan said, taking his brother's vacated seat with a sigh.

"I didn't say otherwise," Winkler said.

"Who's this?" Ezekiel Tanner glared at the two Dominic Pruitt brought into his private study. Like Obediah, Ezekiel had chosen to decorate the large room with the heads of exotic animals, plus three taxidermic werewolves in human form. Dom was glad they were dressed. At times, Zeke left them naked. Two were female, one male.

"New allies—an associate put me in touch with them," Dom smiled.

"Not human," Zeke got a good scent off the visitors.

"Of course we are not human. That is the worst insult. Do not offer it again or you will much regret it," one of them sniffed.

"What can they do for us?" Zeke growled at Pruitt. He didn't like threats of any kind and considered setting some of his wolves on these two.

"We can give you all of the young ones inside the village you are targeting, in exchange for one of them," the other guest answered while Dominic Pruitt searched for a suitable answer. "You must overlook my brother's impatience," the visitor spoke again. "He grows tired of this chase."

"And you are?" Zeke frowned at both of them.

"I am Baltis, King of the Dark Elemaiya," came the reply. "And this is my brother, Prince Beldris. I understand you need some youth within your ranks. Rest assured we will deliver, in exchange for the one we hunt. With a bit of assistance from you and yours, of course."

"What do you mean, you relayed messages for him?" Matt Michaels was angry enough to spit. Wildrif had been sequestered inside the mental hospital in D.C., with specific orders not to allow any visitors or for the staff to repeat anything Wildrif said. The one who'd circumvented that order now quailed before the Director of the Joint NSA and Homeland Security Department.

"Took money," one of Matt's agents dropped a folder onto Matt's desk. "That shows bank deposits. Around half a mil."

"From Howard, no doubt. Now I know how those terrorists knew we were sending someone in at the British Embassy. Did you contact the same one for that particular piece of treason, or somebody else?"

"I called the number Wildrif gave me," Orderly Kelly Tharpe tried to make himself smaller. He was handcuffed and shackled to the chair beside Matt's desk. "Somebody answered. I gave the message Wildrif passed to me."

"And what was that message?" Matt was becoming angrier by the second.

"He said to tell them that if they wanted proof of what the boy could do, to go to the British Embassy at a certain date and time."

Matt cursed. Kicked the side of his desk and cursed again.

"What about the second message. To Congressman Howard?" Matt's agent asked the question, since Matt was still cursing under his breath.

"Wildrif said for him to leave the country. Said that Howard would know what he meant and would pay."

"Is Wildrif still at the hospital?" Matt looked at his agent.

"He was ten minutes ago."

"Call. Have him transferred to the maximum-security facility in Colorado. Do it now. Nobody talks to this guy, nobody listens to this guy. Got it? Move."

Ashe hadn't gone far. He'd stopped a quarter mile from the beach house and stood on the sand while waves sloshed around his feet.

Briefly, he wondered what would happen if he hopped to the horizon, using his newly discovered talent.

He wasn't planning to tell anyone about it, yet. It would just be another reason to keep him under surveillance. Trace had stepped out to the deck after Ashe left the others behind. No doubt to keep an eye on Ashe and make sure he didn't get away.

Sharp hearing was always a plus—it let Ashe know many things. He'd heard Trace close the patio door behind him; even heard the creak of the chair when Trace settled into it. Shaking himself, Ashe turned to go back.

~

"I think I'll ask Dawn to come for a visit," Denise said, looking over the postcard while she drank coffee at Adele's kitchen island. "There's plenty of room at the house. She might enjoy being close to the gulf for a change."

"That's a great idea." Adele smiled. "Do you have her number?"

"I do." Denise pulled out her cell and flipped through the phone list.

~

"I know I gave you bogus news before, but I just found out that Dawn Smith is coming for a visit and Randy has vacation time, so he's coming too." Sali called Ashe again while Ashe sat in front of the computer inside his office, working on a few small assignments for Winkler.

"Sali, aren't you supposed to be working?" Ashe asked.

"Break time, dude."

"When are they coming?" Ashe asked, plugging in a password and revealing all sorts of sensitive information on a Savings and Loan.

"Coming in on Saturday. Leaving after the full moon. Mom talked Randy's mom into running with us."

"That's nice, dude. Gotta go. I think I just uncovered graft and corruption." Ashe hung up on Sali, ran out the door and was knocking on Winkler's office door in seconds.

"What is it?" Winkler was getting off the phone as well.

"Mr. Winkler, I think you ought to see this." Winkler rose and followed Ashe down the hall.

"See—this bonus was paid in December. And then a duplicate amount was issued in January, another in February, and once each month since then," Ashe pointed out. "It wouldn't have made me suspicious, except for the amounts."

"Yeah. I can see that a million dollar bonus in less than a year might be a little out of a vice president's league," Winkler agreed, leaning over Ashe's shoulder to examine the figures on the screen. "This is a small S and L. I wonder how this was hidden?"

"I don't know," Ashe shrugged. Winkler whipped out his cell and placed a call. Ashe listened in while someone at the FBI was given information on somebody. It wasn't a low ranking somebody, either.

Winkler had more contacts than anybody knew, Ashe figured. He wondered how large Winkler Security actually was and if Winkler held government contracts. *That's likely a big whopping yes*, Ashe thought to himself. Yet another thing he didn't plan to tell anyone.

"We'll find out soon enough," Winkler clapped Ashe on the back. "Come on, kid. Come have a glass of juice or something."

Ashe ended up having a snack in the kitchen. Jimmy, the cook, made a sandwich for Winkler and handed Ashe a small bowl of pretzels after Ashe said he didn't want a sandwich.

Jimmy didn't talk much at all. Ashe knew the cook was werewolf. Jimmy was short—barely five-four or so. He was also the only werewolf Ashe had ever seen who shaved his head.

"Thanks, Jimmy," Ashe crunched into a pretzel.

"No prob, kiddo." Jimmy grinned at Ashe. Ashe couldn't help but grin back.

~

"I was asked to give this to you," Tony Hancock walked into the media room shortly after sundown, handing a manila envelope to Ashe, who stared at the vampire.

"What is it?" Ashe had avoided speaking with the former Director of the Joint NSA and Homeland Security Department.

"I had to pull a few strings to get this, and the Head of the Council has already seen it, as have I. That's what you get. All you get." Tony's face was shuttered, showing no emotion.

"You have a habit of avoiding direct questions?" Ashe said before he thought. Winkler, who'd just walked in, burst out laughing.

"Nailed you, Hancock," Winkler chuckled.

"I'll uh, just go to my room and look at this," Ashe stood, tapping the envelope against his chest.

Ashe's bedroom held a desk and chair. Settling into the chair and turning on the floor lamp beside it, Ashe opened the envelope. Three loose pages were inside. He pulled them out carefully. The pages appeared to be a computer generated copy of a handwritten manuscript. The top page made Ashe draw in a breath.

The contents herein, being an excerpt of Ekdi H'Morr, the Book of Prophecy belonging to the Elemaiyan Race, as translated by, and that part had been redacted. There was nothing there except blank space.

"So, I don't need to know," Ashe muttered, feeling a bit of anger. Were they afraid he'd attempt to find the translator? He flipped the cover page, anxious to learn more.

The Elemaiya, Bright and Dark, are a varied and talented race, Ashe read. *Formed at one and the same moment, they are halves of a whole. Once they were a single race, although they have forgotten this,* was handwritten on the page.

Their talents are many, although any one of them who holds more than two talents is considered uncommon, and the few holding four or more are among the royalty of the race. The talents are thus, from most common to extremely rare:

Gating—this ability belongs to all Elemaiya and is not included in the number of talents assigned to any individual. Gating is essential as an ability, as it enables the Elemaiya to travel from one world to another. Some worlds have multiple gates; a few have none at all. This talent, and the ability to sense when a gate is near, appears to be instinctive.

Telekinesis—this talent presents in varying degrees of ability. Many are able to move a feather about. Few may lift something heavier than that. The rarest and most talented might lift extremely heavy objects.

Illusion—the ability to make objects or people appear to be present and solid. Some of the higher talents will see through any illusion but it is still useful at times, making an enemy believe there are more foes present. If done properly, an enemy will see the specter as real and attack. A few very talented in this ability will make their illusions appear to move naturally. A fine talent, often present in the military faction.

Relocation—this enables the individual to move from one place to another almost instantly. It is generally short range, however, and more than two relocations in a single day tend to tire the individual, so it is reserved until needed. A few can relocate more often, but that is uncommon.

Acute Hearing—this is useful in the guards protecting royalty, as it allows them to detect approaching danger.

Mindspeech—the individuals holding this talent are separated from those considered common among the race. While nearly all have Telekinesis or Relocation skills, roughly half have mindspeech. There are castes within the races, and mindspeech demarcates Low from High Caste. Mindspeakers, holding none of the higher abilities, belong to the Middle Caste. Holding mindspeech and any of the remaining, rarer talents marks the individual as High Caste.

Compulsion—a useful and uncommon gift, enabling the one talented in this way to compel others to do their bidding. If one holds this ability, it must be used sparingly against his fellows; else it will bring about animosity.

Manipulation of the elements—fire, water, air and earth, or solid matter. Of course, these are the elements as determined by ancient beliefs and not based in current scientific fact. It is believed that a very talented individual might burn oxygen from the air, or form water using the same method. Perhaps to create air from water as well, or manipulate solid objects. Manipulation of solid objects is the rarest of this particular ability. One with that talent has not come in a very long time, and none is now known to exist.

Shapeshifting—a rare gift, endowing those holding such talent with the ability to take the form of an animal. They cannot be distinguished from the actual animal, by either sight or scent. Humanoid Shapeshifters still hold a bit of their other scent. Shapeshifting Elemaiya do not.

Misting—this gift is among the rarest of talents. None can perceive the Elemaiya in this form, except in the most unusual of all cases. The holder of this gift can slip through the smallest of spaces. Legends surround this ability, but those will be discussed at a later time.

Foresight/Prophecy—this talent is the rarest of all and individuals blessed with it are highly prized by the ruling houses of both Bright and Dark.

"Where's the rest?" Ashe looked at both sides of the last page. There was nothing more. *They're withholding it*, he thought. He then read the list again before counting. He held five of the talents. At least five. It made him think about the gates on Earth, too, and he wondered where they were located.

If he could discuss this with Sali, an entire universe of possibilities might open up. He could ask Tony Hancock, though. Maybe he'd know, since he was an eighth Elemaiya. Ashe raced out of his bedroom and into the strangest sight he'd ever seen.

The beach house was different. The furniture different. Things were in different places. The air almost seemed tangible as it flowed around him. He saw Winkler, looking much as he still did, only dressed in an older style.

Ashe stared at the woman from the photograph that hung in Winkler's Dallas office. She'd come to life and now stood beside the table in the breakfast nook. She was arguing with Winkler about something, and then lifting a metal-framed dining chair, twisting it easily in her hands before tossing it on the floor and stalking away.

"Holy cow," Ashe said, his words breaking the spell. Winkler now stood before Ashe, calling his name.

"Dude, that woman just twisted a chair into a pretzel," Ashe stared at Winkler. Winkler hauled Ashe from the room immediately.

"What did you see?" Winkler hissed. "Tell me!"

"Th-the woman in your picture—in Dallas? She was here. Only everything was different. She bent a metal chair like it was clay." Ashe felt breathless.

"Come on." Winkler pulled Ashe through the front door and away from the house. "Ashe, I don't know how you saw that, but that happened more than twenty-three years ago," Winkler said.

"Who was she?" Ashe whispered. He felt shaky over the whole experience.

"Lissa. Ashe, if you haven't figured it out yet, she was vampire. Female vampires are so rare they almost don't exist. I was a fool and didn't hold onto her. Now, only a few werewolves remember her. The vampire race has no memories left of her. Something took those memories, Ashe. Something powerful. *Someone* powerful."

"But the vampires knew about her? Back then?" Ashe watched Winkler's face closely. It was filled with pain.

"Yes. They knew about her. Ashe, don't ever say anything about her to any of them. Weldon and I tried to convince them of her existence, once. After she died. We won't try that again." Ashe knew who Weldon was. Weldon Harper, Grand Master of the Werewolves.

"Did Tony Hancock know about her?" Ashe asked.

"She worked with Tony for a while. A lot of those things the history books say he did? He didn't do them. Oh, he was a hero, all right. But Lissa was better than he ever was."

"And now she's dead."

"Yes. She died a long way from here. She had Elemaiyan blood, too. Ashe, whatever you do, don't throw your life away, all right? Promise me." Winkler's fingers gripped Ashe's shoulders—hard.

"I'll do what I can," Ashe was frightened at the look on Winkler's face. Winkler hugged Ashe after that.

"Come on," Winkler pulled Ashe through the door again. "If you get another one of those visions, though, I'd appreciate it if you'd tell me."

"Okay."

Ashe worked up the courage to talk to Tony Hancock before going to bed. "Can you do anything besides mindspeaking?" Ashe asked. "And do you know anything about gates?"

"I read that about gating," Tony said. He sat on the deck outside the media room, the gulf breeze ruffling his black hair. "There's a gate in the Kansas City area somewhere. I have vague memories of it. And another one in Great Britain, but it's closed."

"Closed?"

"You know, I don't remember how I know that," Tony shook himself. "I remember that my sire died not far from there. Killed with a wooden arrow."

"That's not good," Ashe muttered. His father had explained about wooden stakes, after all. "So that's why you have a surrogate sire? A replacement?"

"Yes. My surrogate sire was stricter. It's like going through five years of your childhood, all over again. A sire is responsible for his vampire child." Tony smiled wryly.

"Did you give them fits?" Ashe smiled back.

"A couple of times. We won't discuss that. You should go to bed, it's late."

"Yeah." Ashe rose from his seat and walked inside the house.

Ashe learned two things by the end of the week; first, that Winkler's son and daughter had been in Europe after finishing their junior year in college but were now on their way to Corpus Christi, and second, that Dawn and Randy Smith would be staying at Sali's house during their vacation.

"Dude, settle down, I'm on the way now. Marco's driving. He wants to know if his bedroom has been given away. If it has, he's staying with us." Ashe grinned at Marco, who was trying to stifle a snicker as they drove through Port Aransas on the way to the ferry.

Sali called Ashe as soon as he'd gotten up on Friday after sleeping late. It was July fourth—Independence Day. Winkler had shooed Marco and Ashe out of the house, sending them to Star Cove for the weekend.

"Mom will have a cow if Marco stays at your house, dude," Sali huffed. "But I could stay with you."

"Then you'd better ask now," Marco said, knowing Sali would hear. Ashe heard Sali trotting through the house, looking for Denise DeLuca.

"Mom, can I stay with Ashe over the weekend while Marco's here?" Ashe almost laughed at Sali's words. Marco didn't hold back the snicker this time.

"Salidar, you'd better ask Adele and Aedan first," Denise's reply came through clearly.

"I'll ask Mom, it'll probably be okay," Ashe said. "We'll be there in about twenty minutes." Ending the call, Ashe watched as Marco maneuvered the Winkler Security van onto the ferry and shut off the engine. The ferry bobbed in the water as Ashe got out. He wanted to see dolphins again, if they were nearby.

"See?" Ashe pointed out the gray backs and dorsal fins of three dolphins sliding in and out of the water.

"I haven't seen any until now," Marco snapped a photograph with his cell phone.

"Cool," Ashe said when Marco showed him the picture. The ferry ride took five minutes, once the boat cast off. "Look at all this traffic," Marco said as they passed a very long line of vehicles on the opposite side of the road, waiting for the ferry to take them onto the island.

"Holiday weekend," Ashe said. "Everybody wants to get to the beach."

"I guess so," Marco agreed. The line of cars was nearly half a mile long with more coming. "I'm glad we're getting off the island before this hits."

"That's probably why Winkler sent us out the door so fast," Ashe said, leaning back in his seat. Sali stood in Ashe's driveway when Marco pulled in to drop Ashe off.

"Come on, I'll look sad when you ask your mother, so she'll let me stay," Sali grinned. Ashe waved at Marco, who backed out and drove to the house next door.

"Salidar, how are you?" Adele greeted Sali after hugging Ashe when they walked through the front door.

"Good, Mrs. Evans," Sali grinned.

"Can Sali stay the weekend while Marco's home? He'll have to sleep on the hard floor otherwise," Ashe said. Sali managed to look pitiful.

"Sali, of course you can stay. Ashe, go make sure the guest room is ready. Take Sali with you," Adele laughed. "There's extra shampoo and soap beneath the sink in the guest bathroom," she called out as they ran upstairs.

Ashe dumped his backpack on the bed before heading next door to the guest room. "What do you think, Sal?"

"I can live with this," Sali grinned at the neatly made bed, dresser and chest. The bathroom was next, and it was fine. "Come over to our house, dude. Mom made cookies," Sali said.

"I'm going to Sali's," Ashe called as he and Sali left the house. Adele waved as they walked through the door.

"Didn't I just see you?" Marco teased when Ashe walked into the DeLucas' kitchen with Sali.

"Can I come in, too?" Cori slipped in behind Ashe.

"Hey." Marco went straight to Cori and gave her a kiss in front of everyone.

"I'm scarred for life now," Ashe laughed.

"What is seen cannot be unseen," Sali nodded sagely.

"If that's the case, then I need therapy," Dori grumped. She'd walked in with Wynn. Wynn was turning a very pretty shade of pink, Ashe noticed.

"Hey, Dori. Wynn." Ashe flushed slightly when he said Wynn's name.

"Have a seat, we've got fresh cookies," Denise hauled a pan from the oven. Cori helped pour milk and they all dug into chocolate chip cookies so warm the chocolate dripped in strings if they were broken apart.

"These are good, Mrs. DeLuca," Ashe said, finishing off his first one.

"Thanks. Sali, you get two," Denise eyed Sali sternly. Sali had his hand halfway to the plate for a third. He frowned and drew his hand back, sneaking a third cookie when his mother turned away.

"Come over to the house and get in the pool," Wynn said after the pile of cookies disappeared. "Ashe, you have to get in this time. You didn't before." Wynn's blue eyes smiled at Ashe. Ashe was ready to do anything Wynn asked at that point.

"Can bats get wet?" Sali asked innocently.

"Dude," Ashe flipped Sali's ear.

*S*he agreed to get in the pool after Cori slathered his back with sunscreen. Sali made a big deal out of rubbing lotion all over Wynn. Cori and Ashe helped Dori out with the protective sunscreen before sliding into the pool.

Marco got a volleyball game going, with Cori, Marco and Dori against Sali, Ashe and Wynn. Ashe didn't know how much he could take, watching Sali steal a kiss from Wynn occasionally. Dori just turned her head and refused to watch.

"Hey, no kissing during volleyball, it delays the game," Cori teased after the third time. Ashe was glad she had the courage to speak up; he was worried that Dori would get out of the water, she looked so angry.

"Okay," Sali looked sheepish.

"Look who's here," Sharon O'Neill opened the patio door and allowed Larry and Jeff onto the deck. The two who followed them made Cori growl low in her throat. Chad and Jeremy had come, too. Cori never let her panther take over like that. Never. Ashe felt the same way, but he couldn't produce his echolocation squeak while human, no matter how hard he tried.

"Cori, we're civilized," Marco had his mouth at Cori's ear, speaking so softly only Ashe could hear. Ashe forced himself to relax. Maybe Chad and Jeremy had developed manners. And maybe the sun would rise in the west the following day.

"Come on, we'll take on all six of you, since you'll be playing with girls," Jeremy laughed. Marco held Cori back. She was ready to turn and go after Jeremy.

Cori's panther was larger (and more determined) than Jeremy's wildcat, and Ashe knew who would be the winner in that fight. Hayes walked through the patio door while all three girls (and Ashe) glared at Jeremy.

"I'm coming in," Hayes, dressed in swim trunks and a T-shirt, grinned and pulled his T-shirt over his head before jumping in. He splashed water over everyone and effectively defused the situation.

"All right, five against six," Larry declared, sending Ashe, Wynn and Sali to the other side to play with Marco, Dori and Cori.

"Trade places with me, Ashe," Dori had her hands on Ashe's waist, moving around him in the water. "You can get the higher stuff from the back."

"All right," Ashe stepped backward, allowing Dori to move to the front. She wore a pretty, pink bikini, Ashe noticed, her dark blonde hair hanging down in a wet ponytail. She also had tiny earrings in her ears that matched the bikini. Ashe blinked a time or two before shaking himself and settling in to play.

"Here's someone to even things up," Sharon O'Neill was back with Jackson Pruitt. He waved at the crowd, slipped off the Hawaiian shirt he wore over a swimsuit and slid into the pool with the other five opposing Ashe's team. It did even things up but Cori, Marco, Ashe, Sali, Dori and Wynn were on a mission. Jeremy had hurled the insult, as was his way, and there was revenge to be had. Ashe's team won by two games when they finally came out of the water for lunch.

Denise DeLuca, Lavonna Anderson and Ashe's mother had brought sandwiches, Sharon handed out towels and everybody was wandering around or sitting on the deck, a towel wrapped around them and eating ham, turkey or tuna salad sandwiches.

"They're having a fireworks show in Corpus Christi tonight,"

Marco said, sitting beside Ashe on the deck. Cori settled down beside Marco, allowing him to play with her hair. Dori sat in a chair behind Ashe; Wynn and Sali were in deck chairs beside her.

"I love your mother's tuna salad," Dori patted Ashe on the back.

"Thanks," Ashe turned to grin at her. "Tell Mom. She loves compliments."

"Mrs. Evans, I love your tuna salad," Dori said, loud enough for Adele to hear.

"Thanks, Dori. That's really sweet of you," Adele smiled.

"Are you driving us to the fireworks show tonight?" Sali asked Marco.

"I could, if the parents are okay with that."

"I heard they're shooting them from a barge out in the water," Cori said. "So the show should be amazing. We could watch it from that spot just off the bridge going into Corpus."

"We'll have to take the long way around," Marco said. "The ferry was backed up when we came through this morning."

"I wouldn't mind seeing fireworks," Marcus DeLuca walked out on the O'Neill's patio and grabbed a sandwich.

"Then we can carpool and get everybody there," Denise smiled at her werewolf husband.

"I want to wait until Aedan is awake," Adele said.

"I want to wait for Nathan," Sharon O'Neill agreed.

"Mom, I'll come with you and Dad," Ashe said.

"I'll ride with Ashe and his parents," Dori offered. Rides to Corpus Christi were sorted out quickly.

The afternoon was spent either in the pool or lounging on the O'Neill's deck with snacks and soft drinks. Jeremy had finally settled down, after a few serious glares from Marcus and Marco. He knew better than to push the Packmaster or his oldest son.

"Ready?" Aedan asked as he slid into the driver's seat of his SUV.

"This is a nice ride, Mr. Evans," Jackson Pruitt ran a hand over the leather seat in the back.

"Thank you, Jackson. Now, did anyone forget anything?" Aedan asked.

"I think we're good, Dad," Ashe replied. He was squeezed into the back seat of Aedan's SUV between Dori and Jackson. Aedan put the vehicle in gear and backed out of the driveway.

Parking was nearly impossible to find. Aedan ended up leaving the SUV in the parking lot of a bait shop about a quarter mile away. Lawn chairs were carried and unfolded at a good spot.

People were everywhere, making Ashe feel slightly agoraphobic. Aedan, too, watched the crowd carefully. Ashe realized his father had done that always, he just hadn't noticed it so much until he was older. He also knew his father's sense of smell was nearly as keen as any werewolf's.

"Here you are," Marco, Cori and the others found Ashe's small group and began unfolding lawn chairs. The night was beautiful and clear, with a quarter moon hanging low over the waters of Corpus Christi Bay. The air was thick with moisture, but nobody seemed to mind.

"I haven't seen fireworks in a long time," Nathan said, standing on the opposite end of the small group from Star Cove. Ashe realized that Nathan stood at one end, Aedan at the other, and Marcus was behind, taking up that position. Marco, too, stood at the front, just off center so he wouldn't block Cori's view.

"Why didn't I see that before?" Ashe breathed.

"See what?" Dori had sat beside Ashe.

"I'll tell you later," Ashe patted Dori's arm. The fireworks began shortly afterward and Ashe couldn't have said exactly when it happened, but by the last fierce display, when it seemed the sky was lit with all colors of bursting rockets and falling stardust, Dori's hand was clasped firmly in his.

～

"Ashe, what are you doing?" Adele walked onto the back deck Saturday morning. Sali was in a deck chair, shirtless and wearing only sunglasses and a frayed pair of cutoffs. He watched Ashe while grinning hugely. Ashe, sitting cross-legged on the deck, tipped a glass of milk so Dori, in her ocelot form, could drink from it.

"Dori climbed over the fence. She's thirsty," Ashe said, watching Dori lap the milk. Her ocelot was beautiful, with stripes and spots evenly distributed over fawn-colored fur.

"Dorilou, what are you doing?" Lavonna Anderson was looking over the fence to see where her youngest had gone.

"She's having milk, I think," Adele frowned at Ashe, who shrugged amiably. Dori licked her whiskers, growled softly in thanks and leapt from the deck to the top of the fence before jumping down into the adjoining yard.

Ashe heard the back door of the Anderson's home open and close. Sali snickered. "I still have half a glass of milk here, wanna wear it, dude?" Ashe turned to Sali.

"Do not point the deadly Dori-contaminated milk in my direction," Sali laughed. Ashe was standing in a blink. Sali was over the fence and in his yard seconds later while Ashe flapped after him as the bumblebee bat. "Oooh, I'm so scared," Sali was waving his arms and doing a creditable imitation of Principal Billings.

"Ashe Aedan Evans, stop that this instant," Adele had to hide her laugh as Sali now ran around the DeLuca's yard, flapping his arms wildly while the tiny bat fluttered over his head.

"This is too good," Marco was outside the DeLuca's house and recording the incident on his cell phone.

"Salidar, what are you doing?" Marcus was now standing behind Marco, a cup of coffee in his hand.

"Oh, my gosh," Denise walked out of the house and started laughing.

"Sweetheart, don't laugh, it just encourages him," Marcus said dryly, and then began laughing as well.

"Hello?" Dawn and Randy Smith joined Marcus, Denise and Marco on the deck. "Is that Ashe?" Randy asked, watching Sali run around the yard, still flapping his arms in mock fear of the tiny bat.

"Yep. Welcome home, bro," Marco slapped Randy on the back.

"I've missed this," Randy sighed, settling into a deck chair. "Land of the free, home of the weird."

~

"So, working for a Chicago newspaper, huh?" Ashe asked later. Ashe had come over to the DeLuca's home to talk with Sali, Randy and Marco.

"It's not glamorous, by any means," Randy sighed, stretching his legs out on the ottoman inside the media room. "I get the assignments nobody else wants. Like going down to the abandoned narrow gauge rail tunnels beneath the city and checking out dead rats. Some people are worried that the tunnels may be flooding, and that's not a good thing. That's caused problems in the past."

"Man, I thought rats were good swimmers," Ashe said.

"They are. That's why everybody is so upset. They've got experts doing rat autopsies, to see if they drowned," Randy said. "If they drowned, that means the tunnels were full of water. Repairs could cost a lot."

"Dead rats aren't a bad thing. Maybe they shouldn't look a gift horse in the mouth," Sali shuddered. "I hate slimy rats."

"Sali, they're not slimy. Not all the time," Ashe teased. "Besides, don't those wolves in Alaska eat rats?"

"Those are wolf-wolves, not werewolves," Sali tossed a corn chip at Ashe.

"Oh. *Now* I get it," Ashe rolled his eyes.

"This is the best stuff, and I can't ever write a damn thing about it," Randy grumbled.

"You know it will get us killed," Marco said softly.

"Yeah. I know that for sure. You think I'd take chances with my mother's life? I won't ever say anything. Or write anything. Been down that road before, remember?"

"How's Trajan?" Marcus sat on the sofa next to Ashe.

"Fine. Up and around the second day like nothing happened. Back to slave driving in the weight room on the third day."

"You lifting weights?" Sali stared at Ashe.

"Yeah. Trajan thinks I'm too skinny, so he's determined to build me up."

"Ashe is running three miles a day with me," Marco nodded. "Trajan's orders. We work in the weight room first, and then go for a run before breakfast. I think Ashe is looking better."

"But Sali's always been the pretty one," Ashe grinned. Sali threw more corn chips.

"Marcus," Denise walked into the media room where all of them had gathered. Ashe jerked his head around—his skin was suddenly tingling. Denise sounded frightened.

"Denise, what is it?" Marcus was on his feet already.

"Ben Billings is outside and he's issuing a challenge." Denise was twisting her fingers nervously.

"He can't go to wolf if it's not the full moon; he has to fight as a human."

"I think he knows that, Marcus. He has a gun."

Ashe muttered a word that might upset his mother. *Mr. DeLuca, I'll get the gun, you get Principal Billings,* Ashe sent. Marcus gave the briefest of nods. Everybody else was up and following Marcus from the room when Ashe turned to mist and went straight through the roof.

Micah Rocklin, Marcus' Second, was already out in the DeLuca's yard, attempting to reason with Billings. The werewolf Principal was waiting just off the front porch, pointing a pistol at the door of the DeLuca home.

"Don't try to talk me out of it, Micah. I deserve to be Packmaster. Should have done this a long time ago," Billings was hissing, spittle flying from his mouth. Ashe had never seen the Principal like this before. He sounded crazy, and that wasn't like him. Angry and biased, yes. Crazy—no.

Coming down now, Ashe sent to Marcus. He zipped down and only forming hands, snatched the gun right out of Billings' hands just as Marcus stepped outside the door. Hovering overhead, then, Ashe watched as Billings stared first at his empty hands and then at Marcus. Billings growled.

"I don't know what kind of tricks you're up to now, DeLuca, but your time is over," Principal Billings snapped.

"Ben, you don't want to fight me. Not like this. Go home. If you still want to challenge, we'll do it on the full moon, all right?" Marcus had his hands out in a placating gesture.

Billings cursed. Ashe was shocked—he'd never heard the Principal say words that foul. "I'll fight you here and now, Marcus. You're just scared to fight me—admit it. Whenever there's an execution, you let me take it. You're weak and you don't want to get your hands dirty."

"Ben, go home. Think about this. We'll settle it on the full moon," Marcus repeated his warning.

Ashe, from his high vantage point, watched Marcus' hands. They were prepared to strike. The yard and the street beyond were filling up with people—mostly werewolves, Ashe realized.

This was Pack business. Marco held Sali in a tight grip on the front porch and Micah was standing next to both boys. Greta, Micah's wife, was there with them, too. Denise DeLuca went to stand beside Greta, who put an arm around the Packmaster's wife.

Among those gathered, Ashe saw Chad Hollis and Jeremy Booth, talking softly together. Ashe couldn't make out what they were saying. Dawn Smith was also there and surprisingly, Randy had gone to stand beside her.

"I'm not backing away or going home with my tail tucked between my legs, Marcus. This is going to be finished today. Then I'll have a few words with the Grand Master and this will be a wolf only community. Like it should have been in the beginning." Billings was putting up his fists.

"Ben, for the last time, go home. Now. As your Packmaster, I'm telling you to wait for the full moon to shine on a challenge." Marcus carefully observed every move Billings made.

Benjamin Billings, Ph. D., werewolf, Principal, lunged at Marcus.

His blows never landed. Marcus had his opponent's neck snapped in a blink—Ashe heard the bones breaking from overhead. Billings fell in a heap to the grass and Ashe, feeling ill, flew straight to his father's bunker, dumped the gun on the floor and then went to heave in the bathroom inside his bedroom.

"I take it you saw that," Marcus was inside Adele's kitchen later, talking to Ashe. "Where's the gun now, Son?" Marcus might have wanted to touch Ashe, but he was worried that Ashe might not want it.

"It's in Dad's bunker," Ashe muttered, letting his head drop into his arms at the kitchen island. Adele stood nearby, wearing a worried frown.

"Only the ones inside the house knew about the gun, Adele," Marcus turned to Ashe's mother. "So we won't have much damage control for Aedan and Nathan. I've already told the others to keep quiet about this. Denise and Marco won't be a problem, they knew already. Micah and Greta know. The rest we'll deal with later. Ashe, if I'm challenged outside the full moon, the fight is human. You're allowed weapons, but you have to give your opponent fair warning. At least two days. That wasn't fair warning, and he had plenty of opportunity to back away and meet me later. He chose not to do that."

"I know," Ashe whispered, lifting his head and staring at Marcus.

"Ashe?" Aedan knocked on Ashe's bedroom door before walking in. Ashe was sitting in his favorite spot on his bed; his back pressed to the headboard; short, white socks on his feet. Ashe had chosen to wear a pair of cargo shorts that morning. He didn't think he'd ever wear them again without remembering what happened that afternoon.

"Dad?" Ashe looked up as Aedan Evans walked in and sat on the end of Ashe's bed.

"I gave the pistol to Marcus, then Nathan and I took care of a few things. It wasn't much. You did right, Son. Marcus would have been killed in an unfair fight and the Grand Master would have been forced to come and sort everything out. I can't believe that old werewolf went crazy like that."

"That's just what I thought. He wasn't acting normal. I don't know what caused that, but it was scary."

"He didn't suffer. Marcus was trained to kill quickly and cleanly by the military. He was Special Ops, but he doesn't like killing. That's why he allowed Billings or one of the others to take executions when necessary. That doesn't mean he won't fight if he must. He holds his position because he can."

"I'm not questioning that. I just feel that Billings might have been pushed into this, somehow. Otherwise, it just doesn't make sense." Ashe picked at his comforter.

"I'm not going to argue with you on this. I know what happened the last time." Aedan stood. "But if ye need to talk, or just to be with somebody, I'll be up all night, and your mam won't be doin' much in the way of sleepin' either." Aedan's accent had come through. Ashe liked the lilting speech when his father used it.

"I know, dad. I think this is something that has to go away on its own, but I'll let you know."

"Good. You're me baby boy, Ashe, and don't ye be forgettin' it." Aedan stole from the room.

Ashe's cell rang half an hour later. Winkler was calling. "You all right, Ashe?" Winkler asked.

"Yeah. It was just a shock, that's all."

"If you need to get away, you can come here. My kids came in, but they won't bother you if you need peace and quiet."

"Yeah. I think I'll be okay, but I'll let you know." Ashe said good-bye and hung up.

～

"Usually the family has a private service," Sali whispered. Ashe was playing a mind-numbing game on his laptop close to midnight and Sali had sneaked into Ashe's bedroom.

Ashe knew Sali's memory had already been adjusted. Sali thought Marcus had taken care of the entire incident. This time, Ashe didn't mind so much. Now, Sali was giving Ashe information on what would happen to their former Principal.

"But Billings doesn't have any family here," Ashe agreed.

"Yeah. So Dad is going to let Mr. Dodd handle it, and anybody that wants can go. Shirley Walker says they can bury him on her property—there's a couple others buried in the same spot already."

"I can't believe he challenged," Ashe sighed, shutting down the game. "He was smarter than that. There's something else behind this, dude."

"Ashe, I don't know what it could be. Dad says Billings was old—almost one-ninety. He thinks he just went crazy."

"Well, he might have been crazy; I'm not arguing that point," Ashe agreed. "But I think something made him go crazy."

"And the weekend was great, until that happened."

"Yeah. When will they have the service?"

"Tomorrow. There's no place to keep him," Sali pointed out.

"Yeah." Ashe recalled that the body of James Johnson, the seventeen-year-old werewolf who was killed three years earlier, had been kept inside a walk-in refrigerator in the O'Neill's barn. Ashe shivered at the memory.

"Dad won't go. It's tradition not to recognize a challenger after the challenge. So we'll be home."

"Marco and I will go back to Winkler's tomorrow night."

"I know. And we have to go back to picking fruit on Monday." Sali didn't sound pleased about that.

"Sali, be careful out in those groves. And keep an eye on Dori for me, okay?"

"Sure."

~

"This is what our spy was able to get," Pruitt showed Ezekiel Tanner the video sent by cell phone. One of King Baltis' guards also watched what had been sent.

"Are those hands? Coming out of nowhere?" Ezekiel drew in a breath as the pistol was snatched away from the grasp of the challenger and then disappeared, as did the ghostly hands. Baltis' guard hissed as well. "I must inform my King," he said, and rushed from Ezekiel's study.

"I hate those guys," Dom Pruitt huffed when the Elemaiya disappeared. "The sooner we get rid of them, the better."

"If that is the one he wants," Ezekiel was running the video back to watch it again, "we may have a tussle over it. Do you see the possibilities, here?" Ezekiel lifted an eyebrow as he looked at Pruitt.

"Yeah. If that one can carry a gun away without being seen, imagine what else he might carry."

CHAPTER 13

"My King, I had to rest. My apologies for arriving at this time," Rend bowed before Baltis, out of breath and breathing with difficulty.

"No matter, I was not asleep," Baltis sighed. Both Dark Elemaiya stood inside an underground chamber hollowed out beneath Chicago's streets. "What do you have for me? Or did you merely wish to get away from those foul-smelling creatures?"

"I have news, my King. The one whom we seek? What if you could turn him to our purposes?" Rend gazed at his King's back. Baltis had no view. He had no windows. Instead, he stared at a painting his servants had hung on the newly formed walls of his chamber.

"Why would we need him? We have shapeshifters in plenty. We have always birthed more of those than our Bright cousins."

"My King, the one working as spy for those creatures sent images to them. I have good reason to believe that the boy is a mister." If Rend wanted his King's attention, he had it then.

"Perhaps half." Marcus answered Micah's question regarding how

161

many had gone to Ben Billings' service and burial. "And I'm not sure I understand why Dawn and Randy went, but that's not my concern." Marcus ran a hand through short black hair.

"I'm not sure why Marcie and her boys went either," Micah sighed. "Perhaps it's a morality lesson for her sons or something."

"I'm not sure I want to know, either way," Marcus said.

"Ready?" Marco stood in the doorway of Ashe's bedroom, watching while Ashe zipped his backpack and slung it over a shoulder. Sali sat at the foot of Ashe's bed, watching Ashe prepare to go back to Winkler's beach house.

"Yeah. Come on, Sali." Sali rose and followed Ashe. "Time to go, Mom," Ashe met his mother at the foot of the stairs.

"Honey, I almost wish you could stay home for a few days," Adele said.

"I know. We'll be back Friday night."

"Full moon," Adele reminded, hugging Ashe.

"No worries," Ashe nodded, squeezing his mother's shoulders before letting go.

Sali walked out with Marco and Ashe, watching both of them as they climbed into the borrowed Winkler Security van. Ashe waved at his friend as Marco backed out of the driveway.

"It was the best of times, it was the worst of times," Ashe quoted the Dickens classic.

"Yeah." Marco was in complete agreement as they left the Star Cove addition behind and drove toward Aransas Pass and the ferry. This time, the long line of vehicles was waiting to get off the island, so Ashe and Marco were one of only four vehicles riding to Port Aransas.

"Have you met Winkler's kids?" Ashe asked as Marco drove off the ferry, the van thumping over the gangway and onto solid pavement.

"Yeah. They're okay. Wayne goes by his middle name, because he's named after Winkler, and Wynter can be a bit of a diva at times, but she's all right, too."

"What happened to their mother?" Ashe thought to ask. Nobody had mentioned her at all.

"Kellee is the biggest jerk," Marco sighed. She's remarried now, to a werewolf Second in Ohio. She only asks to see Wayne and Wynter if she wants something from Winkler. Money and stuff."

"Aren't they old enough to decide if they want to see their mother?" Ashe asked.

"They'll be twenty-one in August, and that's when Winkler can stop supporting Kellee, according to the agreement he made. Kellee is probably fit to be tied over it, because she can't bug Winkler after that. Not with any leverage, anyway. Word has it that Winkler paid for the huge house she's living in, there in Cleveland. Her husband owns a small construction firm, so it's likely he didn't buy it."

"Sounds like daytime television," Ashe grinned.

"More than you know," Marco said. "Want ice cream before we hit the beach?"

The small ice-cream shop in Port Aransas only had a few customers inside. Ashe and Marco ordered a cone each. Ashe whipped out his cell and dialed Winkler's number.

"Ashe?" Winkler answered.

"We're at the ice-cream shop in Port A. Want anything?"

"Yeah. Bring a half gallon each of chocolate, strawberry and rocky road," Winkler's smile came through in his voice.

"Will do," Ashe said and ended the call. Marco paid for the ice cream, placed the bag in the back of the van and drove the few remaining miles to the beach house. Winkler, Trajan, Trace and two others were waiting when Marco and Ashe brought the bag inside.

"Ashe, this is Wayne and this is Wynter," Winkler introduced his twenty-year-old twins to Ashe, who smiled and took offered hands.

"Shapeshifter, huh?" Wayne asked.

"Look," Marco hauled out his cell phone and replayed the video he'd taken of Sali waving his arms while the bumblebee bat flapped overhead.

"That's tiny," Wynter breathed, watching as well.

"And extremely handy," Winkler said, chuckling at Sali's antics. "Ashe has echolocation skills like that. He can detect you from half a mile away."

"And he's so cute," Trajan slapped Ashe on the back. "Get your shorts on. You haven't gone running for two days. We'll work extra hard in the weight room tomorrow, too."

"You enjoy this, don't you?" Ashe said.

"You know it. Marco, to the beach!" Trajan pointed toward the sandy stretch behind Winkler's beach house.

"I'll come, too," Wayne said. Minutes later, Ashe, Wayne and Marco were jogging southward along the sandy strip between the gulf water and a line of beach homes and condos. "Heard you had a little excitement in Star Cove," Wayne breathed, running between Ashe and Marco.

"Yeah. Dad took care of it," Marco replied.

"My dad says it was out of character," Wayne went on.

"It was, in a weird sort of way," Marco agreed. "Never saw Billings go off like that."

"I think something set him off, I just don't know what it was," Ashe offered.

"Either way, he was buried this afternoon. As a human," Marco ended the conversation regarding Principal Billings. "How's school? What about the vacation in Europe?"

"School's okay. Europe ditto. Gran and Grampa went with us to Stonehenge, and then walked around with us in Edinburgh and Paris. We got to go out alone sometimes, too."

"Maybe I'll ask my dad to send me when I graduate from high school," Ashe said.

"What does your dad do?" Wayne asked.

"He's security for the community. Part of it, anyway. He's vampire," Marco answered for Ashe.

"You're one of those. I heard there aren't many that the Council allowed."

"Somebody said there were twenty, I think," Ashe huffed out a breath. "And I don't understand that."

"I heard the Council keeps a tight grip on everything vampire," Wayne said. "But you might know more about that than I do."

"Not likely. They don't hand out much info," Ashe said. "You can always ask Tony Hancock, when he wakes up."

"You don't mess with Tony," Wayne offered sagely. "You don't want to mess with any Council Assassin."

"What? He's an Assassin?" Ashe almost stopped running.

"Yeah. Heard his surrogate sire is, too. You don't get away from those guys if they come after you."

"I feel comforted. Don't you Marco? Don't you feel comforted to know that if they send a vampire Assassin after you, you're toast?" Ashe was grumbling and he knew it. "And it's doubly comforting to know that a vampire Assassin is only steps away while you sleep."

"Ashe, your dad's a vampire. Why are you so concerned?" Wayne asked.

"Let's just say it's inside information." Ashe turned up his speed and loped away from Marco and Wayne.

"I don't know what set him off," Marco told Winkler later. "Wayne let it slip that Tony is an Assassin for the Council and Ashe just took off. I didn't know he could run like that."

"Marco, there's a lot you don't understand about the vampire race. Hell, there's a lot *I* don't understand. And I'll have a talk with Wayne. He should never have let that information out. Ashe has enough to worry about."

"What are we not understanding?" The object of discussion, Anthony Hancock, appeared in Winkler's kitchen, watching while Marco dipped out a bowl of rocky road ice cream. "I used to love that stuff," he sighed.

"We're not understanding anything about congress and the price of fossil fuels," Winkler said. "And Ashe has enough to worry about without vampires, werewolves and alien races breathing down his neck."

"With his ability, he has a responsibility," Tony said.

"Hancock, he's sixteen. What were you doing at sixteen, other than playing in a dojo somewhere and giving your parents fits?" Winkler started dipping out ice cream for himself.

"That about sums it up," Tony agreed amiably.

"Did you eat all the strawberry?" Ashe walked into the kitchen.

"I don't think anybody's gotten into it, except Wynter," Winkler grinned. Tony Hancock stood nearby, watching as ice cream was dipped into bowls.

"Do you miss it?" Ashe asked the vampire.

"Yeah. But I hear that goes away after a while. A few hundred years or so."

"That information you gave me? How much did the Council hold back?" Ashe opened the carton of strawberry before grabbing a bowl and spoon.

"That's classified," Tony said.

"Is it? The world gonna implode if I read a fourth page?" Ashe scooped ice cream, a determined set to his mouth.

"Marco, out," Winkler snarled. Marco took his ice cream and left the kitchen quickly.

"Kid, I stopped trying to figure out why the Council does anything," Tony said. "And yes, they might think the world will implode if you read any more."

"That's the story of my life," Ashe's blue eyes gazed coolly into Tony Hancock's gray stare. "Ashe doesn't need to know anything. But he can haul his butt here and there so everybody else gets what they want."

"Kid, that's the way the world works. A few are in charge, the rest of us toil and scurry. And I'm practicing patience right now. If my sire were here, compulsion would be laid and that would be the end of it."

"Yeah? Sounds a little despotic to me." Ashe placed the container of strawberry back in the freezer and grabbed his bowl. "I'll eat this out on the deck," he said, nodding at Winkler.

"This will not be a competition, to see who ends up with him," Tony's growl was almost as good as Winkler's best snarl. "His father is a vampire and required permission from the Council to become a parent."

"Is that why they gave permission? To see if any of the kids turned out to be something they could leisurely take if they wanted? Hancock, even you know that's wrong. When you were turned, you asked for it. You were dying in the rubble of a bombed hotel in Paris. Are you going to ask that kid before you rip his throat out?"

"Nobody will rip his throat out, it's dangerous to turn anyone that way," Tony snapped. "And I won't be the one selected, if it comes to that. It'll be somebody older, with more experience. I've never tried it and honestly, I have no desire to do so."

"They'll send one of those old bastards, then."

"Nothing has been decided. And you're right, he's only sixteen. The rule, as you well know, is eighteen at least."

"How quickly after that are they going to conscript, Hancock? Do you think I'm stupid? That I can't figure out why the Council will assign one of their few Assassins to cool his heels with a werewolf?"

"They sent me because they trust me and I'm not so ancient I have nothing in common with a sixteen-year-old. In their eyes, at least."

"You think you have something in common with Ashe? Do you? He's struggling, Hancock. He's trying to come to terms with his father's placement of compulsion every time the inhabitants of that community see him do something that's considered secret. You didn't see the look on his face when he found out they'd handed the credit to me for rescuing that girl in Amarillo. I had almost nothing to do with that part of it. I just supervised the rounding up of Tanner's rogues afterward."

"If we don't conceal him, the Elemaiya will be all over him," Tony was beginning to show anger. "One side will kill him, the other will likely get him killed, sending him out to do this or that. We need him. We can accomplish so much with his talents."

"Provided he's under Wlodek's thumb."

"I don't know that for sure. Wlodek hasn't said anything."

"Yet."

"I don't see anything happening for a few years unless there's an unfortunate accident."

"I hope I don't see any unfortunate accidents," Winkler gave Tony a hard stare.

"It won't be because I wanted it," the tips of Tony's fangs showed.

"Hey, now, no growling and hissing," Trajan walked in and slapped Tony on the back, breaking the tension.

~

"What were you talking about before—reading another page?" Marco asked.

"Some stuff on the Elemaiya. I get the idea I was supposed to get a lot more, but I got three pages. That's it," Ashe poked his ice cream with the spoon in frustration. "I guess they think it'll be awful if I know more than I do."

"Did you talk to your dad about it?" Marco asked.

"No. There wasn't any time, what with everything happening over the weekend."

"Why don't you talk to him now? He's up," Marco grinned.

"Yeah. Think Winkler will be upset if I take ice cream into the bedroom with me?"

"He does it all the time, dude."

"All right. I'll call my dad. See what he says about all this." Ashe rose from his chair and walked into the house.

~

"Dad, I forgot to tell you about this. I can scan it through the computer—it's only three pages," Ashe spoke to his father by cell phone.

"Go ahead and send it, Son. I think I'd like to see this." Aedan was surprised to hear from Ashe.

"All right." Ashe walked into his office and powered up the computer. The scanning was complete a few minutes later. "Did you get it?" Ashe asked. By that time, his mother had joined his father inside Aedan's study.

"Aedan, look at this," Ashe heard his mother's voice clearly as the information popped up in an email to his father.

"I wish we'd seen this earlier, but that's neither here nor there. I don't think I have to warn you not to let any of this get out, and whatever you do, don't let anyone you don't trust see anything other than what they've seen already, all right?"

"Sure. I sort of figured that out already."

"I know you're cautious. Just be doubly so, all right? Is Anthony Hancock still there?"

"Yeah. I may have pissed him off earlier, though."

"While he may have more patience than a lot of vampires I know, that patience isn't limitless. Tread carefully, all right?"

"He has mindspeech, Dad. Did you know that?"

"I did know that. I trust you'll come straight to me if there's a problem in that area? I'm older than Hancock, by a long way."

"I'll keep that in mind," Ashe muttered.

"The older ones can place compulsion on those younger. Nathan and I are both older than Hancock. Remember that. Son, whatever you do, never let them know you're not susceptible to compulsion. They don't like it when they can't handle someone like that."

"I will." Ashe was shocked to be getting information from his father like this. That spelled one thing—Aedan Evans was worried.

～

"My Queen, our spies have reported. We have watched our Dark cousins for a while, now. Baltis is sending some of his to a place in the country of Mexico. They tell me the nearest city is called Juarez. A violent place, it seems. I have taken the liberty of sending some of our own there, and we now have better information. All it took was a bit of bribery to a politician who has escaped pending charges against him. All his assets have been frozen, so compensation from us was quite welcome. He informed my spies that an attack is planned, just before the full moon. Somehow, they gained information regarding our intended raid upon the community at the full moon and plan to usurp our attack. I also received other valuable information."

"And what is that, Sapphire?" Friesianna gave her Sentinel a cold stare. Was one shapeshifter worth all this trouble? She was about to step back and allow the Dark Ones to take him.

"The boy is a mister," Sapphire announced triumphantly. "We hold hard evidence of this fact. The spy for our cousins sent images of this, and it is rumored that the boy may have other talents. I know not exactly what those might be, but he is a valuable property and those creatures our Dark cousins have allied with have designs on him as well. They intend to wrest him from beneath Baltis' nose and use him for their own illicit purposes."

"Baltis will kill them—he has no living misters. All of them disappeared years ago, for reasons unknown to me." Friesianna settled her silk dress around her, lounging gracefully upon her throne. Had she a mirror, she might have checked the position of her crown. Instead, she struck as haughty a pose as she could. "Find out what else the boy can do and bring the date of the attack if you can. I command that you and your brothers do what you must to take what rightfully belongs to us. The boy is becoming more useful by the hour."

"Of course, my Queen." Sapphire bowed low and rushed away.

"I did not let her know we have other spies," Sapphire informed his fellow Sentinels. "It was a stroke of luck finding the quarter-blood, but now it is difficult to get information from him. Who knew that humans would lock him up so tightly that he would not be allowed visitors? Would that we had a mister at our disposal—that would give us everything we need. Unfortunate it is that the Foreseer is Dark and only quarter-blood—the Queen will never allow him within our encampment. Rabis gives the Queen only what she asks for and nothing more. I question his loyalty at times."

"The Queen sent Rabis away centuries ago when his prophecies failed to tell her what she wanted to hear," Emerald pointed out. "Now that Hilbah is no more, she was forced to call Rabis back. I cannot say that I would have the most positive of attitudes under such circumstances."

"You speak treason," Ruby snapped.

"He speaks truth. Just as Rabis spoke it in the beginning. However, we are all committed to our Queen, are we not? We must do her bidding and no other, as she instructs. We may speak the truth among ourselves, as brothers and Sentinels." Diamond looked at all of them. "It will be good, will it not, to have a mister and shapeshifter at our command? We hold the skills to force his will to ours. As does the Queen. He will do our bidding and with his help, we will crush the Dark Ones. It is time they recognized which race will survive."

"Then we must position our troops. Do we attack in Mexico, after they have acquired the boy, or do we preempt and take him in Texas?" Sapphire asked.

"I say we wait until they get him away from his parents and the others in that community who seek to protect him," Diamond said.

"I wish to consult Rabis," Ruby whined.

"No! Consult Rabis at your own peril. He will report to the Queen. She will have no difficulty with our decision, once the final outcome is to her liking. I follow my brother Diamond in this. Let the Dark Ones think they score a victory against us. We will be waiting for them and take the boy when they do not suspect. And if those rogue creatures think to prevent it, then they will be most sorry, I assure you," Emerald smiled. "We will call in our best troops. They will be ready to follow us quickly, should the need arise."

"Have you given a thought to whom the boy's parent might be?

Will she object to his treatment? He is High Born; else he would not mist or shapeshift."

"We will make sure they do not object," Diamond clenched his fists. "The Royal House is all but gone, destroyed by the predations of our Darker cousins and a few, well-placed assassinations, here and there. At the Queen's command, of course."

"Of course," Sapphire agreed. Diamond was firstborn of the brothers, and often acted as assassin for the Queen. Sapphire was next, followed by Ruby and Emerald. Their parents were dead—killed by Baltis' Destroyers. They certainly wanted revenge and would stop at nothing to obtain it. "We will protect our Queen and bring about the downfall of Baltis and all his subjects."

"We strike on Friday, the day before the full moon," Ezekiel informed his werewolf troops. "We know where the groves are and most of the older children are working there. They are our targets. We have no use for the younger ones. Our compatriots, here," Zeke nodded to the two Elemaiya standing in a corner of his trophy room, "will grab the boy they want—he works elsewhere. We'll go in full daylight so we won't be fighting vampires. Pruitt, I want you and Rutherford to go with our guests to take the shapeshifter boy."

Pruitt, sitting not far from Ezekiel, nodded his understanding. He and Rutherford were Zeke's most capable and deadly among the rogue werewolves. It was their job to take the Elemaiya down, once they had Ashe in their possession.

A rendezvous point had been agreed upon—in Rockport, a small town north of Star Cove. Three boats would be moored there, ready to take the entire party out to a larger ship anchored at sea.

Zeke figured the parents and the Grand Master's werewolves might not suspect they'd take them that way, expecting the kidnapped children to be transported by vehicle or plane. Ezekiel had many contacts in the drug world and most of those contacts had a fleet of boats at their disposal.

"What if we meet up with any of Shirley Walker's wolves?" One of Ezekiel's werewolves asked.

"Kill them. I'm handing out the assault rifles. They won't likely be armed if they're nearby. No witnesses, got it? I don't want anybody left alive who can identify any one of you."

"What about me? I can handle a gun just as well as the next person," former Congressman Jack Howard spoke up. "I think I wouldn't mind doing a bit of murder." He cracked his knuckles pretentiously.

"Howard, it amazes me that you could actually convince people to vote for you," Ezekiel snapped. "You'll stay here. You get caught in the states; I won't be forming a posse to rescue any part of your sorry ass. Stay here, you're safer."

"Then take me along to guard the boat while you're off it," Howard suggested. "Surely you can't argue with that logic."

"Fine. You stay with Julio and guard the ship. Julio, if he steps a toe out of line, shoot him." Ezekiel nodded to a grizzled rogue who grinned, showing missing teeth.

"Hey, wait just a minute," Jack Howard huffed.

"Howard, you ceased being important to me when they froze your assets. Right now, you're as useful to me as lips on a chicken. Stay out of my way—you'll live longer. Any questions? You all know the plan?" Zeke looked at those gathered around the room.

Nobody said anything. "Good. We'll travel by land to the gulf, through Matamoros. The boats will be waiting for us south of the Las Palomas Wildlife area. Be ready to carry your gear on foot for a little way. We leave tonight."

CHAPTER 14

"Ashe, I convinced Tony to give me a copy of what you got," Winkler called Ashe to his office after breakfast. Winkler had a copy of the three pages in his hand when Ashe sat in front of Winkler's large desk. "How many of these things can you do?"

"My dad doesn't want me to discuss those things," Ashe said. "And I really couldn't say. I haven't tried most of them." Ashe had been thinking about the one regarding Relocation. When he'd played around with that ability, he'd done it repeatedly, without tiring. The information on the pages made it sound as if the Elemaiya wore themselves out after doing it two or three times, so they held it back for emergencies.

"Kid, this has me worried. Do you think the Elemaiya know exactly what you can do?" Winkler's forehead was creased in a frown.

"I hope they don't know anything except about the bat. That's all Dad will allow, except with Marcus, Marco, Marco's mother and Micah and Greta Rocklin. Well, Nathan, too. And Cori knows. That's it. The rest of them think I'm a wimpy shapeshifter."

"Three years ago," Winkler sighed, "I hoped we'd gotten the leak, after you pegged Paul Harris. Now I'm worried that someone else might have taken over his spot, or was working independently as a spy. It bothers me that somebody seemed to know Wynn would be traveling to Amarillo to visit relatives. And somehow, their mutant creature was headed right for Cloud Chief when he killed that human boy." Winkler stood and raked fingers through his hair.

"You think somebody told him where to look?" Ashe was frowning now. "That he didn't just track us down?"

"Ashe, when you're in this business, you have to look at all possibilities. Honestly, I was keeping an eye on Ben Billings, but he's taken himself out of the game. So, if there is a leak, then it wasn't Ben. Or if he was involved, then he's conveniently out of the way."

"Mr. Winkler, that wasn't Principal Billings. Well, it was him, but he wouldn't do something like that. What if somebody placed compulsion? Forced him to do that? I don't think Dad or Nathan would even consider it, but what about another vampire?"

"Ashe, you read these pages," Winkler held up the copy he had. "The Elemaiya—some of them, anyway—can do that too. I just can't figure out why somebody would tell him to make a challenge."

"Yeah. This is so confusing," Ashe sighed. "And now he's dead. Is this the way it feels?" Ashe studied Winkler's face. "You have someone you consider an enemy, and when he dies under unusual circumstances, it's—just weird."

"Weird is a good word. Mixed emotions best describes how I feel. Billings was old school. He remembered too well the race war between vampires and werewolves. Back then, we were trained to track and kill. Weldon and Wlodek knew both races were headed toward extinction. They hammered out a peace agreement. So far, it has held. There are a few on both sides who don't like it, but most of us see the sense in it. We both hold to our own laws, and both races have a law against killing humans. Mostly it's to keep the races hidden. If my sources are correct, the vampires don't place compulsion for unethical reasons. Your father and Nathan are trying to protect you. I know that's a little hard to accept right now, because you have talents that most people only dream about."

"Next time you rescue the girl, hand her over to your best friend while somebody else takes the credit and see how that feels," Ashe snapped.

"Ah. I think I'm beginning to see." Winkler huffed out a breath. "Ashe, I'm sorry about that, but I don't see any way out of it now. We all want life to be fair, and it so seldom is."

"What does not destroy me makes me stronger? Is that what you're trying to say?"

"Spoken like a true dead philosopher," Winkler grinned.

"Mr. Winkler, I've been thinking about the vampires who got permission from the Council to have children. I wonder if it's given permission recently. The big drawback in having a vampire father is that I never get to see him during the day. Mom and I go shopping alone most of the time. If Dad goes, it's late at night. If anything happens during the day, he doesn't know until he wakes. Like Principal Billings' challenge. It frustrates him, it frustrates me and it frustrates Mom. She won't ever say it, but there have been times—like when I got shot—that she really needed him and he was asleep."

"Ashe, Tony told me last night that the Council has shut down the experiment with vampire children. That's what it was—an experiment. Those reasons were cited. Children are a huge responsibility, and I can only imagine that the vampires have had a terrible time dealing with kids who could walk in the sun. Mates, too. The Council hasn't given permission for twelve years. I think you were among the last to be born. Nathan having two children is almost unheard of."

"Yeah. I think you're right. What did you want me to work on today?"

"Actually, I'd like some files cleaned out in my computer system. I'll hand my desk over to you and let you take care of a few things. I have a list of files here that I want deleted." Winkler lifted another paper and waved it at Ashe before setting it on his desk and moving away. "I have some errands to run in Corpus today, so if you need anything, ask Trajan."

"All right." Ashe traded places with Winkler, watching as the werewolf walked out of his office before settling in to delete files.

~

"I got flowers?" Dori stared at the pink roses Mr. Dawkins dropped off. He'd been manning the guard kiosk located outside the gate and signed for the delivery. Lavonna had shown them to Dori the moment she got home from working in the groves. "Who are they from?" Dori sniffed a delicate pink bloom.

"Read the card," Lavonna smiled. Dori lifted the tiny envelope from the bouquet and opened it.

"It says *Happy Monday—Ashe*. They're from Ashe. This is so cool! Wynn didn't get flowers!" Dori was hugging the card to her chest and bouncing on her toes with excitement.

"I'm not surprised Ashe sent flowers," Lavonna laughed.

"So we found out who the Lothario was?" Cori walked in from the deck.

"Here, read for yourself," Dori passed over the card and sniffed another pink rose. "They smell so good."

The doorbell rang. Cori went to answer, finding Wynn on the porch. "Come on in, Dori's having a fit about the flowers Ashe sent."

"Dori got flowers?" Wynn was in the kitchen quickly, cooing over the pink roses and reading the card. "He sent you flowers 'cause it's Monday?" Wynn sighed. "That's so romantic."

"Do you think I should call?" Dori looked at her mother.

"It's polite, to let him know you got them," Lavonna said. Dori pulled her cell phone from a pocket in her jeans and dialed Ashe's number. He picked up right away.

"Ashe, I got the flowers. They smell so good. I love them."

~

"Somebody sent somebody flowers," Marco teased. He, Ashe, Wayne and Wynter were dressed for a run on the beach before dinner. Ashe was standing on the deck dressed in shorts, running shoes and an old T-shirt when Dori called.

"Did you like the color? I saw your pink bikini and earrings and thought you might like pink," Ashe said, coloring a little. Marco stood nearby, listening to the conversation and smirking.

"I love pink, Ashe. These are the first flowers I've ever gotten. Thank you."

"Great. I'm glad you like them," Ashe was now fending off Marco, who was grinning and trying to flip Ashe's ear. "Dori, I have to go. Marco wants to get a run in before dinner. I'll talk to you later, all right?" Dori agreed and hung up. "Dude, I can depants you the next time you're kissing Cori in front of the entire universe," Ashe threatened Marco.

"You think you can? You have to catch me first," Marco grinned and took off, running down the steps to the deck and then out to the beach, Ashe hot on his heels. Wayne and Wynter struggled to keep up. Ashe was keeping up with Marco easily. Running was easier for him now, and the weight lifting with Trajan was showing some results. "Man, now I have to give Cori flowers, just to keep her happy," Marco grumped good-naturedly as they ran.

"Hey, slow down, some of us are out of shape," Wayne jogged up beside Ashe. Wynter was still running gamely behind.

"Trajan can fix that," Marco grinned. He slowed down anyway.

"I'll be in the weight room in the morning, I promise," Wayne sounded out of breath.

"Hey, slow down a little more," Wynter called out. Ashe slowed his stride and soon he was running alongside Wynter, who was very pretty, with black hair and nearly black eyes. Ashe thought the twins favored their father quite a bit.

"So, one more year in college, huh?" Ashe asked conversationally.

"Yeah. One more year of marketing and business. Dad has a PR firm, but he wants me to keep an eye on things for him. I think he's got somebody in mind for me, too, but I keep telling him that I won't marry anybody unless I like them."

"You haven't met him yet? That sounds odd." Ashe watched Wynter as she concentrated on her running, long black hair tied in a ponytail and swinging as she ran.

"It's not odd. He had somebody picked out for Aunt Whitney, too, only she eloped with Sam Sheridan. I hear there was quite a bit of growling and snarling over that."

"I don't think Winkler would be happy if somebody foiled his plans," Ashe grinned.

"You have no idea," Wynter rolled her eyes in exasperation. "So I promised my dad I'd at least meet the guy and then tell him exactly what I thought of his choice."

"I got grounded the last time I talked back to my dad," Ashe muttered.

"I was seventeen when I told Dad that. I was grounded for a week." Wynter smiled.

"What about your grandparents? Are these your mother's folks or your dad's?"

"Mom's mother and her second husband. Davis is no relation, but he's the best grandfather. Dad's parents are both dead."

"That's too bad. I don't have any grandparents. I always wondered what it would be like to have some." As soon as Ashe made the statement, he remembered the email he'd gotten from the one claiming to be his grandfather. He wondered still whether he should believe what he'd received or if, as the message had indicated, he shouldn't trust it at all. Shaking himself, Ashe came back to the present. "I didn't see Trace when we came in last night."

"He didn't come in. Trace was visiting his friend Eric," Wynter said. "Eric came down for the weekend, so they rented a condo down the beach."

Ashe blinked for a few moments. "Trace is gay?"

"Yes. Does that bother you?"

"Does Eric treat him well?"

"Yes. He's werewolf, too. They're a small minority, but they do exist."

"As long as Eric cares about Trace, I have no problem with that. Trace is a good guy." Ashe nodded determinedly.

"Is it just Trace you don't have a problem with?" Wynter asked.

"Nope. People are people. They love other people. What difference does it make? Dad told me a few years back, when he explained about the birds and the bees, that everybody deserves love and respect. He says there are gay vampires and shapeshifters. He didn't know about the wolves, but he figured there had to be some."

"I might like to meet your dad sometime," Wynter said. "I've only met a few vampires—Anthony Hancock, now Anthony Rockland. Dalroy and Rhett."

"Yeah? Well, you'd probably like Nathan Anderson, too. He's more laid back than my dad, I think. If something makes my dad angry, he's angry right away. Nathan thinks about it for a little while before making a decision. Probably a good thing, since he's Cori and Dori's dad."

"So, Wynter let the cat out of the bag," Trace sat next to Ashe on the sofa after dinner.

"Is it supposed to make me feel different about you?" Ashe blinked at the taller werewolf.

"I hope not." Trace grinned and ruffled Ashe's hair.

"Did you have a hard time in school because of it?" Ashe asked.

"You have no idea," Trace nodded. "And then to find out I was werewolf on top of that? Trajan and my parents kept me from going crazy."

"Are your parents still alive?"

"Yeah. Still live between Waco and Fort Worth. Still grow peaches, pears and pecan trees, plus a few other things. I followed Jason around as soon as I could walk, I think. He's like my second dad."

"Discussing the joys of youth?" Tony Hancock walked in. Ashe stared at him for a moment before everything shifted. Just as before, when he'd seen Winkler and the woman, the air around Ashe seemed to shift and shimmer. He saw Tony with a blond man nearly the same height. The blond man appeared to be teaching Tony something, gesturing with his hands while they both sat in a study decorated in French period furniture. The desk was ornately carved and gilded. Louis XIV came to Ashe's mind as he stared at the image before him.

"Ashe—Ashe? Buddy, where are you?" Trace was shaking Ashe as he came back to the present.

"Wow." Ashe held his head in confusion.

"What happened? Did you have another vision?" Winkler was in the room quickly and kneeling next to Ashe.

"I saw Tony and a blond man. I think the blond man was telling Tony something." Ashe looked past Winkler at Tony Hancock. "I saw you in a room filled with French furniture. The blond man was sitting at a gilded, antique desk. I think it was Louis XIV or something."

"You saw that?" Tony had a cell phone in his hand faster than Ashe could follow the movement.

"Who was it?" Ashe asked as Tony dialed a number. Ashe heard it ringing. Someone picked up immediately.

"Honored One, Ashe Evans just had a vision of me—and René—in the past. He described René's study accurately."

"Has the boy had any other visions?" Ashe recognized that voice. Wlodek, Head of the Vampire Council, had come to Cloud Chief three years earlier to attend Old Harold's funeral. Ashe hadn't known who it was until the ancient vampire had driven away with his vampire chauffeur.

"He's had one—of me around twenty-four years ago. It was nothing, just something I was thinking about at the time. Someone's memories must trigger it." Winkler stood up, nodding at Tony. He knew Wlodek could hear his words easily.

"Take the boy from the room," Wlodek ordered.

"But," Ashe looked from Winkler to Tony.

"Come on, let's go find Trajan and Marco," Trace pulled Ashe off the sofa and led him from the room.

~

"He's out of hearing range," Winkler nodded to Tony.

"What else has the boy been doing that I should know about?" Wlodek sounded angry.

"Honored One, that child probably wouldn't tell anyone—he's very tight-lipped. At his father's insistence, of course," Winkler said.

"Of course. Aedan is the same way."

"Honored One, I understand that there is more information to be had than what was handed to the boy," Winkler went on.

"Yes." Wlodek's voice was guarded.

"Then I think you should search through the rest of it, to see if there is anything there regarding something—or someone—called *Ir'Indicti*."

"Will you spell that for me, please? And how did you learn of this?"

"The information came from a quarter-blood Elemaiya who Matt Michaels picked up at Tanner's game preserve. The man seems insane, but he can predict things better than anyone I've ever seen. Matt let me talk to him earlier today. He gave me the spelling of the term, but he wouldn't tell me anything else."

"And where is this person now? What is his name?" Wlodek asked calmly. Winkler knew enough of Wlodek to know he was more dangerous this way.

"His name is Wildrif and he's in the federal maximum security facility in Colorado."

"Ah. Well. Do you know if he is Dark or Bright Elemaiya?"

"He says Dark."

"I see. I will research this, as you ask. If I find anything useful, I will let you know." Wlodek ended the call.

"Wildrif will be dead in a week, won't he?" Winkler watched Tony pocket his cell phone.

"Most likely. Don't try to stop it," Tony said. "If the enemies of the Council learn of his existence, they'll get him out of prison and make him vampire. We had a hard time cleaning out their nest of Dark Elemaiya-turned-vampires the last time. We only turn the Bright Ones. At least they're not homicidal when they wake as vampire."

"I remember—I was there when the army of Dark Elemaiya vampires tried to kill all of us," Winkler huffed. "I know all about the misters, the mindspeakers and the shapeshifter vampires, all bent on destruction. Where we differ is how they were destroyed."

"I know what's in the official records the Council keeps," Tony slapped Winkler on the back. "We don't deal in fantasy, like you do."

"Tony, if it makes you feel better, then believe anything you like." Winkler stalked from the room.

~

"Come on, wimp. Get those weights up," Trajan grinned as he put Wayne through his paces on the weight bench. "Your dad can do twice that—easy."

"Seriously? Dad can do six hundred?" Wayne hissed out a breath.

Ashe watched, leaning against the wall of the weight room. Marco was spotting Wayne—it wouldn't do to let the boss's son get smacked by three hundred pounds. Ashe had worked his way up to one-seventy-five. Now he was determined to do better than that.

"Yep. Your old man can do six hundred, easy," Winkler stalked into the room, acting like a caged wolf. "Come on, get off that bench. I need to work off a little steam."

Trajan put more weight on the bar; Winkler stretched first and then got on the bench. Ashe was completely impressed when Winkler did four hundred to start, and then Trajan added more weight until the six-hundred mark was reached.

Ashe reminded himself that this was the Dallas Packmaster, with one of the largest Packs in the U.S. The Grand Master depended upon him just as much as his official Second; his son, Daryl Harper.

"Okay, I'll work harder," Wayne grumbled when Winkler rose from the weight bench.

"Good. I'm going into town for a Dilly Bar. Anybody want to come?" Winkler grinned. Ashe, Trajan, Trace and Marco loaded into Winkler's SUV. Winkler drove, which was unusual. Trajan or one of the others usually did.

Ashe loaded into the back seat with Trace and Marco; Trajan sat in the front with Winkler. Gene, Gabe and Tony stayed behind with Wynter and Wayne.

Winkler pulled into the parking lot of the Port Aransas Dairy

Queen minutes later. Only six cars were in the parking lot. Ashe smelled the familiar scent of hamburgers, fries and other fast food when they walked inside the small eatery. Before making his selection, Ashe examined the freezer filled with frozen treats, deciding he wanted a soft-serve cone after all.

"What made you want a Dilly Bar, boss?" Trajan grinned as they loaded into the SUV again. Winkler was munching on his ice-cream bar, so Trajan was driving. He'd settled for a limeade drink.

"Because Ashe is too young to go to a bar," Winkler said. "Take us to the beach. We'll drive on the sand for a while."

"Charles, did you find anything?" Wlodek eyed his vampire assistant. Charles had several aliases, but in each of them, the first name was always Charles. He'd been Wlodek's personal secretary/assistant for three hundred years.

As a vampire, and even as a human before that, Charles was eternally curious. He was also discretion itself and capable of doing at least five things at once. Plus, since the invention of typewriters and then computers, Charles was most likely the fastest typist anyone had ever seen.

"I did, Honored One." Charles stood before Wlodek's antique desk. It wasn't Louis XIV—it was older, heavier and made of darker wood. Rumor had it that this was the fifth antique desk that Wlodek had used since becoming Head of the Council—he'd destroyed the other four in fits of anger.

"And what does it say?" Wlodek lifted an eyebrow at Charles.

"You should read this for yourself, Honored One. I need to sit down, I think."

"Feeling faint, Charles?"

"No, Honored One. Feeling frightened."

"Anthony is already in the states, Honored One," Gavin Montegue wasn't expecting a call from Wlodek so close to dawn. He was in Barcelona, tracking a rogue vampire.

"But your vampire child is on another assignment. I want you to bring this Dark Elemaiya to me. I wish to question him before he dies. He is already causing havoc among humans, werewolves and shapeshifters. I can trust you with this. Tape his mouth shut if you have to. Select two others to go with you; I want this done within the week, quickly and efficiently. No trail. Understand?"

"Of course, Honored One. Russell and Will are available, and Dmitri can take over this assignment."

"Good. Keep me advised." Wlodek terminated the call abruptly.

"You wanted to come along, you get to change the tire." Ezekiel didn't have much patience with Jack Howard. The former congressman thought of himself as an outdoorsman and hunter. He was soft in Zeke's estimation.

When a tire had blown on one of the trucks, Ezekiel ordered Jack Howard and two others to change it. Howard grumbled about it the whole time. Sweat dripped off the end of Howard's nose as he rolled the replacement tire toward the front of the transport vehicle. It resembled those the army used to haul troops, with canvas covering the back portion.

The canvas sides had been rolled up to provide airflow for those riding inside. All the passengers currently stood on the side of a dirt track in jungle conditions, while Jack Howard and two others worked to change the heavy tire. Insects buzzed around Jack Howard's sweaty face, making the situation worse.

"How long will we be at sea?" Jack huffed as he and a werewolf positioned the tire on the wheel bolts.

"Three days," Ezekiel said, watching as the other werewolf placed lug nuts on the bolts and screwed them on. The truck was let down after the bolts were tightened, then checked one last time before everyone loaded up and resumed their journey.

~

"I don't know which direction Pruitt went—he won't answer calls from his Second, but I've ordered him to keep trying," Weldon Harper, Werewolf Grand Master, informed Winkler over the phone.

Winkler had walked down the beach a little way so the others wouldn't be privy to the conversation. Winkler could see Ashe wading in the surf near the SUV while the others watched nearby. A half-moon hung low over the water, lighting a pale path toward the east. It would become full in five nights. Every werewolf felt it—it pulled at them the entire week.

"I don't want to send my trackers across the border after him if I don't have a specific location to send them," Weldon added. "If we catch scent of him, we'll go after him for the murders he's ordered."

"I may have some ideas on that," Winkler said. "What are you planning to do about the Phoenix Pack in the meantime? It's obvious Pruitt has abandoned them. If he sticks his nose back in the U.S. now, he knows we'll be all over him."

"I've left the Second in charge for the moment, but I've asked to borrow Dalroy and Rhett again—they're on standby in case we get a hit on Pruitt. We need to find out if anybody knows anything. I'm getting itchy about this, Winkler. You and I know that Ezekiel Tanner disappeared years ago. There was never any concrete evidence that he died in the attack against his father, Zachariah."

"I know," Winkler raked fingers through his hair, unsettling it. "And Obediah always insisted that Zeke was dead, but I never believed a word he said. That was when he was still an official member of the community. I think Zeke and Pruitt are together and working that side of the drug and smuggling ring. Marcella said that Pruitt was going to Mexico at least once a month, remember?"

"That's what got me worried about this to start with. If I had my hands on Pruitt right this minute," the Grand Master growled.

"I'd like to hear a few answers myself," Winkler agreed. "We've gotten a couple of hits on one of his bank cards—he pulled cash from a machine in El Paso shortly after he disappeared," Winkler added. "That spells Juarez to me."

"Home of Drug Cartels R Us and anybody will take a bribe to do anything," Weldon sighed. "I'm afraid to send wolves down there, that's how violent it is."

"I wouldn't go unless it was night and I had vampires at my back," Winkler agreed. "I think Pruitt and Zeke Tanner have been partners for a while, even if Tanner didn't know about Pruitt's attempt to kill me. He could have gotten his son out and left me alone. Something about this bothers me, but I can't put a finger on it. Matt has people working out of El Paso, but if they haven't uncovered Obediah's supply trail before now, they're not likely to. If it's Zeke, he's way too smart for that. They're getting stuff inside the states and not using any conventional means to do it." Winkler toed bits of shell with his snakeskin boots.

"He may be running the risk of exposing all of us."

"Like I haven't thought of that?" Winkler bent to pick up a small bit of shell, tossing it far into the water. The half-moon was rising higher overhead. Ashe, as mist, hovered overhead as well, listening to Winkler's conversation with the Grand Master. The illusion he'd left behind of him wading in the water was working perfectly. Nobody suspected a thing.

CHAPTER 15

"If he can shapeshift and mist, then it is only logical that he has mindspeech." Rabis bowed before the Bright Queen. She thought herself beautiful, but the Queen before her had been more so. Friesianna was subtle and devious. She'd betrayed her way to the throne, courting those useful to her, casting away those she considered weak and ineffective.

Friesianna was also gifted with Le'meruh, a particularly strong form of compulsion, which few could deny. Only a handful had known of her talent before she cast away the former Queen.

Friesianna also wasn't above killing here and there, when it suited her purpose. Rabis had been away, tending to other matters when the former Queen fell, fleeing from Friesianna and her newly acquired Sentinels.

The Jewel brothers, who'd secretly supported her in her efforts to take over the Bright race, were hers to command. Under Friesianna's rule, the Noble Houses were nearly gone, the Middle Caste wasted in battle against the Dark Elemaiya and the Lower Castes viewed as nothing more than fodder in any skirmish.

Children had become rare. Hilbah had suggested the fertility clinics, with unsuspecting human parents raising the half-Elemaiyan children until the Call went out. Then the Dark Elemaiya had uncovered the plot, with disastrous results.

Rabis sighed at the thought. So many innocents had died, thinking they were as human as their adoptive parents. Only one remained who had not been gathered or killed. One, who seemed to be particularly talented. Rabis was afraid to voice his fear—and his hope —where that one was concerned.

"So, mindspeech. That's logical," Friesianna struck a pose as she repeated Rabis' words. Rabis wondered whom she thought to impress. No Nobles were present and only Diamond stood in attendance. The other three Jewels were on some errand or other. "Which of the lower talents do you imagine he might possess?"

"That I cannot see, my Queen. You know I cannot see if there is a cloud of uncertainty about any of those I track with Foresight. We know the Dark Ones seek him out. Now we know that they may take him for their own purposes, since they have no living misters. The uncertainty surely comes from that—which side will end up with our quarry."

"Then we must ensure that he comes to us. Diamond, have you devised a plan to accomplish this?" Friesianna sounded bored as she addressed her oldest Sentinel.

"Yes, my Queen. My brothers are making preparations. Do not fear, we will have this one and he will serve you gladly. I will see to it personally."

"Very good. We haven't had a misting spy in a long while. This pleases me."

"My brothers and I know to place compulsion first. He will come willingly."

"Rabis, do you see this?"

"My Queen, I cannot see past the uncertainty. I regret that I may not be as talented as Hilbah." Rabis bowed again to hide his face. Hilbah was particularly inept. Friesianna had listened to his small lies and flattery, accepting them as true prophecy and foresight.

"I regret that as well. Leave me. I must think on these things. Please keep looking. Let me know if anything changes." Friesianna waved Rabis away.

"As you will, my Queen," Rabis turned and walked quickly through the field. North Dakota was normally Friesianna's choice to place the camp. Many places remained in the wild where none would detect them, but North Dakota was Friesianna's choice. It was also two jumps from the nearest gate. Perfect for the Bright camp.

Friesianna's tent was always assembled first and her throne placed, even before food was served to hungry children. There were only three of those, now. Of the hundreds of half-Elemaiyan children raised by humans, only forty of those remained. Eight were in the camp. One was still out there and targeted for collection. Rabis sighed and walked toward his tent.

"Hey, what are you guys doing here?" Ashe grinned at Dori, who stood in the doorway to his office, Cori, Sali and Wynn right behind her.

"Winkler invited us over to go to the beach after work." Dori came in and leaned against Ashe's desk. She wore shorts and a tank top. Sali wore his swim trunks and a shirt he left unbuttoned. Wynn wore shorts too, but she had a loose shirt on over her swimsuit top.

"Glad you could come," Winkler was in the doorway now. "Jimmy's cooking homemade pizza when you get back. Marco and Trace will keep you company on the beach. Towels are on the deck as usual. Have fun." Winkler walked away.

"Ashe, get up from there and get into your swim trunks, man," Sali said.

"All right. Why didn't you tell me you were coming?" He leaned in to give Dori a peck on the check, making her blush.

"Winkler said it was a surprise. Said you did something cool," Sali said.

"I do a lot of cool things. To which cool thing are you referring?" Ashe was grinning like a fool and he knew it.

"Something on the news today, I think," Sali said. "We were working. We didn't see it."

"Oh. I'm crushed. The hero goes unsung as usual," Ashe said. Winkler had let him watch the news program earlier, which showed photographs of a Savings and Loan Vice President who'd been arrested for bank fraud and a list of other charges. He'd been slipping hidden fees and interest charges onto bankcard statements and reaping the benefits, hiding the money as bonus payments.

"I'll change and meet you on the deck in five minutes." Ashe herded everyone out of his office and shut the door.

"The bad thing about this is we can't play Frisbee like we usually do," Sali grinned as he smoothed sunscreen on Wynn's back. Ashe had already taken care of Dori.

Marco and Cori had walked down the beach a little way. Sali referred to the game he and Ashe preferred to play with the flying disk—Sali catching the Frisbee as werewolf, when Ashe tossed it to him.

"We can do that this weekend," Ashe said, lying back on the beach towel next to Dori. She snuggled against him, making Ashe turn toward her and smile. "I like this," Ashe said and shared his first real kiss with Dori Anderson, lying on a large towel in front of Winkler's huge beach house.

"Grand Master, we've located a compound, and it looks like Zeke Tanner's place," Tracker Clayton Tucker reported on his cell. "If we hadn't had Dalroy and Rhett with us, we'd never have made it. Let's just say there were a few guards trying to stop us."

"I always thought the old bastard was still alive. No doubt he's been working with his brother all this time," Weldon mused. "Please tell me you have Ezekiel in custody." The Grand Master was at home in North Dakota, having a late-night cup of coffee and speaking to his Tracker by cell phone.

"He wasn't here. I understand quite a few headed out with him, wherever he went. Didn't leave that information with anyone here. The vamps already checked."

"Do they know which direction Tanner's bunch took?" Weldon asked.

"Drove east, according to the two who watched them leave. Had three big trucks and an SUV. Nothing uncommon for this area."

"Where the factions are all at war with one another?" Weldon snorted. "They could have gone to attack a rival cartel."

"True. Had weapons, according to the source. Don't know when they plan to come home, either."

"I don't want you staying—all of you could end up dead. I never thought I'd hear myself say that to werewolves and vampires, but that area is too unstable and deaths can be had for very little money. Can you get across the border again tonight? I want you on U.S. soil before morning if possible."

"Yeah, I think we can manage that. Especially if the vamps drive."

"Then give them the keys and hold on. We'll put out a reward on Zeke Tanner and send a bigger force next time. Leave now, Clayton. I trust Grady is also well?"

"Yep. One of the vamps—Rhett? He was grazed by a bullet, but the one who shot him didn't live to tell the tale."

"Dalroy trained him. Dalroy was a Texas Ranger, Clayton. I've not seen many fight like that. Go on, load up and get out of there. We'll work out a strategy for capturing Tanner when you get back. Have those vamps place compulsion that you were never there."

"Already taken care of, boss," Clayton grinned and loaded into the Hummer Dalroy was starting up. "See you in a couple of days." Clayton terminated the call.

~

"Zeke Tanner's alive, we've confirmed it," Weldon informed Winkler, shortly after he'd let Clayton go. He went on to explain what Clayton and the others had found outside Juarez.

"Not surprised," Winkler said. "Too bad he wasn't home when your

Tracker arrived. Dalroy would have gotten him, I think, if nobody else could. He almost took Obediah down, years ago. If the sun hadn't come up, he would have."

"The rather large drawback to being vampire," Weldon observed dryly.

"If they all could do what Lissa did, I'd worry," Winkler agreed. "At least we know we're safe during daylight. If Wlodek could move about during the day, well, that would be flat-out frightening."

"You know he'd be Prime Minister of England if he could walk in the sun."

"There's always that, I suppose. But that might force him to crack a smile now and then."

"That's the frightening part," Weldon said.

"I'm taking Cori out to eat," Marco was dressed nicer than usual when Ashe came out of his office, stretching. He was ready for a run on the beach, but his usual partner had a date.

"What about Trace?" Ashe asked. It was Wednesday, July ninth. Ashe noticed the wolves were getting fidgety over the full moon in two days. "And how does dating figure into the full moon thing?" He lifted an eyebrow at Marco.

"Not a prob, dude," Marco patted Ashe's shoulder. Jingling the keys to one of Winkler's vans, Marco headed for the front door.

"Gotta guard the Winkler, man," Trace grinned when Ashe asked about a run on the beach. "Trajan and Winkler are holed up inside Winkler's suite. How about using that treadmill in the workout room? It doesn't see much use."

"I'll think about it," Ashe yawned wide enough to crack a jaw. He had a hard time covering it with one hand.

"Maybe a nap instead?" Trace suggested.

"I'd really like to have dinner with Mom, I think, but a nap would be okay. Yeah, maybe I'll do that," Ashe nodded.

"See you later, then," Trace walked through the patio doors. He'd come inside for a drink of water before going out to patrol the perimeter of Winkler's beach property. Since Nick's attack, security had been beefed up considerably.

Ashe walked up the stairs and into his westward-facing bedroom, closing the door behind him. Brushing his teeth a few minutes later, he checked his appearance in the bathroom mirror before hopping to the new house in Star Cove.

"Mom, I can do this one," Ashe pointed out the Relocation talent on the sheets his mother held. She'd asked him to explain how he'd suddenly appeared on the doorstep, with no car and no accompanying werewolf guard.

"Honey, that's extraordinary." Adele stared at Ashe.

"Well, it was a shock when I found out I could do it."

"I think we should keep this information to ourselves," Adele added. "I'm not sure it would be a good thing if people learned you can do it."

"Yeah. I think so, too."

"I'll tell your dad. I'm sure he'll want to keep this secret." Adele shoved the sheets into Aedan's desk drawer and locked it again. "Now, what did you want for dinner?"

"I love meatloaf," Ashe said later as he polished off a second helping. "I haven't gotten any since we moved."

"Mr. Winkler might not like it," Adele pointed out. "I'm sure his cook caters to what he wants to eat."

"Jimmy's a pretty good cook," Ashe said. "But he's not my mom."

"Aw, honey, that's so sweet." Ashe hugged his mother when she squeezed his shoulders. "Now, we're going to call Mr. Winkler, and tell him where you are."

"Mom, you just took the fun out of sneaking away," Ashe muttered.

"Honey, he doesn't need to worry that you're just going to disappear; he has a responsibility to keep you safe. We'll tell him you misted over, and I'll drive you back."

"All right." Ashe rose and began loading dishes into the dishwasher while his mother phoned Winkler.

"Yes, I've told him already that he shouldn't disappear like that," Adele agreed over the phone. "I'll bring him back when his father wakes."

~

"Are you kidding? He misted home?" Trajan rolled his eyes as soon as Winkler ended the call from Adele Evans.

"Went home to have dinner with his mother," Winkler shook his head. "I want you to work him extra hard tomorrow, and I'll find something particularly nasty for him to do afterward. Honestly, I'd have gotten someone to take him home if he wanted to go that badly."

~

"Son, I want you to show me this." Aedan had driven to the darkened beach, careful to make sure no tourists were nearby to see. The moon, now very close to full, glittered on the gulf water that reached and drew back along the shoreline.

"See that marker, down there?" Ashe pointed to a beach marker roughly a tenth of a mile away. The tall post was white and easily visible in the moonlight.

"I see it," Aedan nodded. Ashe hopped from the spot beside his father to the marker and then back again, the entire process taking less than a second. "If I hadn't seen that, I wouldn't have believed it possible," Aedan sighed, staring at Ashe. "Never let anyone else know of this if you can help it, and only use it in emergencies. Sneaking away for dinner with your mother isn't an emergency. You should apologize to Mr. Winkler as soon as we arrive, and you can expect some sort of punishment, I think. He promised to keep you safe. He can't do that if you run away and he doesn't know where you are."

"I know, Dad. I was just missing you and Mom."

"The move has been unsettling for everybody. I understand that.

But we have to keep our good sense. Especially after Wynn's capture and the attempt on Mr. Winkler's life, not to mention Jackson's father, who is still hunting for his son, I'm sure. Don't make our jobs harder than they are already. Marcie allowed Jackson to work in the groves with the others, but only after Shirley promised security."

Ashe felt guilty. More guilty than he might have if his father had displayed anger. He was silent on the drive to Winkler's beach house after that. "I'm sorry, Mr. Winkler," Ashe hung his head when he walked into Winkler's kitchen, where Winkler and Trajan were having a cup of coffee.

"Oh, you'll get your punishment tomorrow, never fear. Just don't do it again. Did you think we'd say no if you wanted to see your parents? Ashe, I'm not that terrible. Until you see what I've got planned for you to do tomorrow, that is." Winkler's tight smile didn't reach his eyes, telling Ashe just how angry he really was. Anthony Hancock walked in. Ashe shifted uncomfortably.

"Running away? Not the smartest thing to do," Anthony Hancock pointed out.

"It's not running away if I go home, is it?" Ashe said before he thought.

"Ashe, be respectful," Adele said. She'd not said anything while Aedan and then Winkler had spoken with Ashe, but she offered Tony a hard stare while she admonished her son.

"I will. I'm sorry, Mr. Hancock."

"That's Rockland. Get it right, kid." Tony stalked out of the kitchen.

"Get in bed, Ashe. Since you've already had dinner," Winkler instructed. Ashe, grateful to leave the tension-filled kitchen, had to force himself not to run for the stairs.

"Dude, why didn't you tell me you came home?" Sali hissed into his cell phone. Ashe, feeling brutalized over the incident, called his best friend.

"Sal, I should have asked," Ashe admitted reluctantly. "I just wanted to go home and have dinner with Mom. Like normal. Marco left to take Cori out to eat, and nobody else was available to go run on the beach, so I took off." Ashe wasn't about to tell Sali how he'd gotten home, just that he had. Let Sali think he'd borrowed one of Mr. Winkler's vehicles. He'd had his license for nearly a month and hadn't gotten to use it once.

"Dude, was your mom's meatloaf worth getting into trouble over?"

"Maybe."

"We're replacing the lines for the sprinklers, that's why," a werewolf lawn and garden expert had been hired to work on the sprinkler lines in Winkler's flowerbeds surrounding the beach house. Ashe was digging narrow trenches after raking back mulch and ground cover around short, squatty palm trees and tropical flower bushes.

Sweat dripped off his nose and into his eyes in the muggy morning air as the werewolf showed him where and how to dig the trench. Trajan had already worked him hard in the weight room, and then Marco had forced him to run farther and faster than normal down the beach. Without allowing Ashe to clean up before breakfast, Winkler sent him out to help dig trenches for sprinkler pipes after he ate.

Jimmy had cast a glance at Ashe now and then but didn't say anything while serving up ham, eggs and biscuits. Then, to cap it off, Winkler had taken Ashe's cell phone before sending him out to do manual labor.

"You're too soft, boy. Put your back into it," the werewolf snapped at Ashe. Ashe hadn't worn gloves and blisters were forming on his palms.

Determined not to give the werewolf anything else to complain about, Ashe kept digging, doing his best to ignore the pain. After the trenches were dug, Ashe laid PVC pipe and then screwed in pipe nipples and sprinkler heads. His hands were burning by that time, so he cooled them in the spray when the lines were tested.

"We're done, go ask Mr. Winkler if he has any other jobs for you," the werewolf said, sending Ashe into the house. Grabbing ice cubes from the fridge and wrapping them in a paper towel, he held onto those while he went looking for Winkler.

"Anything else?" Ashe stood in the doorway to Winkler's office. Trajan sat in a chair before the desk, making Ashe wonder if he'd interrupted anything.

"Blisters?" Winkler lifted an eyebrow.

"A few."

"Wash them out, then get something from Jimmy to put on them."

"All right." Ashe turned to go.

"Ashe?"

"Yes, Mr. Winkler?" Ashe turned around.

"Don't do that again."

"Yes, Mr. Winkler." Ashe went off to find Jimmy.

"Not a pretty sight," Jimmy examined Ashe's hands. "A wolf would heal after a good sleep. I hear that's not always the way with shifters."

"Yeah, it takes Mom and me a little longer, usually," Ashe answered truthfully as Jimmy rubbed ointment into his blisters. Most of them had broken during his stint at sprinkler repair. The ointment stung, but Ashe didn't want to show weakness to the werewolf cook. The werewolf lawn worker had certainly thought him weak and beneath his notice.

"Kid, don't ever feel like you have to prove anything to anybody," Jimmy said, squirting out more antibiotic ointment onto Ashe's hands. "You are what you are. We all have strengths and weaknesses. The ones who think you're weak don't really know you. Take this and put more on around bedtime." Jimmy handed the tube of medication to Ashe. Ashe nodded and thanked Jimmy for the help.

Eating dinner later proved to be a tricky endeavor—Ashe did his best to work around holding a fork and protecting blistered skin. Winkler and Trajan both watched Ashe struggle without saying anything.

Tony Hancock walked in and sat at the table without saying anything, either. Jimmy didn't even acknowledge the vampire as he cleared a few dishes away. Ashe rose and took his plate to the kitchen as soon as the vampire was seated.

"What did I do?" Tony glanced at Winkler. Winkler growled low at the vampire.

~

"Cori, Winkler said he misted to Star Cove, but I don't think that's it," Marco said softly over his cell. "The day Nick attacked us here at the beach house, I swear Ashe just disappeared from a spot on the beach and then reappeared on the deck to get Trajan out of harm's way. No way could he move that fast, even as mist. And Trajan let it slip that Winkler got some information from Hancock about the Elemaiya, but I can't get to it—it's locked up somewhere."

"Stop worrying about it. Just be thankful that Ashe was able to save Trajan. I overheard your dad telling Micah that Trajan would have died if Ashe hadn't helped out like he did. Nobody else could get there that fast and Trajan was putting himself in front of Winkler. Besides, you took one of those creeps down yourself. That's pretty good, Marco. Your dad is proud of you."

"Does anybody ever say they're proud of Ashe? Cori, all he seems to do is get in trouble. I might have done the same thing—except I'd have gotten into a van and driven back to Star Cove."

"Marco, you're not sixteen anymore."

"But think about what I did when I was seventeen. I just took off and went wherever I pleased after James was killed. Ashe even got me to the church in Cordell for a funeral. Nobody ever knew about that until now, Cori. Ashe took me inside his mist and that's how I went. Dad might have grounded me for a few days after all was said and done, but Ashe—I don't know."

Cori was in Star Cove; Marco was walking the beach, kicking at loose bits of shell and seaweed in the moonlight as they spoke on their cells.

"Marco, it's close to the full moon and tempers are short. You know that. It'll blow over and Ashe will know to tell somebody next time."

"But who remembers what he does, Cori? You only know because your dad chose to let you know."

"Yeah." Cori's voice deflated. "I think this is why they shut down the project to allow vampires to have kids. Too much compulsion and distrust. Not to mention the other drawbacks."

"There are drawbacks, all right. Cori, you have to promise that you'll remind me if I ever forget any of these things."

"Marco, I could be made to forget, too. I trust Dad, but who knows what the Council could end up telling him to do? They rule the entire race with an iron hand, I think."

"The Grand Master isn't nearly as strict," Marco sighed. "Look, I have to get back before they start looking for me."

"Marco, be careful, all right? And try to keep Ashe out of trouble."

"I will." Marco ended the call and loped toward the beach house.

The boat was a modified, twenty-thousand-ton freighter. It rolled gently with the swells beneath the moonlight. Ezekiel Tanner stood against the railing on deck, gazing westward toward the barrier islands of Texas.

He'd planned this carefully. He knew he couldn't do anything during the full moon—he and the others in his Pack would have to turn and hunt. He intended to do that on St. Joseph Island, located to the north of Mustang Island.

There wasn't much there except dunes, wild grasses, snakes and a few small animals. Tourists came during the day, but it would be deserted come nightfall. If any humans thought to camp out on the island, well, they'd make good hunting for his wolves.

They'd return to the freighter near daybreak on Saturday morning with the shifter and werewolf children in tow. Zeke smiled. This would be so easy. To throw the coast guard and DEA off his trail, he intended to set the congressman adrift in one of the smaller boats after they set sail for Mexico.

The subject of Ezekiel's thoughts walked up. Congressman Jack Howard now stood beside Zeke, staring at the dim lights shining onshore ten miles to the west. "I miss it," Jack Howard said, nodding toward the coast of the U.S.

"Want to go back?"

"I'll spend the rest of my life in jail if I do."

"I'll take that as a no."

"People are such puppets," Jack Howard observed. "So easy to control with a few lies and a little money."

"That's in your world. In mine, it's muscle and money."

"Not all of us can be born werewolf," the congressman pointed out.

"Yeah. We're the lucky ones, all right," Zeke agreed. "Too bad the Grand Master thinks living alongside humans is a good thing. Sad, too, that the rogue vamps didn't win out a few years ago. We'd own the planet now, if they had." Zeke tapped the railing and turned to go.

"What? What are you talking about?" Howard hadn't heard that before. He assumed that vampires and werewolves were satisfied to live among humans.

"Just what I said. You're lucky to be alive, my friend." Zeke said the word *friend* with contempt. A tingle of fear crawled up Jack Howard's spine.

CHAPTER 16

"I believe they will be here," Diamond had procured a paper map from a convenience store. He tapped the spot to show his brothers where the wolves planned to spend the day before hunting during the full moon. "The source says that they did not wish to spend that night caught on board the ship. Too many things might go wrong in such a crowded space."

"They are compelled to run," Sapphire agreed. "That cannot be accomplished aboard such a vessel."

"What will they do with the young ones? There are werewolves among them as well," Ruby asked.

"Cage them, perhaps," Diamond replied. "They will likely employ smaller boats to bring the cages ashore. Those boats will be moored not far from the coast, waiting to pick everyone up afterward. Baltis' Destroyers will likely be there to assist, in exchange for the one we seek."

"Then we must be there to wrest that one away. Are we prepared to take on all the Dark King's Destroyers?"

"They do not have the talents we possess," Emerald scoffed. "We will take them easily, and leave Baltis scrambling to replace them."

"It is our destiny to relieve Baltis of his Sentinels, don't you think?"

Diamond gave his brothers a wicked smile. "If we present their royal talismans to our Queen, she will be most appreciative."

"As bargaining chips, perhaps?" Sapphire touched the square gold medallion on his arm reverently.

"Of course. Those are irreplaceable."

"As are ours," Ruby pointed out.

"Then we must see that ours stay with us," Diamond nodded to his brother. "Think on this—we give the Queen five gifts—the half-blood child with the misting ability and the four talismans of the Dark King's Destroyers? That will be a fine day."

"Shall we position ourselves upon this small strip of land, then?" Sapphire asked. "We will conceal ourselves and wait for those allied with our Dark cousins to bring our target to us."

"Yes. Gather what you need and we will go."

"Ashe, you're different." Winkler settled into the guest chair inside Ashe's office the following morning, cup of coffee in hand. He sipped it while Ashe lifted his head from the work he'd been handed right after breakfast. Ashe wasn't talking to anyone after a bad night with blistered hands and a bout of sleeplessness.

"Ah, still not talking. Well, when you're different, things are handled differently. I know you've probably seen others get away with more while receiving less punishment. I understand that." Ashe bent his head and tapped a few computer keys. "It's not fair, most of the time. Life, that is. Are you going to talk back to me, now? I'll allow it."

"Mr. Winkler, I have no future. But you've already figured that out, haven't you?" Ashe snapped, his angry gaze focusing on Winkler's calm countenance. "I won't ever be able to make my own decisions, will I? The Elemaiya think they own me for some reason, and I figure the vampires and the werewolves are right behind them. Tell me I'm wrong." Ashe got up and stalked from his office, striding through the massive beach house until he reached the patio doors. He jerked one of the double doors open, walked through and slammed it behind him.

"Got it in one, kid," Winkler muttered before rising to go after Ashe.

≈

Sali lifted another crate, passing it off to Hayes, who stood atop the flatbed vehicle, positioning the crates of peaches they'd picked that morning. The truck was nearly loaded.

The driver would have to take that load to the barns to drop it off for shipping before returning for another load. A wind whipped the trees and Sali's hair; a spray of dust whirled into his eyes, nearly blinding him.

"Hey," Dori shouted. The wind picked up again, blowing her hat away. She chased after it, running between rows of peach trees. Sali turned his back to the fierce wind blowing from the west. He never saw what happened, but there was no mistaking the screams and gunshots.

≈

Everything slowed for Ashe. He blinked. And then blinked again. Sali was werewolf, as was Hayes. Larry had turned to his bobcat, Dori to her ocelot. Jackson was nearby, with two others who retained their human shape.

They were facing off against seven large werewolves, all of whom were growling. An adult driver lay in the dust beside a loaded truck, bleeding from wounds to the throat. Ashe knew he was dead.

Others were coming with weapons, but there was no time. Four more appeared from nowhere. They seemed human, except for the delicately pointed tips to their ears. Ashe drew in a breath as those four began to glow. Then they, the seven werewolves and the Star Cove teens disappeared.

"No!" Ashe shouted. Winkler was standing before him, hands on Ashe's shoulders, shaking him.

"Winkler, they have them. All of them. From the groves. We have to go!" Ashe was still shouting.

"What? What did you see?" Winkler was trying to make sense of what Ashe said as his cell phone rang. Cursing, Winkler jerked it from his pocket and answered. Ashe heard a voice on the other end, saying the same thing he'd just explained to Winkler.

Sali, Dori and several others—all teens—had just been kidnapped from Shirley Walker's groves. Several of Shirley's Pack had been shot during the kidnapping.

"They'll come for you next," Winkler growled low as he stuffed the phone inside his pocket.

"Boss!" Trajan shouted inside the house. Ashe, who'd made it to the deck before the vision hit, jerked his head around before lifting Winkler into his mist.

"Micah, they've kidnapped those kids from Shirley's groves," Marcus stuffed a pistol into the waistband of his pants and pulled extra clips of ammunition from a drawer inside his study. "They knew to come in daylight so the vampires couldn't help."

"Where did they go?" Micah had come as soon as Marcus called. Greta and Denise stood in the doorway behind Micah, both frightened.

"No idea. Shirley's Second says the rogue werewolves were joined by four they didn't recognize, and their scent was off. They all disappeared—with Sali and the others."

Marcus struggled to keep his emotions out of the equation. Denise was terrified, he could tell. She was good in a fight as werewolf, but her son's life had never been on the line before.

"Are you going to stay home?" He turned to her with the question on his lips.

"Marcus, don't ask me to do that," she begged. He just nodded.

Marcus stalked out of the house, Micah, Greta and Denise right behind him.

Other werewolves were gathering outside his house, vehicles at the ready. Shirley Walker's groves were the first destination, to find scents. Then Winkler and his security force would join them as quickly as possible to help.

"Pruitt is behind this," Micah growled.

"With Zeke Tanner, more than likely," Marcus nodded. "Everybody," he said, addressing the crowd outside his home, "load up and follow us to the groves. Don't shoot unless you have a clear shot. Turn if necessary, but only if it's necessary. Don't endanger the children, whatever you do." There were nods throughout the gathered crowd. "Load up and let's go." Marcus jumped into the van Micah had already started.

Adele Evans watched, her heart beating triple time in her chest as she saw every werewolf from the Star Cove Pack drive away behind Marcus and Micah. Sharon, Jonas and Wynn O'Neill stood behind her on the Evans' front porch.

Wynn wept softly. Lavonna and Cori Anderson joined them. Cori was pale and gripping her mother's hand tightly. "I wish Daddy was up," Cori couldn't hold the tears back any longer.

"Honey, I wish Aedan and Nathan were both awake," Adele gave Cori a hug.

"Why do they want Dori?" Wynn was frightened, Adele knew. "They got Jackson, isn't he the one they want?"

"Honey, we don't know why they took Dori and the others," Sharon held Wynn against her. "It doesn't make any sense at all."

"Marcie and Jason went, didn't they?" Cori looked up at her mother.

"Marcus wanted werewolves only," Lavonna sighed.

A car drove into the Evans' driveway. "What's going on?" Dawn and Randy Smith got out of the car. "We went to pick up a few things at the store," Dawn added, "and we saw everybody passing us on the other side."

"The kids have been kidnapped from Shirley Walker's groves,"

Lavonna broke down, then. "They took Dori." She dropped to her knees and sobbed.

"What?" Dawn sounded shocked. Randy looked stricken. Adele knelt next to Lavonna and put an arm around her friend. Cori knelt on the other side, weeping with her mother.

~

Trajan was wolf and snapping at two that tried to get past him. Ashe rushed downward and pulled Trajan inside his mist. The two attackers were shouting and hurling fireblasts at the spot where Trajan disappeared, setting the floor and walls of Winkler's beach house on fire.

Get out! Ashe sent to anyone inside the house. *Run toward the front, I'll pick you up.* The desperation came through in his mindspeech as he rose straight through the roof. He could see that Marco, Trace, Gene and Gabe were all running away from the house. Ashe could have wept—Jimmy wasn't with them.

Flying downward when he saw the two assailants appear outside the front door, Ashe had the four werewolf guards gathered quickly before they could be hit with the power blasts the two attackers threw after them.

Then, in a desperate effort, Ashe flew back inside the house, although he could feel the distress from those he held within his mist. Jimmy's body lay on the kitchen floor, a huge, charred hole in his chest. The house was in flames around him as Ashe rose through the roof a second time. He would have wept if he'd been corporeal; the werewolf cook was dead.

I'm taking you to the groves, Ashe sent to his passengers, and using the hopping ability he had, arrived there in less than a second.

The peach grove was crawling like an angry ant's nest when they arrived, and a few werewolves growled while others screamed when Ashe appeared and dropped his cargo in the dirt between rows of trees.

Ashe was angry and wiping tears away at the same time. Winkler went straight to a tall, broad-shouldered woman who stalked angrily among werewolves in wolf and human shape.

"What the hell happened?" Winkler demanded.

"They came from nowhere," a wolf in human form explained. "Right out of thin air. Killed Brett and three others right off and then took those kids. Just disappeared, like that." He snapped his fingers. "There were seven werewolves and four others that looked human but didn't smell human."

"Did they smell a little like Ashe, here?" Winkler pulled Ashe toward the werewolf.

"Yeah. A little like that, all right." Ashe wanted to hit the werewolf for sniffing him.

"And we have no idea where they are now. There's no trail to follow," Shirley Walker was growling, too. Ashe had never heard a female werewolf growl quite like that. He knew immediately how Shirley Walker became Packmaster of the Corpus Christi Pack.

Winkler cursed and hauled out his cell. In seconds he had the Grand Master on the phone, explaining what had happened. Ashe felt impotent rage as he stalked away from the Dallas Packmaster.

They'd taken Sali, Dori and the others. That was unforgivable. He'd hidden from the Elemaiya before. Was afraid of them. What was it his grandfather had said in the email? *Make them fear you, grandchild, and beware the Diamond at the shining.*

His backpack containing the dictionary and the note were burning inside Winkler's beach house. If he found the ones who had done this, he was determined to do just as his grandfather instructed. They would fear him, all right.

Ashe heard every word as Winkler ordered guards to the local airport, bus station and rental car agencies. If there were werewolves passing through, they'd know by scent. Ashe didn't think it would be so simple. His head hurt from lack of sleep and worry. His cell phone rang. Ashe pulled it from his pocket.

"Ashe? Thank goodness. We heard Mr. Winkler's beach house was on fire." His mother was frightened, he could tell.

"Mom, they killed Jimmy," Ashe wiped away a tear.

"Honey, I'm so sorry. Are you all right?"

"I'm fine, Mom. We're at the groves right now, but the kidnappers just disappeared with Sali and the others. There's no scent for anybody to follow. We don't know where they are." Ashe knelt in the dust between rows of peach trees, wishing his parents were there with him.

"Honey, they came after you, too, didn't they?"

"Yeah, but they don't know what I can do."

"Marcus and the others will be there soon. Don't do anything foolish. I wish there were somebody to bring you home."

"Don't ask that right now. I think if there's any way to get them back, I'll have to help."

"He's right, Mrs. Evans," Winkler sighed, stopping beside Ashe. "I wish it were otherwise, but we may need his help. Thank goodness, they didn't set the garage on fire. Hancock will have a fit when he wakes."

"Mr. Winkler, we have to find those children. Quickly. Nathan will go crazy when he finds out they took his daughter."

"I understand that," Winkler said. "I'm just glad Wayne and Wynter flew back to Dallas yesterday." Ashe jerked his head around—he hadn't even asked after Winkler's twins. Winkler placed an arm around Ashe's shoulders, giving a comforting squeeze. "We'll keep your boy as safe as we can."

"Bye, Mom," Ashe said and hung up.

～

"What can Ashe do?" Dawn Smith handed a cup of coffee to Adele after she hung up the phone. They'd all gathered inside Adele's kitchen.

"Dawn, Ashe is more than he seems," Adele sighed. "Thanks." She accepted the coffee and sipped, wishing Aedan were awake for perhaps the hundredth time.

～

"We needed others with us," Yindis whined. "With only two of us, we could not take on all the werewolves at once. We killed one inside the house before the others disappeared before our eyes. We never saw the boy."

"Werewolves do not disappear," Rend growled. He was the eldest of Baltis' Destroyers. They were four brothers, pitted against the four Jewel brothers of the Bright Queen.

"But they did," Terrin agreed. "We both saw. Four werewolves ran before us, and then vanished. We understand the boy can mist, perhaps he gathered them up."

"Impossible. A mister might lift smaller objects, but carrying others? That has never been accomplished." Rend glared at Yindis while he cowered.

They were in a hidden spot on St. Joseph Island, toward the northern end. The southern end was where the tourists visited. Their makeshift camp was shielded from sight by a Dark Elemaiya with that talent.

Altogether, the Destroyers had brought four others. Their King had been most specific—give the allies what they wanted, but under no circumstances should they allow the werewolves to have the target. Slash and the others were placing compulsion upon the young ones they'd taken from the groves. The children sat complacently among the dunes, tall grasses waving around them.

"What do you mean, you couldn't get the boy?" Ezekiel Tanner growled next to Rend. The Destroyer had failed to note the werewolf's approach.

"We never saw him. We only saw the werewolves there," Yindis muttered. He hated werewolves. Wanted nothing to do with them, foul creatures that they were. They would likely get him killed, too—his King would not understand his failure to collect the boy.

Zeke Tanner cursed. He wanted to wrap his fingers around Rend's neck and squeeze the life from him, then kill the other one after that.

"The others will be gathering. We will make a second attempt," Rend snapped. "All is not yet lost. Slash! Grind! Crush! To me!" He shouted at his brothers.

Time was ticking away. Ashe checked the time on his cell for perhaps the fiftieth time. Marcus and Micah were sequestered with Winkler, Trajan, Shirley and her Second, a werewolf named Carlos, inside Marcus' van.

"Ashe, we'll do our best." Marco sat beside Ashe. Ashe knew he was just as worried about Sali and the others as Ashe was. Trace came to sit on Ashe's other side, offering a bottle of water. Ashe took it, removing the top and drinking.

"Zeke Tanner's behind this," Trace said. "We just found out he's alive not long ago. Figure Dom Pruitt is with him in this. They were after Jackson, but what they wanted with the others is a mystery."

"Zeke Tanner?" Ashe didn't want to give away the fact that he'd eavesdropped on Winkler's conversation with the Grand Master.

"Obediah Tanner's older brother," Marco sighed. "Probably supplied drugs and animals, among other things, and all of it funneled through Mexico."

"How hard would it be to load drugs on a werewolf's back?" Ashe asked. "Nobody's looking for dogs or wolves. They're looking for people crossing the border."

Trace cursed. Rose, dusted off his borrowed jeans and cursed again. "I'll be back," he muttered angrily and stalked toward Marcus' van, where Winkler and the others had gathered.

"That would answer all sorts of questions," Winkler agreed. "He may have wanted Jackson at first, to do this for him. His wolves are aging, more than likely. When he learned there was an entire community of young weres and shapeshifters at his disposal, it was too good to pass up."

Winkler was pacing as he reasoned it out. "Just get the young wolves and the shifters who are large enough to carry drugs across the border and then bring the money on the return trip," Winkler blew out a frustrated sigh. "He could threaten or harm them if they didn't cooperate. Or, if they were willing, he might promise them all sorts of things. They could have money, cars—anything."

"The Grand Master," Trajan handed a cell phone to Winkler.

"Weldon, I think we know why Tanner wanted those kids," Winkler said right away.

∼

Dori watched the others. They were as docile as sheep, now. Her father's compulsion was so much stronger than what these had placed. She still couldn't struggle out of her father's instructions, but this—it had slipped away as quickly as it was laid. Briefly wondering if resistance to compulsion could be built up over time, Dori pretended to be as dumbstruck as the others, whenever the captors looked in her direction.

"We'll watch them," one of the pointed-ears said. "While you change and run. Meanwhile, I'll send two of my brothers back to the groves. Surely, someone there will know where the other is. Compulsion will be placed immediately to discover the truth. We will collect him quickly, have no fear."

"You'd better collect him," the old werewolf growled. Dori shivered. The werewolf looked murderous. Cell phones had been taken away first thing, when they'd landed on the small island. Dori couldn't say exactly where it was, but it wasn't much different from the beach near Port Aransas.

Wishing she had some way of contacting the Star Cove Pack, Dori bent her head and examined the old shoes she'd worn to the groves that morning. She almost jerked in surprise when she heard Ashe's voice in her head.

∼

Dori, right now I wish you had mindspeech, Ashe sent. *We're looking for you. Hang on, baby. We'll come as quick as we can.* Ashe sighed. He'd sent almost the same message to Sali, not knowing if it would get through to either one.

Ashe, I wish I had mindspeech too. Is that what this is? Ashe didn't hide his jerk when Dori's voice filtered into his mind.

Dori, where are you! Ashe demanded.

I don't know. Ashe didn't mistake the quiet terror in Dori's mental voice. *On an island. There are dunes and grass all around us, but we're the only people here. That I can see, anyway. The others are under compulsion. I heard one of the werewolves say something about boats. They're planning to run here tonight at the full moon before taking us somewhere else.*

"Winkler!" Ashe was standing and shouting in a blink. "Winkler!"

CHAPTER 17

"$\mathcal{A}$she, can you take us? We know we have until nearly dawn tomorrow; they won't move them until after the run," Winkler said. Ashe sat inside the van with Marcus, Trajan, Shirley Walker and Winkler.

"Yeah. Do we have a map?" Ashe picked at loose skin around one of his blisters. It made him think of Jimmy, who'd rubbed ointment onto the raw skin the day before. Ashe drew in a shaky breath.

"Stay with us, Ashe," Winkler said, hauling out his cell. In very little time, he had a map of the area pulled up. "Now, they're either here," he pointed out the northern tip of Padre Island, which began just south of Mustang Island, "or on one of these," Winkler pointed out St. Joseph Island and Matagorda Island, north of that.

"I'll take you overhead," Ashe agreed. "Are you afraid of coming with me—as mist?" He asked Shirley Walker. Shirley snorted.

"That's a no," Winkler interpreted. "Come on, Ashe. Let's go. Trajan, stay here and make sure nothing else happens." Winkler nodded to Ashe, who went to mist and gathered Winkler, Marcus and Shirley Walker immediately, rising high above the van and flying eastward, invisible to anyone who might come looking for them.

~

"Bash, Crush, go now. You know what to do," Rend instructed his two youngest brothers. Both nodded to their eldest brother and disappeared.

~

"Trace, Marco, Gabe, Ace, I want you to be werewolf. I get an itchy feeling every time I think about the fact they didn't get Ashe," Trajan said quietly. "If anybody appears from nowhere and it isn't Ashe and the Packmasters, jump 'em."

"All right," Trace replied softly. "Where do you want us?"

"By the van, I think. I'll put a few of the others around it, too. That will make it look like we're guarding something inside. They won't know it's empty. I hope."

"Okay, bro," Trace slapped his brother's arm before shucking his clothing and turning to a tall, black wolf. Marco did the same, becoming the dark-gray wolf, standing somewhat shorter than Trace. Ace, when he changed, became a snowy white wolf. Gabe's wolf was a reddish-brown with a splash of white around the muzzle.

"Trajan, what's going on?" Jason and Marcie walked up when they saw Trajan leading four wolves toward the van.

"Just don't want any extra trouble," Trajan said. "If those things come back, they'll have a fight on their hands."

"Will they find Jack? What are Mr. Winkler and the others going to do?" Marcie's voice trembled. Nobody had seen Ashe leave; he'd misted away from the van. For all the others knew, Ashe and the Packmasters were still inside the vehicle.

"I hope they find them, but I don't know what the plan is. In the meantime, we have to guard the van, I think."

"You think they're after Ashe, too." Jason nodded.

"Possibly. We don't know."

"I'll turn if you want me to."

"Sure." Trajan trusted Jason. Jason handed his clothing off to Marcie before changing to a compact, black wolf. He paced beside Trajan, positioning himself at the front of the van. The others spread out around it, interspersed with a few of Shirley Walker's guards, who'd remained in human form.

Trajan stood beside the door and drew a pistol from the waistband of his jeans—Marcus had left the weapon with him. Denise DeLuca, without saying a word, stepped up beside Trajan, nodded to the tall werewolf and stood at the ready.

"Honey, if you've ever wakened early, now's the time," Adele brushed away a tear. Aedan Evans lay in the rejuvenating sleep all vampires experienced while the sun was in the sky. It was past six and two hours remained before twilight fell, bringing with it the possibility of Aedan's rising. Adele had a number to contact the Vampire Council, and dithered over calling it.

Night had fallen already in England. Adele knew the Council was based somewhere near London, but the exact location wasn't given to anyone except those who absolutely had to know. Besides, Winkler or the Grand Master might have already contacted them. Sighing, Adele brushed Aedan's hair with shaking fingers and rose from the edge of his bed to leave the bunker.

There! Do you see? Ashe sent mindspeech to his passengers, none of whom had the ability to reply. He flew over the small camp, making note of where Sali, Dori and the others sat. Ashe then made a wide turn, taking in the terrain before passing lower, until he was misting through the camp itself.

It would be so easy to gather them inside his mist, but that would allow their captors to escape. Ashe didn't want that. He wanted the kidnappers. He wanted Winkler and the others to take them. Deal out justice. That's what he wanted. Silently apologizing to his friends who sat on the sandy beach between two large dunes, Ashe misted away.

~

The moment Bash and Crush appeared outside the van, they were in the fight of their lives. Attacked by werewolves, both wolf and human, Bash was shot by Trajan right away but gamely fought with Ace anyway.

Bash didn't have the power blasting ability of Yindis and Terrin. He held strong compulsion, but the bullet wound pulled at his concentration. Ace, the white werewolf, had him down quickly, savaging his throat.

Crush, thinking to hop inside the van, met with Trace and Jason before he could get the words of compulsion past his lips. He died, gurgling out his last breath on the sandy soil of Shirley Walker's peach groves.

~

"Those two aren't coming back," Zeke snarled at Rend, who worried for his younger brothers. They should have returned long ago. The sun was slipping toward the horizon, too, which presented a new concern.

How many vampires would come looking for them? Without his younger brothers, they might be able to fight off one or two. More than that and there would be trouble. "What do you intend to do about it?" Zeke interrupted Rend's thoughts.

"I will think on this," Rend replied haughtily. After all, he could take the children they'd already gathered and use them as bargaining chips, though they were of no use to the Dark King.

"Think quick," Zeke snarled.

~

"They must have the camp shielded; I didn't see it until Ashe took us right through the thing," Marcus pulled Denise into an embrace. "We saw Sali; he's all right for now."

"You did the right thing, not taking them now. We need to get our people in there and take those idiots out. They'd have scattered if you'd picked up the kids." Winkler nodded to Ashe.

Ashe was staring at the bodies of two Elemaiya who lay stretched out beside the van. Ace, the white wolf, still had a smear of bright red blood around his muzzle. Trace and Jason sat near the bodies, both wolves guarding the corpses.

Ashe could see the pointed ears of the Elemaiya from twenty feet away. Both throats had been torn out. It made him wonder why he hadn't been born with pointed ears.

"We'll move 'em if that bothers you," Trajan whispered next to Ashe's ear.

"No. I'm okay," Ashe nodded to Winkler's Second. He felt a little queasy, but was determined to overcome it. He might see worse before the night was over.

~

"Sunset is in half an hour," Winkler said. He'd pulled Ashe to a deserted part of the groves to talk. "Let's go get Hancock, your father and Nathan Anderson. I know you can carry them as mist without hurting them in sunlight. The Head of the Council has contacted another vampire who still lives in the area. He'll come as soon as he wakes and gets the message."

"What do you want me to do with Dad and the others?" Ashe had an idea, but he wanted to make sure.

"I'm coming with you. I want you to carry Trajan, Ace, Marcus and the vampires, too. You'll have to send mindspeech when the sun goes down so they'll know what's happening. We'll hover over that camp. Shirley and her bunch will go in with boats north of the camp. I hope it'll send Zeke Tanner and his bunch in that direction. With the moon coming up, all the wolves will be itchy. It'll be a real mess, Ashe. You've never seen a werewolf battle, and I wish you didn't have to see this one. The vamps will be on our side, though, and that will make a big difference."

"But what do you want me to do after I drop you off?" Ashe asked.

"Get the kids. We're asking you to be a grownup, now. I know you pretty much are, but we're throwing things at you that shouldn't be thrown at anyone. Not without a lot of military training beforehand. Pull them into your mist and go straight to Star Cove. The Grand Master is sending as many of the San Antonio Pack as he can to help guard it, but the full moon may interfere with that. They're on their way and should arrive soon."

"But what about Dad and the others? How will you get back? Will there be enough boats?"

"We'll work that out. You don't need to worry about it, all right?" Winkler squeezed Ashe's shoulder.

"All right. Should we go get Mr. Hancock now?"

"Yeah. Do whatever it was that you did before, Ashe. We may be short on time. Drop Hancock in your dad's bunker while we sort this out with your mom and the others left in Star Cove."

"Okay."

Winkler called Trajan, Ace and Marcus over; Ace was still wolf. "Ready?" Winkler nodded to all of them. They agreed. Ashe turned to mist and gathered them up. The hop to Winkler's beach house took little more than a blink. Ashe wanted to shout angrily at the devastation that met them as soon as they arrived atop the detached garage. The beach house had burned to the ground. A police cruiser was still parked out front, as was a fire truck.

Thankfully, Winkler had spoken to the local authorities—the apartment over the garage hadn't been touched. Ashe broke away from his thoughts and dropped through the roof after feeling Winkler's temporary anger and discomfort.

Anthony Hancock lay quite still on a bed inside the larger of two bedrooms. Ashe gathered the sleeping vampire and hopped to Star Cove.

~

"My shields are holding—they suspect nothing," Sapphire reported to his oldest brother. They'd arrived shortly before sunset. The wolves wouldn't run until the moon was high overhead, but that time would arrive soon.

Diamond wanted to stake out the camp and make sure they were prepared to take on the Destroyers and anyone else Baltis had thought to send.

"The boy we want is not among them," Ruby pointed out quietly. They were near enough to see and hear everything going on in the enemy camp.

"What?" Diamond whirled to stare at his brother. Ruby held the sharp hearing that a few of their race still had.

"I overheard them talking—they failed to take him on the first try, and the second try met with failure as well. Likely because only two Destroyers—the youngest—were sent after him. I imagine that he was well guarded by werewolves by that time. We can take them if we surprise them, but if they expect us, it is much more difficult," Ruby replied. "I think they will make a third attempt, once the werewolves turn to run."

"Where are they going? Did you hear that?" Diamond asked.

"Yes, brother. They figure he will be guarded inside his community home. That is where they plan to go. They have two fire blasters with them. Rend will take those two with him, leaving his brother to guard the young ones."

"That complicates things. Very much," Diamond grumbled. "We have no interest in the others. They are useless to us and the Queen will not allow them inside the camp. Besides, Rend is pushing it, relocating a third time today. He has to be using up his energy reserves."

"Perhaps one of the others can transport. Energy blasters are quite uncommon."

"True, but they may be nearing depletion as well. We are fresher.

We will go in behind them, allow them to do most of our work for us and then take the boy—and them—while they are weak. This is becoming so much simpler than we thought," Diamond smiled.

"The Queen will be happy," Sapphire agreed.

~

"We'll take them with us," Winkler spared a few moments to explain to Adele Evans and Lavonna Anderson. "They can feed off the enemy," Winkler waved away Adele's concern.

"Then protect them while they do that; it takes a minute or two," Lavonna snapped.

"Mrs. Anderson, I know you are concerned about your daughter. Ashe will bring her and the others back here while the rest of us take on Tanner's wolves and those Elemaiya filth," Winkler growled.

The full moon was beginning to affect everyone, Ashe knew. He heard it in Lavonna and Winkler's voices. Lavonna would have to turn, just as his mother and the other shifters would. Cori stood beside her mother, her face pale, her eyes focused on Ashe. Ashe reached out and gripped her hand.

"Ashe, let's go," Winkler commanded. Ashe dropped Cori's hand and became mist.

~

Somehow, Ashe knew the moment his father and the other vampires wakened inside his mist. Anthony Hancock, however, was the one with mindspeech. He cursed initially, before demanding answers.

Zeke Tanner's werewolves and a few Elemaiya kidnapped Sali, Dori and the others from Shirley Walker's groves, Ashe explained as best he could. He didn't hold all the information, but he held enough.

Winkler, Dad, Mr. Anderson, Marcus, Ace and Trajan are here with you. The others are coming by boat. I think Mr. Winkler plans to trap Tanner's wolves between both forces when they turn to run, Ashe added. He hovered briefly over the enemy camp—he could see Sali and the others, still sitting on the sand below. And then he gasped.

What is it, kid? Tony Hancock asked.

There's another camp with four more Elemaiya, and I think they're shielded from the others, Ashe moaned. They hadn't been there before. Where had they come from?

The other side, no doubt, Tony Hancock replied dryly. *Kid, you're hotter than we thought. Why don't you drop us off farther north, beyond that big dune down there?* Ashe turned slightly to glimpse the dune Tony Hancock meant. The tall mound was covered in grass and creepers. It might be home to a few snakes as well. Ashe pointed that out to Tony Hancock.

Snakes don't like vamps. We're not vulnerable to the poison, he added. *They usually hightail it away from us.*

Like most normal creatures should, Ashe couldn't help adding.

True, Tony agreed. *Drop us off on the other side. We'll wait for the big furry turning,* he joked.

I hope Winkler bites your butt for that, Ashe muttered and misted toward the dune.

"I will bite your butt for that," Winkler hissed at Tony the moment Ashe released him from the mist.

"Don't mess with a hungry vampire," Tony hissed back, showing his fangs.

"Ashe, we have to wait until those wolves turn," Aedan said quietly.

"Dad, you can take—you know, if you have to," Ashe offered blood to his father. His father had never asked that of Ashe before.

"No, Son. There'll be plenty available later. We can wait for a little while." Nathan, listening to the conversation, agreed.

"It's close," Winkler fidgeted. Ace, who was already werewolf, paced around the small group restlessly. Trajan and Marcus came out of their clothing and turned. "Gotta go," Winkler muttered and made the turn. He was a powerful black wolf, with only his golden eyes glinting in the moonlight.

"Kid, turn us to mist, those wolves are coming this way," Tony snapped. Ashe had heard it too—the first howl from Ezekiel Tanner's Pack, before they began running in his direction.

Ashe had all of the wolves and vampires turned to mist quickly, and rising up, watched as Tanner's Pack raced around the dune. As soon as they'd passed through, Ashe dropped his cargo on the sand and watched briefly as the vampires and werewolves raced after the others. He turned to mist again, his goal of gathering up the younger werewolves and shapeshifters of the Star Cove community foremost in his mind.

They'd all turned—except Jackson—and were sitting quietly between the dunes, just as they'd done earlier. Ashe figured that compulsion had been placed. While he'd been distracted by Winkler, his father and the others however, most of the Elemaiya guards had disappeared, as had the four others hidden nearby.

Suddenly frightened, Ashe zipped through the camp, gathered the kidnapped teens and hopped to Star Cove while the lone Elemaiya guard shouted behind him.

"I hear 'em," Trace said. They'd cut the engines to the boats, allowing their momentum to slide them onto the sandy, shallow water beach along the western edge of St. Joseph Island. "Everybody, get out and turn. We fight tonight," Trace whispered, knowing that the sensitive ears of the werewolves around him would pick up his voice.

Micah turned right next to him. Shirley Walker and her wolves followed Micah's example. Trace, having the most control of all of them, waited until the very last. He nodded to the vampire who stood nearby.

Kyle was the only vampire living in the Corpus Christi area. Ten wolves had also come from the San Antonio Pack, and Trace turned to them.

"I know this is an unusual order, but these are unusual circumstances," he said to them. "Work with Kyle. I expect all of you to meet me here when it's over. Got it?" One of the wolves dipped his head. "Good enough," Trace acknowledged. "Let's go."

∼

Two houses were already on fire. The shapeshifters were fighting an invisible enemy, it seemed. All of them had turned and Lavonna, in her lioness form, stalked the street. Cori's panther crept stealthily beside her mother.

Adele's falcon flew overhead, shrieking whenever something moved beneath her. Wynn and her mother—unicorn and palomino mare—were guarded closely by Jonas' eagle, who flapped overhead. He was prepared to dive and strike if anything threatened his wife and daughter.

Larry Campbell's parents, Bill and Jennifer, in cheetah and leopard form, stalked the northern side of the road, sniffing for anything unusual. Six werewolves from the San Antonio Pack, Amos Thompson in his white buffalo form and several other shifters patrolled the neighborhood as houses continued to burn.

When another fire blast was launched, Lavonna and Cori raced to the spot where it originated while Adele screamed angrily overhead.

∼

"My shield is holding, but that may not last," Yindis panted. He was nearly stretched to his limit. The power he'd expended already would have him recuperating for weeks.

Terrin had set three houses on fire after they'd determined the target wasn't inside. Rend cursed his source—they'd failed to reveal which house was the target's. Then he cursed himself for not asking the question.

Truly, he'd never planned to come here in order to take the quarry to the Dark race. If they revealed themselves, the shapeshifters would attack. Rend wouldn't mind killing them, but he didn't want to expend the energy. He still had to locate the quarry and carry him to the King, after all.

Diamond watched his Dark cousins as they searched. Few knew that one of his talents was seeing through shields. He could see through this one easily. His brothers depended upon him to tell them what the others were doing.

"Foolish, to set the homes afire," Diamond muttered to Emerald, who walked beside him. They'd already dodged the mare and unicorn and easily fooled the eagle who flew over their heads—Sapphire's shields were among the best. "It tells them they are here."

"Stupid," Ruby agreed. "Better to stay shielded and search that way. If the boy is here, he will only hide better. It's a very good thing I can see the mist of others."

"You have not had much practice at it, since our last mister died years ago," Sapphire grunted.

"I have not lost that talent," Ruby snapped. "We never lose what we are born with."

"Very true. Stop bickering and pay attention," Diamond commanded. "Follow them to that house. They seem to be paying an inordinate amount of attention to it," he added.

"Tell us where the boy is!" Rend shouted at the only human left inside the Star Cove community.

Randy Smith had backed against a wall in Marcus' den, unsure who or what was demanding he tell them something. He had no idea that these were Elemaiya—nobody had explained anything to him.

All he knew was what Adele and Lavonna had told him and his mother—that the Star Cove teens had been kidnapped from Shirley Walker's groves. His mother had been quite upset about the whole thing, but she hadn't explained it, either.

Randy cursed silently over the fact that he was human and would forever be kept away from werewolf, shifter and vampire business. He did have one last trick up his sleeve, though, if the one threatening him came just a little closer.

Mom! Ashe screamed mentally as he hit the street in front of his home, releasing the Star Cove teens from his mist. Ashe could see the other shifters, all patrolling the streets that surrounded the canal.

Several boats bobbed in the water, moored to this dock or that. Ashe had no time to speculate over who'd succumbed to the lure of the gulf water. He had to warn them that something might be coming their way.

That's when he saw them. He was too late—three houses were on fire and four Elemaiya had just spotted him standing in the street.

There was no way to tell which wolf was Tanner. Winkler fought like a demon, taking down anything in his path. Aedan, Nathan and Tony were death on anything they could catch, and with vampire speed, that proved to be quite a lot.

Tanner had emptied his compound, almost, bringing more than fifty wolves with him. He was taking no chances with this. The advantage Winkler and his forces had was the age of Tanner's bunch.

They were slower. That didn't help, however, when the Elemaiya came. Somehow, reinforcements had arrived. Fifteen had appeared and immediately began to battle the werewolves and vampires. Winkler and those around him braced for the worst and went to work.

"My Queen, you did not ask and I did not think to look for them. I assumed you sent them," Rabis was on his knees and bowed low before Friesianna. "But I held no information back when you asked."

"I realize this, you fool. Are my Jewels still alive? Are the extra troops they called to them assisting? I must know this quickly," Friesianna snapped.

"Yes. At this moment, they are," Rabis' voice was muffled. "But there is a cloud about them. This does not bode well. Perhaps the ones who answered Diamond's call will pull your Jewels back from a foolish decision."

"What foolish decision?" The Queen was now standing and shouting.

"My Queen, I do not know—everything is fluctuating around them. An effect of the Dark Ones being so close," Rabis muttered. "You know if we are engaged against them, we cannot see the outcome."

"I know that," Friesianna snarled. "My poor Hilbah is dead as a result."

"I am most sorry for your loss, my Queen."

"As you should be. Be gone. Only come again if you have news."

"Yes, my Queen." Rabis rose and backed away quickly.

"Get back!" Ashe shouted at Sali and the others, who were running in animal form toward parents or their homes. He was ready to gather them again as mist—the four Elemaiya were striding quickly in their direction.

Ashe was sure the enemy believed their shield made them invisible to him as well as everyone else. Ashe could see right through it. While he struggled to form ideas on how to defeat the attackers, the vision hit. Ashe was unprepared for what he saw.

Thin strands of light and darkness flowed around him as Ashe stared at Randy Smith's image. Randy was backed against the wall in Marcus' den—Ashe recognized the room easily.

An Elemaiya with flame red hair threatened the young journalist. Three others, each shielded, were also prepared to attack. Randy held a knife in his hand, ready to fight the only Elemaiya he could see.

Before he could stop himself, Ashe hopped to Randy's side to prevent his death a second time. The moment he pulled the human inside his mist, another vision hit Ashe.

This time, it was of the street outside, where the four Elemaiya descended upon the teens and shapeshifters who were unable to see them. One brushed against Jackson Pruitt, who growled. Then, to Ashe's horror, Jackson turned to werewolf for the first time in his life and snapped at an invisible foe.

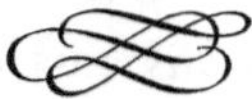

CHAPTER 18

*E*merald's talents included fire blasts. He did not hesitate, hurling energy bombs against the young werewolf. Ashe, mentally screaming Jackson's name, flung himself toward the four Elemaiya who were now creating chaos outside.

The four Dark Elemaiya raced out of the house, searching for the human who'd disappeared. Once they reached the street, they were confronted by their Bright foes. Diamond and his brothers had chosen to reveal themselves after the attack on Jackson Pruitt.

Yindis and Terrin did not hesitate. The air around them became thick with the smell of burning as they hurled fire blasts, not only toward their Bright cousins but at the shapeshifters as well. Ashe, terrified for everyone inside the community, dropped Randy in the attic of the O'Neill's home and raced toward the battle.

The shapeshifters had gone mad. The moon shone high overhead; they were under its influence and an enemy threatened. It was instinct to fight, no matter what the odds. *Think fast Ashe,* he whispered to himself. *Think fast.*

The Elemaiya were fighting while Tanner's Wolves attempted to escape. Winkler went after a grizzled gray wolf, only to leap back when a blast blew a huge hole in the sand around him.

Tony Hancock had been knocked down by the same blast but was up again, fangs out and eyes red as he raced toward the one who'd created the explosion. The air was thick with smoke—anything that could burn was already on fire.

Winkler had lost track of Aedan and Nathan. He could hear Shirley's wolves, the rest of his guards and the Star Cove Pack howling and snapping from the other side.

The battle had turned against them, however; the Elemaiya had opened a gap and now Tanner's wolves were escaping into the gulf. Some were swimming away. Winkler hoped they wouldn't get far—waves were higher and harder to swim through during the full moon. He went after another wolf that was wading into the waves.

"They're gone!" He heard someone shout. Winkler jerked around and stared in shock. Every Elemaiya they'd battled had suddenly disappeared.

"The wolves are swimming away!" Aedan shouted, racing forward. Winkler turned toward the gulf and the escaping werewolves, determined to reach them if he could.

Lavonna Anderson's lioness had one of the Elemaiya on the ground, mauling him. Another Elemaiya turned to help, prepared to level a fire blast at the attacking lioness.

Ashe had to do something quickly. Casting about desperately, Ashe focused on the first thing—the nearest thing—to the impending murder. A boat lifted out of the water and slammed into the Elemaiya, even as he prepared to hurl a fiery blast of energy at Lavonna. The one she attacked screamed as she bit his throat.

Another Elemaiya rushed to help. Adele Evans' falcon shrieked and dived downward, flapping in the face of the attacker. He turned his attention to the peregrine falcon, preparing to eliminate her. Ashe lifted a second boat from the water and tossed it at his mother's foe, knocking the Elemaiya to the ground.

There were consequences, however, to Ashe's desperate actions; the four Bright Elemaiya had made themselves invisible to the community again. Ashe saw they were now walking toward him, still believing that they were invisible to him as well. Ashe stood, shocked, to see that one striding ahead of the others had eyes that shone brightly white in the moonlight—like *diamonds*. Ashe turned to mist immediately.

"Where is he?" Diamond turned to Ruby. Ruby stood, spellbound. The boy had disappeared and even his talent of seeing mist failed to detect him.

"I can't see him," he shouted at Diamond. Diamond cursed.

"Strengthen your shield," he commanded. Sapphire did as requested.

Winkler knew if he swam any farther, he'd never make it back to shore. He turned and paddled toward St. Joseph Island. Trajan and Ace were already swimming ahead of him after coming to the same conclusion. Three werewolves had escaped. Winkler hoped that Tanner wasn't one of them.

The vampires—all four of them—were piling up bodies of werewolves with help from Shirley Walker's Pack. Sadly, some of their own were among the pile to be buried.

The rogues would be taken by boat and buried at sea. Winkler trotted onto the sand after coming out of the water and went to sniff among the dead. Gabe was gone. He'd lost both werewolf brothers. Gene, too, was among the dead. Winkler lifted his head and howled mournfully to the moon overhead.

Dori, stay back. Keep Cori and your mom back, too, Ashe sent desperate mindspeech.

Lavonna was sniffing the air, trying to locate the four who'd disappeared. They were enemies and she was determined to destroy them. She'd taken one down. Surely, she could take another. She and both her daughters had come perilously close to the four Elemaiya. Ashe knew that the one with bright eyes had to be the Diamond his grandfather warned him about in the message.

Dori's ocelot bumped against her mother's lioness, but Lavonna ignored her daughter, coming closer—so much closer, to the four. They'd killed Jackson Pruitt—his body lay empty of life on the street.

Two other werewolves were also dead—they'd raced toward Jackson the moment he'd turned, thinking to protect the youth. They'd perished in the effort. Ashe could see the crumpled wolves from where he stood.

If he didn't act quickly, Lavonna, Cori and Dori would be just as dead. His mother's falcon, flapping overhead, was also a target. Ashe became corporeal and shouted.

"We need to take a boat back to the mainland—Marcus' wife is wounded," Aedan knelt next to Winkler's wolf—he knew Winkler by scent. "A few others need medical attention as well. I'll send them back with Shirley's nurse—they can be treated in Star Cove."

Winkler dipped his head to indicate he'd understood. Trajan was back to human again, though he still hadn't found clothing. He was following Trace toward the boats—a trip would have to be taken and bodies weighted to keep them at the bottom of the ocean.

Shirley and Winkler's wolves would be carried to Shirley's groves and buried come daybreak. Winkler, using scent, was sorting out the ones for burial and Tony, Nathan and the Corpus Christi vampire were helping.

"I wish I knew why they all disappeared like that," Aedan added, meaning the Elemaiya. "Doesn't make any sense at all."

~

If Ashe thought he'd have problems dealing with the four, his worries were only beginning. Twelve more Elemaiya appeared right behind them. Lavonna growled low, as did Cori.

"Hey!" Ashe shouted again. "I'm the one you want. Over here!" Diamond turned his bright eyes back to Ashe. He'd been about to attack the lioness, but she was of no consequence. The boy was right in front of them.

"Get him," he shouted, pointing at Ashe. Three thought to hop to Ashe's side. Ashe was faster, hopping to one of the two remaining boats moored in the canal.

"Here I am!" he shouted and waved, causing all sixteen Elemaiya to turn in his direction.

"On my command," Diamond hissed, "we relocate. To that boat." He jerked his head toward Ashe. "There are enough of us—he's relocated at least twice. That should have exhausted him. He won't be able to do it again. Go."

~

Randy had finally found his way out of the O'Neill's attic, gone through the house and made his way outside. He arrived on the street just in time to see Ashe standing on a boat tied to a dock in the canal, waving at more than a dozen of the pointed-eared enemy.

Randy opened his mouth to warn Ashe, when all of the enemy disappeared from one spot and reappeared upon the boat where Ashe stood. "No!" he shouted instead, as all of them scrambled to get their hands on Ashe. That's when the entire canal burst into fire.

It wasn't an ordinary fire, either; the flames reached twenty feet or higher, burning with an intensity that pushed the Star Cove residents backward.

Randy had never thought to see water burn, but he did that morning. Gaping at the worst sort of miracle imaginable, Randy listened to the screams of the enemy. Fortunately, they didn't last long.

Honored One, the email message read, *we arrived at the prison to take the one indicated, only to learn he escaped an hour before we arrived. I know you will have retired before receiving this message, but we will remain in the area and search for clues in case you wish us to track him. It is most unfortunate, I feel, that he is now loose. We laid compulsion on two of the guards, and what they tell us is frightening. Let us know how you wish for us to proceed —Gavin.*

When Aedan arrived in Star Cove an hour before dawn, it was to find Adele, wrapped in a robe and waiting for him inside her kitchen. Randy and Dawn Smith, Lavonna, Cori, Dori, Wynn, Sharon and Jonas all waited with her.

Adele had been crying; Aedan saw that right away. Dori and Cori, too, were sniffling. "What happened?" Aedan was weary—he and Nathan were exhausted and that was most unusual for vampires. They seldom wearied except under the most extreme and stressful of circumstances.

The werewolf nurse was next door, tending to Denise DeLuca; Sali had been waiting for Marcus and the others when they arrived.

"Aedan, I don't know how he did it, but Ashe lured sixteen Elemaiya onto a boat in the canal and then he set the water on fire. Everything in the canal is gone, burnt so completely there's nothing left. Including our son." Adele burst in tears again.

Ezekiel Tanner cursed at Jack Howard when Howard failed to lower the boat's ladder fast enough. And then cursed again when he almost didn't have the strength to climb up the narrow aluminum steps.

"What happened?" Jack Howard demanded when Zeke climbed over the railing and began to limp toward his quarters.

Zeke Tanner called the Elemaiya many unkind names. Described them in the worst possible terms. They'd failed him miserably. Of the army Tanner had taken ashore with him, he was the only one left.

Several of his wolves had swam away with him, but they'd tired before reaching the freighter. Zeke hadn't stopped to help, watching them sink as he paddled past them. He'd returned to human form upon reaching the boat, so he could call out for the ladder to be lowered. Jack Howard happened to be the one there to perform that task.

"So, we have nothing," Jack Howard muttered. Zeke used up the last of his strength to knock the former congressman unconscious.

The end